BIGGER THAN US

A HIGHER ELEVATIONS NOVEL

JODI PAYNE

BA TORTUGA

Bigger Than Us
Copyright © 2021 by Jodi Payne & BA Tortuga

Edited by LC Hinson

Cover illustration by AJ Corza
http://www.seeingstatic.com/
Cover content is for illustrative purposes only and any person depicted on the cover is a model.

ISBN: 978-1-951011-67-3

Published by Tygerseye Publishing, LLC, November 2021
Printed in the USA

BIGGER THAN US

Jodi Payne & BA Tortuga

When Daniel McCaverty gets the call that his best friend and mentor up in Vermont has cancer, he expects to have plenty of time to go help. He never expects that Adam will be gone before he gets there, or that he will suddenly be in charge of Adam's two small children. He's a loner, an artist, and a wanderer. What's he supposed to do now?

Mitchell Brown is a white-collar kind of guy. Organized. Careful. He has a plan in place for Adam's kids long before Daniel arrives, and is shocked when Daniel is given custody. But for Vicky and Emory, he's willing to put his hurt and confusion aside to help Daniel figure things out, to make the whole situation work.

Daniel and Mitch have to deal with a tidal wave of grief while getting one kid started in school, and keeping up with their work. But they're going to have to figure out their unexpected attraction to each other if they're going to build something together that's bigger than either one of them alone.

THE HIGHER ELEVATION SERIES

All true standalone titles that can be read in any order.

Bigger Than Us

Keeping Promises

Home Free

Heart of a Cowboy

To our wives.

1

"Jesus, Adam." Daniel McCaverty had made it through the five a.m. flight from the Sunport, through Dallas and O'Hare. He'd made it through baggage here in Burlington and through the fucking line at Enterprise. He'd managed to drive about a mile before he looked around this place that was familiar but not, and had to pull over, sobbing against the steering wheel while the radio played.

Daniel hadn't understood when Adam had called last month and said, "Kiddo, I've got cancer". He'd thought, oh, surgery and chemo and radiation. It would be tough with the kids, but he could come out after he'd delivered his last canvases. He would help for a few weeks and, one day, they would laugh together over how Adam's thick black and silver hair had been gone during that terrible time.

That was what was supposed to happen.

Not a phone call early in the week that he'd missed because he was up on Angel Fire, and there was no signal. And then when he'd called back three days later, scared at Adam's voice, Adam's words, Adam's goodbye, it was over.

Fuck him. He hadn't understood.

Adam had told him not to worry.

He never once thought Adam would actually die.

After the storm had passed, Daniel pulled back onto the road, making the trip to Adam's neat house. He'd helped Adam and Tina with adding a bathroom and another bedroom one summer. Another year, they'd put the deck on. He'd painted the nursery—first with Adam and Tina, then with Adam alone.

Little Vicki would know him, but the baby? Shit, he'd been brand new before Daniel had left to work for a few months.

"What the fuck happened, Adam? Seriously. Nobody dies from cancer anymore! It's all about surviving. Don't you fucking watch commercials?" His words echoed in the car, and he rocked with the intensity of them.

He could almost hear Adam snort at him, saying "You can't believe everything you see on TV, Dan-O."

Yeah. Yeah, like he even owned a TV. That was what he got for trying to be ironic.

He pulled into the long driveway, the Escalade rumbling through the ruts. Someone needed to grade this before winter.

The trees around Adam's place were turning colors, some of them already orange and red like fire. That, he'd seen before, but Daniel hardly recognized the man sitting on the front steps. It had to be Mitch Brown underneath the beard and the baseball hat, but the last time he'd seen Adam's business partner, Mitch had been clean-cut and in a sharp suit and tie.

Damn.

He probably looked like a wild man. He hadn't bothered to change from his work clothes, and his jeans were spattered with paint. Daniel parked and opened the door of the SUV. "Mitch? Hey. I—Hey."

Mitch looked up and stood slowly.

"Uncle Daniel!" Little Victoria dropped the hula hoop she'd been playing with and ran toward him full tilt.

"Vicki. Baby girl. C'mere." He opened his eyes, the sweet little black curls shining in the fading sun. "I missed your pretty face."

"You came! Daddy said he had to go, but that you would come, and you did!" She squeezed him tight, little five-year-old arms circling his neck.

"Of course I came." He should have come earlier. Sooner. Weeks ago. He blinked hard, fighting his tears.

Mitch cleared his throat. "I guess you had a long trip. Would you like some coffee? Vicki, baby, why don't you take Uncle Daniel to the porch?"

"I started at three this morning. Coffee is great. I don't— I'm sorry, man. Y'all had been friends a long time."

"Yeah. Um...yeah. Not as long as you. I know this—it was pretty shocking and...hard."

"Uncle Mitch fixed the porch swing." Vicki pulled on his hand, tugging him toward the porch. "Emory is napping. He sleeps all the time. Babies do that, but it's boring."

"They do, and it is. Do you still like those genie toys? I have a color book of them in my backpack."

"For me?" Vicki smiled at him like he'd hung the moon, as if she hadn't just lost her father. Five had to be so complicated.

"Yeah, for you. I'll grab them in a second." He'd brought a suit bag and his backpack.

"Have a seat, I'll get us some coffee." Mitch disappeared into the house, leaving him there with Vicki.

"Did you know my daddy died?"

"Yes, ma'am. I just found out last night. I came straight away."

"He was really sick. He slept a lot, like Emory." Vicki climbed up on the porch swing. "He missed you though. He told me so. I knew you'd come."

"He was my best friend, and you're my god-girl. Of course, I came." *Jesus, Adam. Why didn't you tell me how bad it was?*

She patted the swing next to him and leaned hard once he sat. "Good." She sighed and flopped over, lying her head in his lap.

She was asleep by the time Mitch came back with two mugs of coffee. "She's been waiting for you. Adam's—" Mitch bit his lips together and shook his head, handing him a mug before sitting in a rocking chair. "The promise was important to her."

"I came as soon as I knew. I had no idea it was so bad."

"Well, to be fair I don't think he really believed it would be so fast." Mitch's voice was rough and dry. Anyone could see how tired he was. "I should have just called. He wanted to do it himself, but I should have. It's just that I was here with the kids and helping him deal with his doctors and I... I'm sorry."

"I am too. I would have come to help. You have to know that. I would have come." He wasn't a shit. He loved Adam and these kids to death.

"You know Adam. He was private, and he didn't even like me helping. I think he wanted people to remember him healthy." Mitch sipped his coffee and tugged his ball cap down lower. "This is...so fucked up."

"Yes. More than. Did he—is your business stuff okay?" He knew Mitch and Adam had run an advertising agency, but that was really all he knew about that.

Mitch shook his head. "I don't know. We have good people working for us, so I'm going to hope, but these last few weeks I haven't... I checked out of work."

"I can only imagine." He sort of wanted to give the guy a hug. More than that, he wanted to leave, find a hotel room and drink. He wouldn't, because obviously Mitch had been working his ass off dealing with shit and needed a hand, but that didn't alter his wanting.

"I'm just going to try to look ahead now. The kids need that. I need to get them a new routine. It's a couple of weeks late but I can still get Vicki into kindergarten, and I guess I'll find a nanny for Emory. They need some stability. Then I can get my head back to work."

"Wow. Kindergarten? Already? She's just so little..." Surely she wasn't that old yet, right?

"I know, but she turned five in July. I remember Adam saying at one point that he was going to sign her up but he... didn't." Mitch glanced at him under the brim of his hat. "So, how's the...your art going?"

"It's good. I got my last show in on time." He always felt weird talking about his paintings. He always had. It just felt strange.

"So that's going on now, without you there?"

"Yes. My manager deals with the sales and the galleries. I just paint the canvases. I spend most of my time searching for the right environment to inspire." It was an oversimplification, but it was still true.

"Sounds nice. Where did you fly in from?"

"Albuquerque. I was up on Angel Fire. I called as soon as I got signal. I didn't know. I wouldn't have—" He wouldn't have missed saying goodbye.

"I was with him when he called you. He said he knew you were busy doing what you loved. It made him smile. He didn't—" Mitch cleared his throat, and when he spoke again his voice was even rougher than before. "He didn't call anyone else. Just you. I'm sorry, I haven't really processed any of this, I just—these kids are so important. I'm just a little tired."

"It's okay. You can be—whatever you need to be. I'm serious. You can feel whatever you have to." He didn't know how else to do it.

Mitch glanced up, blue eyes searching his. He wondered what they were looking for. "Thanks. I appreciate that. I do."

Daniel stroked Vicki's hair. "You poor baby. You had to lose both your folks, didn't you? Well, you got people that love you more than the world. Don't you worry."

Adam had obviously intended for Mitch to take the kids, so he'd send money and stay as long as they needed. He wouldn't let them hurt for anything.

"It sucks. It just sucks. But they have me. You. Friends. They have people. I didn't."

The baby started wailing somewhere inside the house. "Emory. He'll be hungry." Mitch hauled himself out of his chair.

"Do you need help?" He wasn't sure he could move. Hell, he didn't want to go inside that house.

"Yes. Stay right there with Victoria." Mitch touched her cheek, then headed for the front door. "That's the deepest sleep she's had in days. I'll bring Emory out once he's fed."

"Okay." He swung with her, singing for her, random songs that he knew. He spent a lot of time in life singing along with the radio. This much he could do.

2

Mitch changed Emory's diaper and his clothes too, cleaning up after one hell of a blowout before he took the gurgling baby boy downstairs for dinner. "That diaper was seriously offensive, Mister."

Emory grinned at him and patted his cheek, blowing little saliva bubbles.

"Tonight we have chicken and carrots in a jar, which is slightly less exciting than the beef and potatoes in a jar you had last night." Mitch sat Emory in his high chair and tossed a handful of Cheerios on the tray to keep him happy for a few minutes.

That was apparently so exciting that Emory immediately dumped a handful of them on the floor.

Yay.

"Listen, you stinker," he teased, grinning at the baby. "If you do that again, I'll feed you the plain peas you had for lunch yesterday. Remember those? Those made you cry."

Emory giggled. Mitch appreciated that. He didn't feel much like laughing himself, but he was glad someone did. Dinner went relatively well, and Mitch followed it with a handful of cut-up strawberries, which Emory gleefully made a total mess with.

Man, both of the kids looked just like Adam. He could even see it in Emory at seven months old. That was good. They looked like each other. Family.

Daniel came into the house, carrying Vicki. "It's cold out there. I'm going to take her to the sofa."

Cold? It was gorgeous out there. He understood though. Daniel was from warmer places. "You want to just tuck her into bed?"

"Will she want supper do you think?"

"If she wakes up, maybe." He shrugged. "We haven't exactly had a schedule the last couple of days with everything going on." He and Vicki were having snacks in the middle of the night last night.

"Oh cool. I'm good at going where life takes you, so I get it."

Going where life took him? What did that mean?

Mitch grabbed a damp rag and started cleaning Emory up, wiping his face and his tiny hands. "This guy eats everything but peas. Can't say I blame him."

"No peas, huh? You've gotten big, bugabear! You'll be playing T-ball soon." Daniel held Vicki easily, like she weighed nothing.

"Yep. All he needs to do is learn how to walk." He lifted Emory out of his chair. "Are you hungry? I was going to throw a sandwich together. There's turkey and roast beef."

"Sure. Whatever. I'm the antithesis of picky. I even eat peas." Daniel shifted Vicki over and held the other arm out for the baby. "I'll take them to the front room."

Relief washed over him as Mitch put Emory into Daniel's arm. He took a deep breath and actually felt...

lighter. "Thank you so much. I'll be right out with sandwiches."

"Sure." Daniel nuzzled into the baby's shoulder. "God, bugabear. What the fuck are we all supposed to do now?"

Then Daniel headed into the living room.

Good question.

Mitch had a plan for the kids—for school and for the house. He had the beginning of a plan for what to do about the business. But neither of those plans took emotions or grief into account. It was a way to move forward, but he had no ideas for healing. He didn't think there was such a thing.

One thing at a time, though. Right now all he needed was a scheme to put sandwiches together. Bread, meat, mayo and mustard, cheese, lettuce, tomato. He had two big sandwiches in a matter of minutes. Go him.

He grabbed sodas—a Coke for himself and, on a hunch, a Dr Pepper for Daniel. They were Adam's favorite. He tucked the drinks under one arm and brought it all into the living room.

Vicki was sleeping on Daniel's left leg, while little Emory played peekaboo, the baby laugh goofy and wild.

"He has the best laugh. And I swear it pops up at the best times. Every time I was ready to scream today, this guy would laugh and make everything else just seem... unimportant." Mitch sat a sandwich down where Daniel could reach it and opened the Dr Pepper for him since he didn't have both hands free.

"He's a hoot. I came down when he was born, and he was just a shot of sunshine from the get-go." Daniel tried to hold his smile, still playing peekaboo, but the words were husky.

He remembered. Mitch hadn't seen much of Adam then; he'd held down the fort at work so Adam could take some paternity leave. "I know Adam was glad you were here. I think he was a little in over his head at first and didn't want to admit it."

"He wanted this baby so bad. He swore he could do it without help, and I just—I had to come out. He was my best friend. I owe him my whole life." Daniel took a shaky breath, then gave Emory a raspberry on his belly.

"I don't think I know that story—I mean, how you two met and everything." They'd only met a couple of times before, but Daniel had always seemed quiet, a little bit of a tough nut to crack. But the emotions they were both working through made the man seem more...real, somehow.

"No?" Daniel's expression softened, and it fascinated him, how this gruff man could be so emotive. "I met Adam at a summer advertising class. He was teaching in Arlington. He did my critique and blew my ass out of the water, just tore me up and asked me what the fuck I was doing in commercial art. By September I'd left school, and I was living in a trailer in Napa."

He laughed. "I guess I can see how that was inspiring, but if it had been me I think I would have lost it."

"Yeah? I just sold every single thing I owned to buy canvases and paint, Adam bought me the little trailer, and off I went. I sold my first painting on the side of the road."

"He was proud of you. He talked about you a lot. He'd show me the pictures you'd text him. He loved your work." It seemed important to tell Daniel that, even though he knew it might be hard to hear right now.

"He did. He believed in me, when I was beat up and robbed, when I was lost and broken down, when the first gallery owner called me a hack. He believed. So I believed."

He nodded. Adam believed in a lot of people. Their

business was full of small, local clients that Mitch had entertained doubts about at first. Adam had made him a believer too. "Yeah. It was a gift. His gift."

"Yes." Daniel closed his eyes for a second, but that was all. "Thank you for the sandwich."

It would probably taste better if Daniel took a bite.

"Hey, buddy." He got up and took Emory from Daniel. "You want to show Uncle Daniel how you can't quite roll over yet?" He set Emory on a mat on the floor. "Eat your sandwich, man. I bet you haven't eaten today. And tomorrow's...a tough day. You're going to need it."

"Yeah. Yeah, I'm—Yeah." Daniel closed his eyes again and took a deep breath, picking up his sandwich.

He sat on the floor with Emory and ate, just letting the silence fill the room for a while. Funerals sucked. This one was going to be especially hard, because it wasn't just the cancer, it wasn't just the kids, it wasn't just the business or their friendship. Someone was going to have to fill some very big shoes. Probably several someones. Him. Maybe even Daniel.

Daniel ate carefully, looking around the room like he was trying to memorize it.

"Did you...if you want anything, something you think he'd like you to have, you should...you know." God, this was so fucking hard. "And the kids...you should come visit. I hope you do. They should know you."

Daniel looked utterly horrified. "Oh god. No. No, I don't want anything. It's all for them. Everything. I'll start sending money too. I was just... I don't know. Looking for him? Are you going to—Will you live here with them?"

He didn't need money. Adam had left plenty, but he wasn't going to argue details tonight. "Yeah, that's my plan. I've been staying here anyway since Adam left the hospital.

He had a nurse during the day, but he needed someone to help with the kids...all their things are here. It made sense."

Mitch had no idea how the whole custody thing worked. He planned to talk with the lawyer who was executing Adam's will. He'd probably know.

"But seriously. Take something. And please visit."

Daniel shook his head. "I can stay as long as you need me. I'm willing to help. I'm their godfather. I love them. But I don't want anything. I don't need anything at all."

He wasn't going to argue with help. Not for a week or so at least. Mitch wasn't too proud to admit he was exhausted. "Thanks. That's... I appreciate that."

"Any time. I promised Adam I'd take care of them. I meant it." Daniel sighed softly. "Can I stay here, or do you need me to grab a hotel room?"

"Stay here. Please. I made up the guest room—well, I put a set of sheets and a couple of towels on the bed for you. That's as far as I got." He'd never ask Daniel to stay in a hotel. Adam considered the man family and would probably haunt him from the grave if he even considered it.

"Thank you. I appreciate it."

Vicki woke up and looked at Daniel, frowning deep. "Daddy said you would come."

"I did."

"When is he coming home?"

God, this was no fair at all, but Daniel just smiled at her. "Oh, my angel girl. His body was so tired, and he had to leave us. His soul is here though, and his love is everywhere around us."

He felt the tears try to come out, partly because this was so heartbreaking but partly because he was so relieved there was someone else here to answer that question for him.

Daniel was good at it too; he had good words, and Vicki looked at him like she believed him.

Mitch looked down at Emory, but that was a mistake because a tear escaped and landed on the baby's onesie. He covered the dark stain with his hand.

"His soul?" she asked, and Daniel nodded.

"We—all of us—have a soul. That's the part of us that makes music and art and laughing and loving and all. That part of him is in you and in the baby. It's in me and Mitch. It's in the house and the ground and the sky." Daniel winked at her and opened his arms. "Come here, you. I need a hug like crazy."

Vicki snuggled right into his arms and hugged him. "Uncle Mitch says hugs make him feel better too. Daddy gives the best hugs ever."

"Oh, I don't know, angel. I think your hugs could heal the world."

"Uncle Mitch needs one too." She kissed Daniel's cheek, slid off the couch, and hugged Mitch hard.

"Always, baby girl. Thank you." She was right. It did make him feel better.

Daniel sat there, eyes on Emory, watching him wiggle and coo. It was weird, the joy in the midst of all this sorrow.

"Vicki, baby. Why don't you take Uncle Daniel upstairs and help him make his bed in the guest room?" He and Daniel needed to stop staring at each other and pretending this was okay for the kids. It was killing him. Daniel was as exhausted as he was, anyway.

"I can do that." She turned around and held a hand out to Daniel. "You remember where the guest room is? I can show you if you forgot."

"I do. I'll have to bring in my bag."

"Did you bring paints for us?"

They headed away, and he could hear the soft rumble of Daniel answering her.

Oh, thank god. This was so much easier alone; he didn't have to pretend he had his shit together. He scooped Emory up off the floor. "Hey, little man. You don't care if I'm a basket case, do you? No, you don't." He bounced Emory in his arms and was rewarded with another beautiful smile. "That's right. You don't care as long as I keep talking like a goon, right?"

Emory laughed and kissed his chin.

This was better. Just him, the baby, and his frayed fucking nerves.

3

"What? What did you just say?"

Daniel blinked at this dude in a suit. He'd just held Adam's daughter in his arms as they all said goodbye, and this guy had just said... No.

"Talk to Mitch. He's the will guy." Daniel didn't do...legal shit.

"Well, yes. I will need to speak with both of you. Apart from the children, you're the only two named in Adam's will. Is there somewhere we can talk?"

"Now?" Mitch had Emory in a stroller and was rocking it forward and back, keeping the baby amused.

"Well, I think this is something Daniel needs to hear before he...makes any plans to leave town."

"Well. Okay, uh. Hang on." Mitch waved a young woman down and talked to her quietly. She nodded, listening and then finally came over to him.

"Hey, Vicki. You remember me? I'm Ruby. I worked with your dad and Uncle Mitch."

Vicki nodded, but she seemed wary.

"Vicki, baby, Ruby wants to take you over to that park right there to run around for a bit."

Her eyes lit up. "I can come back when I need a hug?"

Daniel nodded. He'd ended up sleeping with Vicki and the baby last night, just to give Mitch a break, and today she'd needed a lot of hugs. "You can get a hug *anytime*."

"'Kay! Love you!"

"Love you, angel."

"Thanks, Ruby." Mitch nodded to her, and Ruby took Emory's stroller, following Vicki toward the playground.

Daniel looked at the lawyer guy. "I don't intend to walk away and leave Mitch in the lurch. I wouldn't do that."

The lawyer blinked at him. "Uh. Well, it sounds like you might be in for a surprise. Mitchell, Adam left his stake in the business and its assets entirely to you."

Mitch nodded, tucking his hand into his dress pants. "I knew that, Steve. He and I talked about it. I'm sure whatever he left to Daniel—"

"Adam named Daniel sole and full guardian of Victoria and Emory."

Mitch stared at the lawyer—Steve—and then shot a look at Daniel. "What?"

"Adam left the house to Daniel as well. The children have trusts, and my firm will handle those until they are eighteen. Daniel, you and I can—"

"Wait. No. Wait. This is wrong." Mitch looked like someone had stabbed him in the gut. "Daniel?"

He didn't understand. Daniel just didn't understand. "You read it wrong."

That had to be it. He loved these babies, but Mitch was going to raise them. You could *see* that Adam had told Mitch that.

Steve sighed. "I promise, I did not. I'm sorry if it's not—"

"This is bullshit. Why didn't you just tell me, Daniel?" Mitch looked at Steve. "How do I fight this?"

"I—fight it? They're Adam's last wishes, Mitchell. Why would you want to?"

Emotions were swirling inside him, so Daniel grabbed onto the one he could deal with—fury. "What the fuck do you mean, tell you? I didn't know a goddamn thing about any of this. I didn't even know the son of a bitch was dying!"

Mitch rounded on him, giving it right back. "I have been living in his goddamn house for weeks taking care of him, the kids, the house...me! Me, Daniel. You'd have known if you'd picked up the goddamn phone!"

"I couldn't! I was working up in the mountains, and—" He stopped, his heart just cracking in two. Okay. Okay. What was he supposed to do? How did he deal with this? "Do we have to do this now? Like right now?"

"No." Steve said quickly. "No. Come to my office in the morning. Take some time to cool off. Do you...maybe I should find someone to take the kids for you tonight?"

"No. Jesus, Steve."

"Well, you're a little hot under the collar, Mitchell."

Mitch froze, then took a deep breath. "You're right. I'm sorry. We'll come to your office in the morning."

"See you both then. Go easy, gentlemen." Steve gave them a nod and walked away.

Daniel just walked straight to the park, to the little girl who had lost her daddy. He didn't understand—not any of this—so he didn't try. He needed to take her with him to the art supply store. That would help. It had to. Adam promised him that the art itself would never let him down.

He walked up to the girl whose name he didn't remember right now. "Thanks for watching her. I got it."

"Uncle Daniel!"

"Angel girl!" He smiled, praying that it hid whatever he was really feeling. "Do you think we could go buy paint together?"

"Yes! I want to paint. What about Emory? Can he stay with Uncle Mitch so it's just you and me?"

The girl had Emory's stroller. "I'll take him over. You two have fun."

"Let's go tell Mitch where we're going." He didn't want to, but he wasn't an asshole. He wasn't.

He followed the stroller, Vicki's hand in his. "Do you mind if Vicki and I go to the art supply store?"

"You don't have to ask me. I'm sure she'd love that. Do you want me to watch Emory for you? I can...put him down for his nap."

Ruby dropped off the stroller and gave Mitch a wave. It didn't take a genius to feel the tension in the air.

"Dude, right now, one way or the other, no matter what tomorrow brings, we need each other. Can we call a truce until eight p.m. or something?"

Mitch sighed. "Yeah. Sorry. I'm not really mad at *you*. I'm just...mad."

"I bet. I'm confused. Really confused." Because he didn't understand. He was totally willing to raise these babies, yes, but Mitch... Adam wasn't mean. What had happened? "And sad. So I'm going to take Vicki to eat hamburgers and buy canvases."

"Enjoy. I'm going to take Emory home—uh. To your house. And listen to him laugh." Mitch leaned over and touched Emory's nose, and that giggle filled the air.

He didn't have a house. He hadn't ever had a house since the day he left home. He had a trailer with some of his shit. Still, that wasn't Mitch's fault. "I'll see you at the house. Come on, angel. We need to make art."

It was the only thing that would save him.

4

Emory went down for his nap like the perfect baby he was. A little snack, some warm jammies, and he was out like a light.

Mitch stood in the doorway watching him sleep for a while and then started to wander, poking his head into Vicki's room and then into the master where Adam had spent his last days. The hospital bed was still in the middle of the room facing the view of the changing trees behind the house out the bay window. Someone was coming to get the bed midweek sometime; Mitch had written it down and put it on the fridge.

The funeral had been just what Adam wanted. Small and quiet, country music standards mixed in with a couple of folk hymns, a burial in the tiny cemetery on the edge of town.

Just what Adam had wanted.

This will was just what Adam had wanted too, but Mitch couldn't make any sense of it. Why leave a house and children to a nomad? Even if they were best friends. Just like family. Why do that to Daniel? And why take them from

Mitch, when he understood exactly what it felt like to lose both parents?

He didn't understand. But then he didn't have to, did he? He just had to follow the rules. Make sure everything was... just what Adam wanted.

He didn't want the house. He didn't want the money. But dammit, he'd been in these kids' lives from the start. He knew them. He had changed their diapers, rocked them to sleep—who was Daniel, in the great scheme of things? Some Santa Claus artist who sent weird, inappropriate presents?

God. Who was he kidding? Daniel was special to Adam. More than a friend, really. Adam talked about Daniel affectionately.

The rental car pulled up, and Vicki hopped out, dancing around in the driveway as Daniel unloaded. The man looked like a hooligan—long coppery hair and a full beard, tattooed arms, tiny wire glasses perched on his nose. He was in suit pants still, but the dress shirt was gone, replaced by a Ski Vermont t-shirt.

Something about it made him smile. Maybe it was the touristy t-shirt, maybe it was the little glasses. Mitch hadn't really looked at Daniel before, not seriously. Daniel had always been passing through, just in for a couple of nights, not someone he'd ever had the opportunity to get to know. He was always just under the radar.

Mitch left the window and looked around the room one more time before heading downstairs to see if he could help. Or feed someone. Or...something.

"Uncle Mitch! Uncle Dan-O bought us paints to work out our feelings. And we have fried chicken and fries. And ice cream."

"Good. We have some big feelings to work out, don't

we?" He looked at Daniel, noticing the dark green eyes for the first time. "Thanks for the food. I was just thinking I could eat."

"I know when I'm caught up inside, sometimes a little grease loosens it up." Daniel gave him a tentative smile, and that expression of confusion might be permanent.

"If you say so. I just like fried chicken." Mitch knew his smile was just as unsure, but at least they were smiling and not shouting anymore. He grabbed a couple of bags. "Back room where the light is?" Adam had a little studio back there, though it hadn't seemed like he used it much.

Daniel nodded. "I helped build it. Drove a nail through my hand." Daniel held up one hand, showing off a crazy round scar.

"Oh, damn. I bet that hurt." Vicki squeezed right between them and ran toward the back room. They had a talk coming, but he'd heard Daniel loud and clear. After eight o'clock. Vicki's bedtime. "You got a lot of stuff, huh?"

"Enough to do some work, and let Vicki get some shit out, you know? Do you paint? You're welcome to work with us."

"I don't. I...sing a little though. Play guitar." He sang more than a little. He did covers on Thursday nights at a wine bar in town. Or he used to...before Adam got sick and everything extra had to get put on hold.

"He plays 'Yellow Submarine!' "Submarine'!" Vicki started singing and unpacking art supplies.

He chuckled, nodding. "I've been teaching her Beatles songs."

"Oh? 'Golden Slumbers' is one of my favorites. I'd love to hear you play sometimes. I love music."

"Well, let's eat, and then I can play while you guys paint your feelings." He tried another smile. His fingers itched for his guitar now, because it would feel good to play.

"Yay!" Vicki bounced and hollered. "Daddy! We're going to play and paint! We're going to show our souls!"

Mitch watched her. "God. I kind of wish I was five."

"I know it's not the answer to everything, but—I want her to be able to believe." Daniel's whisper was broken, cracked, and agonized.

"Yeah. Believing in things is important. Knowing she's loved is important too." Daniel had that part down for sure. Maybe Adam wanted him to focus on the business and Daniel to focus on the kids? He was still looking for reasons, there had to be one.

"Dinner, Miss Victoria. Before it gets cold." He shooed her toward the kitchen and followed her back through the house.

She stopped before they got there and hugged him hard. "Dan-O says you need extra hugs today. I love you, Uncle Mitch. Lots."

"Dan-O is not wrong. I love you too, baby." He bent over and rubbed her back, trying not to fall over, honestly. She had his legs wrapped up tight.

She held on for a few long seconds, then she let him go. "I'm hungry now. Okay?"

"Yes. I hear the chicken calling us. You hear that? Bawk!" He scooped her up and tossed her over his shoulder. Her laughter chased them down the hall.

She and Emory were the best things about Adam, and they were here, and they needed him. He and Daniel were just going to have to figure it out.

The plants in his apartment would be glad to see him.

The chicken was delicious. He was curious where Daniel had found it. Must be somewhere near the art supply store.

He'd meant to ask but by the time he got the kitchen cleaned up and found his guitar upstairs, Daniel and Vicki were already heavy into painting.

He understood instantly as he walked into the room that he should keep his distance. The floor was tarped, as well as the wall behind them. Daniel had even tied up some of the curtains and tarped a couple of the windows. This was serious painting.

Or maybe just painting with a five-year-old; he didn't know. He loved art, he even knew a little about it, but he didn't understand the process of painting.

"This looks pretty intense." This back room was more of a sunroom, with lots of natural light, a flagstone floor and a garden feel. Mitch took a seat in the doorway, feet resting on the two steps that led down into the room.

"Painting is hard work. Sometimes it's messy."

"Vicki, you're rocking that garbage bag smock. They're all the rage I hear." Mitch started playing, just noodling and warming up his fingers. He hadn't played in...weeks at least. Maybe a month or more.

"It's a little hot," she complained mildly.

"Sometimes you have to suffer for your art, baby." He winked at her.

"You want me to open windows?" Daniel asked her, and she shook her head.

"It's time for art."

"You heard the lady." He kept plucking away softly, but he was watching Daniel now, who was preparing paints and finding just the right angle for his easel.

Soon, the painting started, and it was this wild, mad moment, with Daniel driving paint into the canvas. Mitch was fascinated, but what was even more stunning was Vicki, who painted like she was furious.

He understood that. He was furious too. That was a lot of emotion for a little girl, though. He felt a little uncomfortable watching them, like he was intruding on some private ritual, so he went back to his guitar to see if he could work through some of his shit too.

When Vicki finished, she screamed and punched the canvas, beating on it and crying. Daniel gave her a minute, and then grabbed her up, holding her and rocking her gently.

Mitch set his guitar aside and slowly went over to them. He touched Vicki's hair and hummed to her, helping Daniel to calm her until she was nearly ragdoll limp, exhausted and dozing in Daniel's arms.

"Better for now, huh? Better than nothing."

"Better. Better for her. She'll sleep." Daniel's eyes looked hollow. Vicki wasn't the only one who'd let out some emotion. "You want me to clean her up and tuck her—"

Emory chose that moment to wake up from his nap, wailing like he'd been making art too.

"I'll deal with her. I got her." Daniel lifted her up and hummed as she muttered. "Come on, angel. Let's go."

And he'd get the baby. No problem. Mitch lived for stinky diapers. He put his guitar away and left it in the living room before heading upstairs.

He had to wonder if Daniel was less used to dealing with an infant. Vicki? She was the one Daniel absolutely got.

Not that it mattered. Daniel was going to have to figure the baby out because Mitch was moving out in the morning. This wasn't his house, and they weren't his kids. and he wasn't going to stop being mad about that any time soon.

He did have a business to run, though, and clients who had been patient while he was unavailable, so he'd just get back to it.

Emory reached for him, wailing, begging him to fix whatever was wrong.

"Oh, I've got you, little man. You're okay. You smell worse than my college frat house bathroom after a party, but you're still cute." He set Emory down on the changing table and took off the offensive diaper. "Jesus, man. You know how to make a mess." He grinned at Emory though, talking in that weird voice the kid loved so much.

Emory settled and babbled at him, pure joy in the expression. This little boy truly loved him.

"Are you hungry? Maybe a nice warm bottle will put you back to sleep." He and Daniel could have their talk in front of Emory though; it was Vicki they needed to be careful with.

Poor thing. He'd never seen anything like that little five-year-old's outburst. It was stunning and raw in that way only a child could be.

He finished getting Emory dressed and headed downstairs, poking his head back into the studio on the way to the kitchen. Man, they had a mess to clean up.

He glanced at Daniel's painting, seeing a picture of Adam, just like he had been six months ago—whole, healthy, laughing.

He nodded, not that anyone could see him, but that was right. To remember him that way. That was the father of a brand-new baby, the business partner that was pulling out all the stops to convince him they should take on a little wine bar as a client.

Yeah. He approved.

"Bottle, right?" He plopped Emory in his chair when they got to the kitchen and started warming up water for formula.

"She let me clean her up. She's exhausted." Daniel came

wandering in and picked up the little one. "Jesus, you're just so tiny…"

"That was some righteous anger. Pretty heavy stuff for a little person. I bet she sleeps all night. I'll have his bottle ready in a minute." Daniel didn't look that awkward with the baby. He'd cleaned up too, Mitch noticed. "You okay?"

"No." Daniel looked at him like he was crazy. "Nothing about this is okay. None of it."

"No, I—sorry." He went back to making Emory's bottle feeling awkward and stupid for asking. "I just meant… I don't know what I meant. At the moment. After the whole— I like your painting."

"Thank you. It's how I remember him. I didn't know. I had no idea. I swear to god. I assumed I would need to make money and help."

He nodded. "I guess it's the other way around."

"What?" Daniel looked utterly confused.

"I'll be the one giving *you* a check every month." He tested the formula on his wrist. Adam had taught him that trick.

"What for? I don't understand." Daniel seemed to be saying that a lot.

"Daniel. I'm going back to my apartment. Tomorrow morning. This gig is yours now. Adam left me the business and that's… I'm going back to work." He offered Daniel the bottle.

Daniel took the bottle, opened his mouth, then closed it and turned and left, taking the baby and the bottle upstairs without a single word.

"Fuck."

Somehow it was okay for Mr. Nomad to send money, but when he offered he got the cold shoulder? Okay.

He hated this whole thing. It made losing Adam a

hundred times worse. The kids needed someone steady; they needed *him*, in fact, but that wasn't what Adam wanted and no matter how he spun it, it made no fucking sense. The best he could come up with was that Adam had wanted Daniel to have a solid home, whether that was what Daniel wanted for himself or not.

He heard the baby crying, and under that he heard low sounds that answered Emory's sobs.

Emory should have a face full of bottle, so what could he be crying about? He headed for the stairs. He was still here tonight. He'd just make sure Daniel was okay and then go pack.

He opened the nursery door, seeing Daniel sitting on the floor, sucking air, face red as a beet, while little Emory fought to understand what was going on.

"Daniel?" He hurried in and sat on the floor too. He hadn't seen it himself before, but he thought Daniel might be having a panic attack. He took Emory and put the bottle in his mouth, calming at least one of them. "Daniel. Hey. Breathe. You're okay."

Daniel looked at him, wide-eyed, the expression pure pain, just this wild, utter panic that was painful to see.

"Hey." He sat Emory down on his crossed legs so he could free up one hand and squeezed Daniel's shaking fingers. "Okay. Everything's fine. Slow breath, ready? Like this." He breathed in slowly and blew it out, then did it again. "Come on, Daniel. You've got this."

Daniel sucked in shuddering breaths, clinging to his fingers like a drowning man. "Please. I feel like I'm going to shake apart."

"I think this is a panic attack. They happen. You're going to be okay, but you need to breathe and try to calm down. Okay?" He looked down at Emory, who'd made it halfway through the bottle. Maybe a little more. *Come on kid.* He'd seen Emory suck one of these things down in no time.

He kept breathing. In slowly and out, eyes locked on Daniel's.

"I'm so sorry. I don't... I don't know what to do, and I know that you hate me, but I didn't do this to you."

"I don't hate you. I don't blame you either. I don't understand why Adam made this decision, and I'm angry about that. And frustrated. I don't hate you." Emory fussed, picking up on their crazy vibes, but that meant he'd finished his bottle. He let go of Daniel's hand so he could put Emory in his crib. "Hang on."

"Can't we—can we have a truce? I don't know how—I mean, I will. I won't desert them, but I don't know anything. I don't have family, siblings, nothing."

A truce? What did that mean? He gave Emory a few good pats and got a nice burp, then set him down in his crib. Not ideal, but nothing was right now. "Let's talk downstairs."

Daniel nodded, slowly uncurling from the floor where he'd landed. It looked like he hurt to move, honestly, and that Mitch understood.

He slipped an arm under Daniel's elbow. "Easy. Just take it slow." He'd get Daniel downstairs, get him some water or...whiskey.

"I didn't mean to fall apart," Daniel whispered. "I'm sorry."

"Don't apologize. We need to talk. I thought I was doing you a favor by bowing out gracefully." Daniel was good with Vicki. She needed that energy Daniel had.

"When I thought things were opposite, I was willing to stay as long as you needed help. Please, if you can, stay for a little while. We don't know for sure what the damn will really says without reading it." Daniel was beginning to breathe fast and light again.

"I'll stay." That was easy enough; he'd been here for weeks. What was a few more days? He hadn't promised anyone at the firm he'd be back yet. "Okay? I'll stay, so breathe and then we can talk this out."

"Thank you. They love you. You're their family. I'm not mean."

Mean? This goofy nut of an artist? Not hardly.

"I don't know if I'm really their family yet, but I've been acting like it for a while, and I feel like I am. I know you are for sure. Vicki adores you; she was literally watching out the window for you the day you arrived. God, was that only yesterday?" He must still be exhausted. It felt like a week.

"It couldn't be. It had to be a week. Maybe longer." Daniel sagged, the desperation and sorrow aging the man by the hour.

"Are you all right? You better go sit. Let me get you some water." A panic attack had to be exhausting. Daniel had looked like he might fly apart for a second there. Mitch filled a couple of glasses with water and followed Daniel out to the living room.

"I'm sorry. I'm not usually a freak. I just... I spend a lot of time alone in the mountains doing my job. I didn't understand."

He took a deep breath and handed off a glass of water once Daniel sat. "Okay. Look. Let's start over here. All I want is for Vicki and Emory to feel safe and know they're loved. Either of us is perfectly capable of that."

"That's what I want too. I want to take care of them—like their souls, you know? Adam saved my life, and I told him I would do anything for my godbabies. I meant that."

"Good. When Emory gets up from his nap, you can have

that diaper." He shot Daniel a sideways grin. "I'm going to have to get back to work soon, but... I can stay here for a while longer and help out. There's plenty of room, and it's not a long drive to the office."

"I appreciate it. I don't know anything about this life. I will. I can figure it out, but not now."

He understood. He'd had a few weeks to process this eventuality. Daniel had just found out about Adam. "I don't want to see that damn lawyer tomorrow. I know we have to, but he's obviously more reality than I'm ready for right now."

"Why do we have to? Is anything going to change? Can't we just order pizza, watch cartoons, and love on the kids?"

"Well, there's the firm..." But what was the lawyer going to tell him? He owned Adam's shares, and he had to do all the work now. Did he need a lawyer to tell him that? "No, you know what? Screw the lawyer."

"Cool. A down day—pizza and cartoons and pajamas. Vicki will like that. Does Emory like things yet?" God, that clueless thing was irritating and adorable all at once.

"He likes it when you talk to him like he's a good puppy. He likes dancing. He likes his bath. He does not like peas. I'm not joking. They'll end up all over you." A down day. He wasn't sure he knew how that worked anymore.

"I can understand liking to dance. I think peas are fine. They're a nice green."

Mitch nodded, watching Daniel. The guy just looked worse than he felt. "We're going to have to do some practical stuff after tomorrow. Food shopping and... Vicki needs to get into school. Emory has a checkup at the pediatrician in a couple of days. They're coming to pick up Adam's bed." He had to clean out the master bathroom, it was full of medical aids and bedpans and...and there was that cabinet full of Adam's meds in the kitchen and...

He took a breath. "Jesus, now I'm going to have a fucking panic attack." He wasn't really, but the to-do list of things he really didn't feel like dealing with was long.

"Yeah. I'm a hard worker. I've dealt with a lot. Nothing like this, but some stuff."

"I'll—we'll get through it." At least he wasn't doing it alone.

"Yes. I'm trying and willing. That's important."

He put a hand on Daniel's shoulder and gave it a squeeze, unsure at this point who needed reassuring more. He couldn't lie though; that small connection felt good. "It is."

Daniel turned and hugged him, holding him for a long, slow bit. He didn't have much choice but to let Daniel hold on, and it was awkward at first, but he ended up hugging Daniel back eventually. They breathed together, both of them taking comfort in one another.

"I didn't realize how much I needed a hug."

"Yeah. Shit has sucked for you. I'm sorry. That's awful."

He shrugged. "It's not about me. I wasn't the one dying of cancer. I'm not a little girl who's lost her father."

"No. You're the good friend. the person left behind to pick up the pieces." Daniel sounded like he understood, more than he ought to.

He nodded. "There are a lot of goddamn pieces too. I told him if I'd wanted to deal with kids, I'd have had some. I miss him though. You know what he told me? He said it was like his cancer. You don't always get to choose life; life chooses you."

"Yeah. Yeah, you know he wouldn't have chosen this. Ever." Daniel sighed softly, staring down at his feet. "I care about him a lot. He was the first successful artist I met in person."

"He cared about you too. He believed in you. He loved your work. There's some upstairs in the master bedroom."

"Yeah. He did. I feel like I've been thrown out of an airplane."

Mitch picked up the remote, turning on the living room surround sound. Music grounded him when he was feeling like that. He settled back into the couch and patted his shoulder. "Put your head down. You're exhausted." Not that he wasn't, but Daniel needed some time to breathe.

"Thank you. I know you didn't have to be nice to me." Daniel leaned—and the man smelled like something herbal and odd. Not unpleasant, just odd.

"I don't have anything to lose by being nice, and a lot more to gain." Like the kids. He needed to stay on Daniel's good side if he wanted to be in their lives. But, Adam's will aside, he didn't think it would be too much of a hardship. Daniel was a good man. Kind. Creative. And he couldn't fault anyone who loved Adam's children.

Obviously Daniel was willing to do what he needed to for them. Hopefully at some point the fact that Adam chose Daniel and not him would make sense. For now, it was starting to sink in at least, and Mitch was less angry and more confused.

He felt Daniel relaxing, getting heavier against his shoulder. He turned up the music a little and tried to just be in the moment, appreciate the company.

5

Daniel propped in the doorway of the baby's room, terrified he'd miss it if Emory woke up in the middle of the night and woke Mitch.

The man already thought he was a waste—which he was, but only accidentally. Mostly he was just clueless.

Still, he was on night duty, so he was watching. Surely this was okay.

Emory sighed, and Daniel crossed the room in a few hurried strides, ready to jump into action. The baby was still and sleeping though, and he exhaled, shaking his head. How was he supposed to know when the kid needed him? Vicki was easy; she'd just tell him so. But this guy?

Maybe he could just sleep right here on the rug. He liked a rug, and his knees felt like jelly.

Just his luck, it wasn't Emory that woke up in the middle of the night; it was Vicki. He heard her voice, and then Mitch's low rumbling answer, thought he couldn't make out what either of them was saying until they walked past the nursery a minute later.

"Daddy gives me water before bed in the blue cup with the pink lid. I like the white straw."

"Okay, baby. Let's see what we can find you."

"And you didn't sing to me before bed." Vicki's tone was indignant.

"Well, you fell asleep early, remember? After painting?"

"I want the blue cup."

"I'll look for it, okay? But if I can't find it, I know where the pink one is." Mitch was doing his best to stay patient, he could tell, but he could hear the tension just under the surface.

"No! I want the blue one!" They passed the nursery right about the time Vicki raised her voice.

"Shhh. Vicki, the baby and Uncle Dan-O are sleeping."

"Dan-O's not. I went to his room first, and he's not there."

"He's...what? Okay, one thing at a time. Let's get you water." Mitch scooped her up and carried her down the stairs.

He followed close behind, not wanting to startle anyone. "I was checking on the baby. I'll help."

Mitch glanced back at him and gave him a nod. "We're on the hunt for a blue cup."

"The one Daddy gives me. It has a pink lid."

Mitch nodded. "It seems to be important."

"Okay. I'm on it. Blue cup, pink lid. Is there a straw?" He started in the dishwasher. That's where dishes usually ended up, after all.

"I like the white ones, there are a bunch over here." Vicki crossed the kitchen and opened a drawer.

"It's not in the dishwasher. I loaded it tonight." Mitch opened a cabinet over his head. "You okay?"

"Yeah. I was trying to make sure the baby was okay. I

worry about him crying." He kept searching for the cup. Blue cup. Pink lid. Blue cup. Pink lid.

Mitch snorted. "That's all he does, you know. Cry I mean. And eat, poop...laugh. But a lot of crying. It's okay." Mitch opened another cabinet and a bunch of cups fell out. "Oh, Sh—*wow*."

"Indeed. Sh-wow. Are any of these your cup, angel?" What did he know? He wanted to give Mitch a break. Go him!

Vicki leaned against him. "Blue cup!"

Mitch pointed to the counter. "Pink lid. Hallelujah."

"White straw. Are you a water or a milk or a juice person, Vicki?"

"You have water at night Dan-O."

Well, okay then. "Sounds great. Ice?"

"No, please. Too cold." Vicki handed Mitch her straw, and he stuck it through the lid and handed it back, then started cleaning up the plastic cups that had fallen out of the cabinet.

Daniel filled her cup up and screwed the lid on. "Are you ready to come back to bed now?"

"Okay." She held her arms out for him to pick her up. "Was the painting okay?"

"It was perfect. I am so proud of you. You let yourself feel and make art." He helped her head upstairs. "That's so hard, and you are so brave."

"I was mad. And sad. I hate cancer."

"Cancer sucks," Mitch agreed, following behind them.

"It so sucks. You, though? You're amazing." Absolutely breathtaking, and he loved her so much. He loved the baby too, but abstractly, like you loved family.

"I love you, Uncle Dan-O." Vicki hugged him around the

neck and kissed his cheek. "Uncle Mitch, is it okay if Uncle Dan-O tucks me in?"

"Of course, baby. Whatever you want." Mitch slowed up in the hall upstairs, stopping by Emory's room.

He headed into her bedroom and pulled the covers back. "I love you, you know that right?"

"I know. Daddy said so too." She climbed back into bed, took a sip of her water and handed him the cup.

"Where does it go? Here on the nightstand?" She nodded, and he put the cup down. "Should we sing tonight or read a book?"

"Read." That was a definite answer. She tugged a book out of her nightstand and handed it to him, then scooted down into the covers. "Uncle Mitch sings. You read to me, okay?" Her eyes were already closing. He didn't think they'd get very far into the book.

"Perfect. Uncle Mitch sings. I read. I got it." He chuckled and shook his head. "Okay, let's see. Once upon a time—"

She lasted through the third page, and then she was out. Boom.

That was when Emory started fussing. Mitch was on it, though, he heard low murmurs and a dim light went on in the nursery.

Lord have mercy, Adam. What the fuck were you thinking, dying on these babies? I would have gone in your place. In a second.

He watched Vicki sleep for a few minutes before getting up and wandering back toward his room. Mitch came out of Emory's room at the same time and they ran into each other in the hallway. Mitch's dark robe made him look a little bit shadowy.

"Hey. Sorry that she woke you. I was trying to let you sleep, but I screwed it up."

"What do you mean? She's five; she's going to wake us up." Mitch's voice was just above a whisper.

"I don't know." He didn't know what he meant. He needed a drink—a drink or a joint or a hug or to talk to Adam.

Daniel hadn't realized how alone—how truly, genuinely solitary—he was until Adam was gone.

Maybe he should go to work. Paint until the pain eased a little.

"Daniel, do you—" Mitch scratched at his beard. "Uh. You should get some sleep."

"Yeah. Goodnight." He couldn't go back in there. He couldn't. "I'm going to grab a Coke."

"Sure." Mitch seemed to be watching him still, but his expression was hard to read in the dark. "Goodnight." Mitch turned and took a few steps away, glanced over his shoulder and then headed for his room.

He didn't know what to do, so he went downstairs to the studio and set to his canvases, sobbing and working out his agony in the only way he knew how.

In sweat, blood, tears, and paint.

6

Daniel was not okay. Fuck, neither of them were, but Daniel was working through something heavy, and Mitch had no idea how to help. He lay awake for a long time before sheer exhaustion knocked him out cold, and he woke up to Vicki tapping on his eyelids.

"Uncle Mitch. Uncle Mitch, wake up."

He put a hand out and pulled his head back. "What's the matter, baby girl?"

"Uncle Dan-O made breakfast. And a mess. And Emory keeps laughing. Get up, Uncle Mitch! It's eggs-es-es."

He chuckled and sat up. "Okay, Vicki. I'm coming. You go on downstairs and eat."

"Hurry up!" She took off down the stairs.

A mess? He didn't care about a mess; he was just thrilled someone else fed the kids breakfast. It was kind of magical.

He hauled himself up, brushed his teeth, and combed his beard. It was time to shave it off. He'd tried it out while he was away from work, just because he could, and it amused Adam to tease him about it. Looking like a Vermont mountain man was completely acceptable, but it wasn't really *him*.

Soon. He'd shave it soon. Tonight maybe.

He pulled on sweats and a T-shirt before heading downstairs. "I hear there's breakfast!"

"Yes, sir. Eggs and toast. Coffee?" Daniel looked like he'd been thrown up on by paint, eggs, and...sweet potatoes?

"Yes, please. And coffee. I'll get it." He grabbed a mug and went to the coffeemaker, passing Emory on the way who was practicing picking up Cheerios and dropping them on the floor. Now that Mitch was closer to Daniel he could see the dark circles under the man's eyes. "Did you get any sleep?"

"I don't know. Maybe. The hour between five and six is a little fuzzy."

He poured his coffee with one eye on Daniel, watching him sway a little on his feet. "Why don't you sit, man? I can manage here. Go sit."

"I made scrambled eggs. There's juice too."

"Thank you. It smells great. Vicki, why don't you pull out a chair for Uncle Dan-O." That should help get him moving.

"I like eggs-es." Vicki went and pulled out a chair, patting the seat. "Sit!"

He scooped a spoonful of eggs onto Emory's tray, then grabbed a slice of toast from the toaster and made a plate for himself.

Emory slammed his fist into the eggs, the curds going flying all over Daniel.

Daniel sat there for a second, then he cracked up, just howling with laughter.

The baby looked rather pleased with himself.

"Ew! Gross, Emory!" Vicki laughed too, once Daniel did, bouncing in her seat.

Mitch grabbed a dishrag and wet it, then went over and started cleaning Daniel up. "Never a dull moment with a baby, huh?"

"No. No, he has an amazing laugh, doesn't he?"

"You too." He brushed the rag over Daniel's cheek. "You have a great laugh also."

"Thanks." Daniel's eyes looked almost bruised, so dark and baggy. "So does beating up the eggs mean he likes them?"

He chuckled. "Who knows? I have no idea. I think it might mean he's full." He stepped back, his bare foot landing in a pile of eggs and Cheerios. Lovely. He brushed off his feet. "Nobody move, I'm getting the broom."

"You should eat. Your eggs will get...cold." Daniel handed Vicki her fork and saved the rest of Emory's eggs.

"Nice catch. I haven't eaten a hot meal since I moved in. Oh, except the chicken you guys brought home. That was warm." He swept and Daniel held the dustpan for him and they got the floor picked up quickly.

"I can make chili and stew and pancakes and stuff."

He smiled. Daniel was so sweet, really. Kind. He understood why Adam had liked him so much. "That sounds great. Maybe Emory will cooperate and let us eat once in a while."

"Emory is a poophead." Vicki took a bite of toast and grinned as she chewed it.

"Actually, he's sort of a poopbutt." Daniel never even hesitated.

Vicki snickered. "Poopbutt!"

Oh boy. "Have fun with that one, *Dan-O*."

"Well, that is where the poop comes out, right?"

"Poopbutt!" Vicki took off into the house, toast in hand. "Poopbutt! Pooooop. Butt!"

Emory squealed in delight and pounded his tray.

Daniel began to chuckle, amusement obvious on the man's face. Oh, mischievous man!

Maybe he didn't need to worry so much after all. Daniel still looked like hell, but he seemed better now that he'd sat for a minute. "You know, you're not the kind of uncle that can wind the kids up and then leave them to their parents. You're stuck with them." He raised his eyebrow over a piece of toast.

"I'm never going to be the one that is good at the rules. I never have been."

"You're going to have to stick to some eventually. You're a parent now."

"Yeah. I don't know why he wanted me."

His knee-jerk reaction was to say he had no idea either. Except that wasn't fair, or true, because the more time he spent with Daniel the more he saw it. The kids would know art, and fun, and joy with Daniel. Maybe that had been more important to Adam than education, discipline, and practicality, which was more what Mitch had to offer.

Though the kids would have just as much love from either of them and, in the end, that was what mattered most, wasn't it?

"I do. And you love them and that's important. We'll figure it out between us."

"Thank you." Daniel reached out and took his hand, squeezing his fingers. "I mean it."

He inhaled sharply and stared into Daniel's eyes, shocked as the touch burned into his skin. Mitch found himself squeezing Daniel's hand in return, not sure what to say, or what to do next.

Christ, he was exhausted and heartsick, and Daniel was kind, if a little clueless, and the connection was welcome.

"You—you're welcome. Thank you for...this." He patted the back of Daniel's hand and then let go. "And breakfast."

"Of course. It was just eggs, but... I'm a little off my game." Daniel rolled his eyes. "Okay, let's be honest. I'm not sure I have a game."

"Yeah, well. Whatever game I'm playing, I keep making up the rules, and they change constantly." He sat in the seat Vicki had left with his breakfast and ate like he hadn't seen food in days.

"That makes perfect sense." Daniel rested his head on his hand, blinking over at him.

"You didn't sleep, and you look it. You do know that you don't have to watch a baby sleep, right? He'll let you know if he needs you, and he's a pretty good sleeper."

"I just—I wanted you to be able to sleep. I feel stupid, you know, and lost."

"You're not stupid, and you're not lost. You belong here." He shrugged and swallowed another bite of eggs. "There's no manual for this shit, you know? And the kids don't care if everything is perfect. You know what they need. Vicki especially, you're amazing with her."

"I love her. I love the little bit, too. I just worry I'll drop him on his head."

"You won't. Not on purpose anyway." He gave Daniel a smile. "Hey. Today is supposed to be PJs and movies and naps and not worrying, remember? Just...us."

"Yes. PJs and movies and pizza. Relaxing together." Daniel offered him a watery smile. "I want us to be good friends."

"I do too." His frustration over Adam's decision had subsided overnight. It would be better for the kids. "I want to be helpful. I want to be in their lives...we should be friends. It's not like it's some awful chore, Daniel. I like you."

He'd developed an odd affection for the artist—Daniel was earnest, and he had a good heart. And if he was honest, the man was easy on the eyes, too.

"Thank you. I—"

Vicki came barreling in, wearing a rainbow tutu and a sequined purple cape with no shirt. "Look! I'm Princess LouLouBelle!"

Daniel didn't even blink. "Dude. Rock on. I love the cape."

He chuckled. "Look at you! Does Princess LouLouBelle like movies? Because Uncle Dan-O and I think we should have a lazy, snuggly, movie day. And pizza later."

"Yeah? Can we watch *Coco*? *Coco* goes to where my daddy is. If I sing lots, maybe I can go too."

"Does he? That's cool. I don't know *Coco*."

"You don't have to go there; your daddy is right here in this house. He hears you sing, watches you paint. As long as you love him and remember, he's still here in spirit." He pulled her over and hugged her. "I haven't seen *Coco* either. We'll watch that first."

"Okay. Is everything going to be all right now?" she asked him, her eyes filling with tears.

"Of course, baby." He glanced at Daniel. He wasn't entirely sure what she meant, but whatever it was, hell yes, they were going to make it all right now.

Daniel nodded like he got it. "Uncle Mitch is here. I'm here. We are going to make it okay, I swear."

"Promise?"

"Yes." God help him, but Daniel sounded like he meant it.

He gave Daniel a nod and then kissed Vicki's cheek. "Okay. Princesses are very sensitive and need shirts to watch movies because it's chilly in the other room. Slippers and a blanket might be a good idea too." He'd start a fire in the stove if it got cold.

Vicki's eyes went wide as saucers. "Oh...we're going to have a slumber party? All of us? Can I bring my babies?"

"Yes, but they might need a spot on the bench, the one by the wall? Because bigger people and your baby brother are going to be hogging the couch." And that was all he needed, to sit on one of her babies by mistake or for Emory to get hold of a doll's hair. That would lead to tears for sure.

Daniel stood with a soft groan and headed for the kitchen. "Let me clean this up, and then I'll bring down blankets and pillows, okay?"

"Hey." He hopped up and followed. "Why don't you go grab a shower? I'll clean up, and then we can all get comfy."

Daniel looked a little bit stunned, not to mention utterly exhausted. "You don't mind? I'll be quick as a bunny. I swear."

"We have all day. Take your time. I've got this." He'd been doing it pretty much alone for a couple of weeks. He could handle another half an hour. "Seriously. It's all good."

"Thank you. I'll be fast. I swear." Daniel hurried off, and Vicki came to him for another hug.

"Dan-O was crying when I waked up. He misses Daddy too."

Mitch looked at the empty doorway that Daniel had just rushed through and sighed. He needed to find some time when the kids were quiet to talk to Daniel. "I know, he does. I do too. Your daddy was special, huh? So many people miss him." He hugged her freely. It was the easiest thing in the world to do and made her feel so much better. "It's going to take a little time, you know? You don't have to be okay all the time. Nobody does. But it will get better very soon, you'll see."

She nodded. "You and Dan-O are here to take care of us. Daddy said."

"That's right. That's my job, baby. And Dan-O's too." Adam said that? Both of them? Why didn't Adam just have a damn conversation with him?

"I was scared that I'd go to a orfage and be sad," she whispered. "Daddy said never ever, that I would have a family."

He hugged her close. "Always. I'm not going anywhere. I'm yours forever." He knew that feeling, being afraid he'd never have a family, and he never really did. He wasn't walking away from these kids for anything. Not even a stupid will. "Daddy loved you, and he was right. You have Daniel and me and Emory. You'll be okay."

She sniffled and nodded. "You and Dan-O and the baby. We're a family."

"We are." Family was what you wanted it to be after all. Okay, time for a distraction. He'd discovered the key to parenting a five-year-old was redirection. "Hey. I need to load the dishwasher and clean up. I really need your help. Can you please bring me all the dishes from the table?" He kissed her and set her on her feet.

True to her nature, Vicki loved to be helpful and ran over to the table. It wasn't a streamlined process, but the kitchen got cleaned up and nothing broke, so he counted it as a win. Emory was getting a little fussy though. "Go get a shirt and your babies and bring them to the den, okay? I'm going to change your brother."

"Okay. I'll be quicky-bunny!"

"Did you hear that buddy? She's going to be *quicky-bunny*." He let her run off and chattered to Emory in that goofy voice the kid liked as they made their way up the stairs, shaking his head. He hadn't planned on kids, and here he was anyway. Adam was right, life chose you.

Daniel was coming out of the guest bath as he came up the stairs, the lean body bare except for a towel. There wasn't a spare ounce of fat on the man.

He blinked at Daniel, not meaning to stare, but staring anyway. "Wow. You're...tan."

"I work naked a lot." Just like that—like it was totally normal.

"Naked...outside. Well, I guess that saves time cleaning up." *What? What the hell, Mitch?* A little tan skin had him saying stupid shit. "I better—you need to—Emory needs a diaper." Good lord. What was the matter with him?

"Oh, you want me to do it? I can. I did one this morning, even though Vicki had to help me with the bodysuit thing."

"Go get dressed." He frowned, because that came out weirdly—more like an order than a suggestion. "You know, before Vicki sees you in nothing but a towel."

Sure. Vicki. Because he wasn't turned on by Daniel in a towel, right? God, he was acting like an idiot.

"Oh. Right." Daniel's smile disappeared, and he slipped through the guest room door, closing it with a soft click.

He sighed and rolled his eyes at himself. Daniel had finally been smiling and he killed the moment. Dammit. He started moving again, heading for the nursery. "Okay, stinky boy. Let's get you changed."

"Dan-O? Can you carry my blanket to the living room?" Vicki asked, and Daniel's door opened, the man totally hidden in masses of huge clothing.

"Sure, angel. You tell me what to carry. I'm your pack mule."

"My blanket and...oh! Can you carry my pillow too?" He watched them disappear toward Vicki's room. He told himself all that clothing was because Daniel was cold, not because he'd said something stupid that made Daniel feel self-conscious. It was Vermont. Everyone not from the north got cold, even in summer.

Emory was his usual sweet self while Mitch changed him and got him dressed, then he headed downstairs to put the baby in the play yard.

Daniel had Vicki piled up in the center of the sofa, her babies and the blankets all organized around her. Daniel was on her far side, and Mitch couldn't even see the man from his place.

He couldn't but feel, as he settled into the couch, that Daniel had done that on purpose. "So... *Coco*?" He turned on the TV, found the movie on one of the zillion streaming channels that Adam had, and started it.

He should have made himself some coffee. He let the movie start and waited for Vicki to be completely engrossed, then hopped up and headed for the kitchen. He tapped Daniel's knee on the way by. "Coffee?"

"Hmm?" Daniel looked up at him, eyes heavy-lidded and tired. "Are you making a pot?"

He nodded. "I am. I'm dying for a cup. Did I wake you? I'm sorry."

"No. No, I was daydreaming. I'd love a cup, thank you."

Olive branch accepted. Perfect. "Great. She's totally in the zone, so she won't move until it's over."

Daniel nodded and stood, following him to the kitchen, rinsing out their mugs from his morning.

"You didn't have to get up. I'd have brought it to you." He grabbed the coffee pot and went to the sink to dump the dregs so he could start fresh.

"Oh. Sorry, I didn't read your clues right. I'll learn."

He put the coffee pot down, took the mug from Daniel and set it down as well, then took Daniel's hands in his. He needed the man's attention; he was so tired, and this was important.

"Daniel. You're doing fine. You don't have to learn my clues. You don't have to defer to me on anything. You don't have to be perfect or have all the answers. You don't even have to have any right now. We're all just making the best of this, you know?" He squeezed Daniel's hands. He hadn't expected to be so caught by those deep green eyes, and he hadn't expected this to matter so much to him all of a sudden. "I'm sorry if I sounded harsh or if I upset you this morning over the towel thing. I'm not really operating at a hundred percent either."

And all that tan skin and lean muscle against a barely there white towel? God, this was so not like him. He looked down at Daniel's hands and smoothed his thumbs over them. "Honestly. I'm sorry. It's all just been…"

"Hard. And you were here the whole time keeping things together." Daniel pulled him into a hug and held him, arms cradling him like he needed this.

It was the least he could do. Adam was family.

He didn't shy away from the hug and leaned in a little, returning it, hands sliding over Daniel's back. Daniel rested hard against him, soft sobs beginning to shake the man, but he never made a sound.

Mitch nodded against Daniel's shoulder and rubbed his back. He got it. He understood. He didn't really know what to say and he was all out of tears himself, but he absolutely knew what Daniel was feeling.

This sucked—for everyone including Adam, for chrissake—and they were going to have to find a way to cope now. Together, apparently.

Daniel straightened up, swallowing hard. "Right. Coffee. Then TV and pizza."

"Onward. Maybe we can sneak in a nap when the kids do." He let Daniel go a little reluctantly and picked up the coffee pot again.

"Sounds perfect. I could use a little nap, and I bet you could too."

"I could sleep for three days I think, but a nap would be a great start." Mitch set up the coffee and started it brewing. "For now? Coffee." He leaned against the counter and watched Daniel. "I bet you're going to miss all the traveling, huh?"

"I don't know. I mean—I guess? But I can make art here, right?"

"You have already. Which reminds me, I haven't had a look at what you did last night. Vicki told me you'd been painting."

"I was. My soul hurts, and I'm confused and scared. It's how I bring myself to rights, you know? Sometimes it's the thing that makes sense." There was such a straightforward honesty there, this odd surety that was so unusual.

"They're just kids, Daniel. I'm pretty sure nobody really knows what they're doing, they just...do it and hope for the best."

"Well, I will do my best. We'll just be crazy artists together, right? Running under the moon and breaking through walls."

He chuckled as the coffee finished brewing. "Maybe leave the walls as they are?"

"Yeah—load bearing is a thing. I remember. Adam and I learned that together."

He winced. "Ouch?" He wondered whether Adam and Daniel had ever been together. Or...fuckbuddies or something. Casual lovers. It didn't seem right to ask, though, it was none of his business. "When you built the sun porch?"

"When he decided he wanted a great room instead of a formal dining. It was...not pretty. At all. Or cheap to fix." Daniel's laugh was soft, bittersweet. "We got each other into trouble. A lot. Tina despaired at the thought that we'd end up in jail together." Daniel's smile disappeared. "If you'd told me that we would lose them both in fifteen months... I mean, Jesus."

Adam's wife had been a sweetheart and balanced all of Adam's energy so well. It was right after Tina's car accident that he'd started helping out with the kids sometimes. Even before Adam got his cancer diagnosis. It was no wonder Vicki followed one or the other of them around all day; she was probably afraid of losing anyone else.

"Yeah. Jesus." Was it too early for Baileys in his coffee?

"Are you religious? Do you know what Adam would want us to tell the kids about Heaven and shit?"

He shrugged. "You're the godfather, you tell me. If Adam chose a godfather for his kids, it's safe to assume he believed in something, but we never really talked about religion."

"Oh. Well, he knows I believe in a universal goodness, that what good we do lives on. Maybe that's enough."

"It sounds good to me. I'm...not sure about this stuff. I'll follow your lead." He didn't know what he believed himself. Something...he believed in something. He just wasn't sure what. He filled their coffee mugs and handed one to Daniel.

"I think that's cool. I'm not sure I trust people that *know* things you can't know."

"Faith is complicated stuff. Personal stuff." He shrugged. "Right now, I believe in this coffee." He took a sip, the warmth steadying him. "And us. We've got this."

"Yeah." Daniel wrapped his hands around the cup. "We'd better get in there before Emory reprograms his See and Say to summon a demon."

He laughed and nudged Daniel. "It could happen."

"I have no doubt. They're both already smarter than me."

"You and me both." It probably wasn't true of either of them, but Daniel had a way of putting himself down and Mitch was never sure how to respond to it. "After you. Time to go sit with the dolls and pretend we're not outnumbered."

7

Daniel felt like he was watching the world through a foggy lens. He'd taken the rental car back, he'd washed his one pair of jeans, and he'd gone to talk to the lawyer with Mitch.

Mitch got the business and control of the kids' money. He got the house and cars and the job of raising the kids. It was fair, he guessed. He didn't really know how to deal with big money—his manager did it for him. Money kind of stressed him out.

So now it was supposed to be normal life and stuff, but he wasn't sure how to manage that. Shit, he wasn't sure how to begin to manage it.

The babysitter had been a good idea though. And so was heading for the bar after their meeting with the lawyer. Mitch had all kinds of good ideas.

"Two Green State Lagers." The bartender set two pints on the bar.

"Thanks." Mitch picked his up. "Here's to...legal shit that probably isn't going to have any bearing on how we handle things."

"Yeah." Daniel clinked their glasses together and drank deep. Oh, beer bubbles. He'd needed that.

"So...this is the beginning of the rest of our lives, huh?" Mitch laughed, turning bright blue eyes on him. "Do you ever feel like Adam is getting the last laugh here?"

"Are you kidding? He's losing his goddamn mind." He had no doubt. None.

"For sure. Bastard." Mitch sipped his beer. "So we need to talk about how this is going to work, Daniel. What you need, what your expectations are."

"Okay." How the fuck was he supposed to know? He guessed that his bank account could feed the kids and keep them in blue jeans. Keep them clean and fed, don't let them die. Beyond that, he had no idea.

Mitch glanced at him. "Do you want me to keep living at the house?"

"Do you want to? I mean, you have a whole life and shit, right?" How evil would he be to be all "please don't go" when this wasn't Mitch's fault.

"Well, I have work, but...the kids are a lot of that life now." Mitch looked at his beer and shrugged. "And you."

"You know you're welcome there. You belong there, don't you?" Way more than he did, if he was honest. He was a wanderer.

Mitch nodded. "Well, I hope I do. I know it's an odd arrangement but... I think it would be easier than trying to schedule things. And better for the kids to have us both around."

Daniel thought that sounded amazing. He wasn't as scared of the baby as he had been—so far he hadn't broken Emory—and Vicki was easy, but he loved the idea that they could help each other a little bit.

"Would you mind if we stopped by my apartment before

we headed home? If I'm going to be living at the house and going back to work I need some work clothes and some files, my work laptop, some other stuff." Mitch's eyes went wide. "Oh. I didn't even ask if you thought you were ready for me to go back to work."

"Well, we won't know until we do it, but at some point we both have to work, so let's do it. If there's a catastrophe, y'all's office is what? Five minutes away?" It made sense.

"More like half an hour. But around here that's a quick commute. So...my place for a minute? Cool?"

"Of course. Whatever you need, huh?" Daniel was easy. He wanted to make this okay. Hell, he wanted to go to sleep and wake up and Adam would be here.

Mitch nodded and gulped the last of his beer. "How's your beer? It's a local brew. Not bad, right?"

"I like it." He sipped again. "Nice and malty. So...tell me something about you. All I know is that you're the best business partner ever."

"Um. Well, you know I play guitar. I used to play on Thursday nights at this bar on Church Street before— before. And I ski in the winter a lot. I was practically born with skis on my feet. I'm from around here—Waitsfield. I went to college in Boston and came back because I love it here."

"I've never skied. I was nineteen before I saw snow, but I've seen a lot of it by now." Adam had never taken him skiing—they'd just never had time, if he was honest.

"Adam and I have taken Vicki. She's a natural. We'll go this winter for sure." Mitch dropped a twenty on the bar. "What do you do besides paint?"

"I like to play cards, I love music, I meditate. Uh... I read quite a bit, and I love puzzles." He lived a fairly quiet life, really. He parked his trailer on a quiet piece of land, painted, moved on. "Oh, I love being outside in the sunshine."

"We have that in common at least. You ready?" Mitch winked at him and slid off his stool. "I've tried meditating, I get so bored. And I don't know any card games."

"No? I love them all—bridge, spades, gin rummy, canasta, hearts, pinochle, whist. I love to play." Daniel stood and followed along behind. "Thank you for the beer, sir."

"My pleasure. You can teach me some card games. You think Vicki is too young? Are there easy ones?" Mitch pulled his keys out of his pocket.

"Crazy Eights. Vicki is ready for that, absolutely. Go Fish too." He amused the hell out of himself.

"Right on." Mitch opened the car door for him. "Count me in."

"I know Adam has a lot of games in that one closet. There are cards in there." Backgammon, chess, Sorry—there were a ton of games.

Mitch closed his door for him after he climbed in and moved around to the driver's side of the truck. "Technically, I'm walkable from here but I'm not sure how much stuff I'm going to pack yet."

"You just point me and shoot me." Daniel felt like he was walking on eggshells because he just didn't know what was right.

Mitch was quiet on the short drive to his place and parked in a tiny private parking lot behind his building. "You want to come in, or wait for me?"

"I can't help from down here..." Was that the right answer? God, he was fucking tired of having to think.

"Thanks. Come on." Mitch smiled and slid out of the truck, leading him to a backdoor and a staircase. The door at the top opened into a tiny kitchen. Mitch flicked on the lights. "It's little, but it's a neat place. Wow. It feels weird to be back here. It's been a while."

"I bet. Would you like me to clean out the fridge? That way you aren't having rotten food."

"I did a lot of that when I left, but I'm still kind of afraid to open it." Mitch shook his head. "I didn't rush out of here, but I didn't expect to be gone this long either."

"No. No, sure you didn't. I promise not to judge. I emptied my minifridge out, because I intended to stay for a few weeks." He tried out a wink. "Point me toward the trash bags."

"Uh..." Mitch pointed. "Under the kitchen sink. Are you sure about this? I mean... I can't promise it's not going to be gag-worthy in there."

"I'm a single dude with a minifridge and a cooler. I know from gag-worthy." He wasn't scared. Hell, he'd seen what came out of Emory's butt. That had been like green, sticky slime.

"All right. Go for it then. Good luck. There's a dumpster at the bottom of the stairs. We passed it on the way in." Mitch shook his head. "Thanks, Daniel. I've got suits to pack."

"No problem." He turned his phone on and got to work, sorting trash from take to the house from ask Mitch. It was straightforward work, and he managed both fridge and freezer in short order. He took the trash load down, then went to ask about whether Mitch wanted the pantry done.

He found Mitch in the bedroom. There was a suitcase out on the bed, packed but not closed and a garment bag with a couple of suits lying on top of it. Along one wall was a huge collection of vinyl records, tall speakers and a vintage turntable.

"Hey! You survived! I'm almost done."

That was a great wall. He did love a person who liked music. "Love your vinyl. That's great. Did you want anything from the pantry?"

"I don't think so. But you know what I want to find? I have this YETI mug. It would be good to have for my commute to work." Mitch looked at the collection, then closed his suitcase. "Yeah, the vinyl is too much to move right now, but I miss it."

"I bet. It's amazing. YETI cup. I'm on it." He started with the dishwasher. Those would be the things Mitch used the most.

By the time he'd found it, Mitch had the garment bag all zipped up and lay it on the kitchen counter. "Did you find it? It's this awful burnt orange color I know, but I like it."

"That's a lovely color." He had gone to school in Austin, after all. He hadn't graduated, but he'd gone. "And I did find it."

"Yeah? Oh. Yeah that's it. It has a lid. Like a travel mug lid? It might be up here the cabinet." Mitch took a step toward him and tripped over the rolling suitcase, tried to catch himself but missed and landed hard, flat on his back on the kitchen floor.

"Oh, Jesus!" Daniel rushed forward and damn near went over too. "Are you okay? Should I help you up? Call 911?"

"I'm...good. I'm okay." Mitch sighed, then lifted a hand and waved for him to come closer.

He reached out to help Mitch up. He didn't want to hurt the man's head, for fuck's sake.

Mitch took his hand and blinked at him a few times, then instead of accepting a hand up, he pulled Daniel down.

And kissed him.

Oh.

Oh, okay.

Daniel blinked, meeting Mitch's eyes in pure confusion, but his body wasn't near as dumb as his brain, so he just kissed Mitch right back.

Mitch let it end naturally, then searched his eyes. "Sorry. That was impulsive. So...if that was cool with you, great. And if not, I'm blaming it on hitting my head, and we can laugh about it on the ride home."

"It was—unexpected, but, yeah. Cool." And wild, a little weird. Hugely sweet, and he wanted to try it again.

"Yeah?" Mitch kissed him again. "Still cool?" When he nodded, he got another quick kiss. "How about now?"

Who knew Mitch was funny? Shit. He started chuckling, tickled as a man with a feather up his butt.

"Well, well, Daniel." Mitch dropped his head back down again and his blue eyes sparkled in the bright kitchen lights. "You're creative, talented, handsome, *and* a good kisser."

"No one's ever said that to me before. Thanks. I'd like to be a good kisser." He wasn't a virgin, but he wasn't in the presence of folks much. He worked, he drove, he got the occasional mutual rub off in an alley.

"Well, you are. Just because no one else has said doesn't make it not true." Mitch tapped his chest. "I better sit up."

"Let me help you." He hauled Mitch up, watching the man's head. "So is it falling or kitchen floors that turn you on?"

"Neither. It was just—whoa." Mitch grabbed his shoulder to steady himself and stood there a second. "Okay. Better. You're so oblivious."

"You are not the first human on earth to accuse me of that..." He was a little in his own head.

"Sorry. It's not an accusation. But I got a babysitter, I took you out after our meeting, bought you a beer, brought you back here where we're finally alone...and you offered to clean out my fridge. So I figured it was a big no. The fall was kind of a...last ditch effort."

"Oh... Oh!" He blinked at Mitch. "I didn't even consider it. I mean, I—" He hadn't allowed himself to even think sexy thoughts. He had been functioning on autopilot. "I'm glad you fell."

Mitch smiled and slid a hand along his jaw. "Me too. And I'm glad it worked." Mitch's fingers tightened just under his ear and pulled him into another kiss.

Daniel spent months and months alone, and he usually had to focus, to remember what it felt like to be aroused, to crave. Mitch was intent on helping him with that, he thought.

Mitch leaned into him. "You okay?"

"I am. Stunned and pondering being hard as a rock." That was as clear as he could be.

One eyebrow climbed slowly toward Mitch's hairline. "Weighing the pros and cons? Because there are cons. But those are all kind of a buzzkill. I'm a pro."

"No. Just trying to catch up." Because he was a little slow, but he wasn't stupid. "Because trust me, I want to catch up. You're happy making."

Mitch laughed and ran a hand through his long hair, all the way to the ends. "Thank you. I would like to make you happy. And I don't want to rush you. I just wanted you to know... I wanted you to notice me."

"I was scared to, I think. To notice, I mean. I didn't know I was allowed to."

"Are there rules?" Mitch's head tilted curiously.

"I don't know. Are there? I more meant I didn't want to offend you, you know? I wouldn't insult you by coming on to you."

"I guess you have better manners than I do, country

boy." Mitch leaned in for another kiss and they were both startled by the phone vibrating in Mitch's front pocket. "Damn. Nobody calls me. I bet that's the—" Mitch pulled back and fished his phone out. "Yep. Babysitter."

Mitch answered it and Daniel could hear Vicki's voice talking a mile a minute on the other end. "Hey, baby girl. Yes, I told you I'd answer if...we'll be home really... Vicki. Baby. Hey, listen to me. We're—yes. We're coming home. Here's Uncle Dan-O." Mitch handed him the phone. "You talk, I'll drive."

"Hey, angel, what's up? We're grabbing some stuff for Uncle Mitch." And macking on each other... He grabbed the box of food.

"Where are you? Are you coming home now? You've been gone a long time. Can you come home now?" Mitch grabbed his suitcase and the garment bag and followed him out. Vicki sniffled into the phone. "Please?"

Sweet baby. He nodded, not caring that she couldn't see him. "Yes. We can. Do you need me to stop and get anything on our way?"

"No. Well. Maybe ice cream. But quick." Five-year-old priorities. "Ali says Ben and Jerry's Peanut Butter Fudge is the best, but I like Milk and Cookies."

"Milk and Cookies ice cream? Sounds perfect. What kind do I like?"

"You? I don't know, silly." Vicki sounded confused for a second, but it didn't take her long. "Do you like chocolate?" Mitch packed the truck and they got moving.

"I love chocolate. Love it." He dared to reach over to hold Mitch's thigh.

Without missing a beat, Mitch dropped a hand from the steering wheel and curled their fingers together.

"Do you like...strawberry?" Oh, this turned out to be a good game. It sounded like Vicki was pretty well distracted.

"I love strawberries, angel, but cherries are my favorite." He stroked Mitch's hand with his thumb, drawing a circle.

"Cherry," he heard Vicki say, and then a soft voice that was obviously Ali. "Ali says there's a cherry one. Cherry..."

"Garcia," Ali prompted.

"Cherry Garcia. You get that one. Emory doesn't like ice cream. It's too cold and he spits it out."

"Are we stopping?" Mitch pointed to the little grocery up the road.

He nodded. "We need Cherry Garcia, Milk and Cookies, and something for you and Ali. Angel, what did you say for Ali? Peanut butter fudge?"

"Yes. She's weird." Vicki giggled, which was a long way from the tears of a few minutes ago.

Mitch pulled into the parking lot. "I'm on it."

Vicki sighed. "Ali says I have to let you drive. You're coming home right? Soon?"

"Uncle Mitch is driving. I am at the grocery store to buy ice cream and then I'm home. We'll have sweets and snuggle, okay?"

"Promise?"

"Pinky promise." He held out his little finger, even if she didn't know.

"Okay. Love you. Bye." Vicki didn't hang up. Ali's voice came over the line next.

"Thank you. She was pretty freaked out that you guys weren't home yet."

"She just needing some time. Thanks for calling. I'll be home in two shakes."

"I've got her. We're going to put Emory down together and then read a book. See you soon." Ali hung up.

"Man, she's wigged." He handed Mitch his phone back. "Four pints of ice cream for us."

He didn't even want ice cream, but if Vicki wanted it, ice cream it was.

Mitch sighed, nodding like he understood. "People she loves keep disappearing on her."

"Yes. So, you and me? We won't." Right? God, he hoped not. He wanted to be her rock.

"Not ever. No matter what." Mitch squeezed his fingers. "You running in or am I?"

"I'll go. Do we need anything else? Text me if you think of anything." He jogged in, hunting ice cream like a man on a goddamn mission.

He had a moment of panic when he couldn't find Vicki's Milk and Cookies, but he finally dug up one pint way in the back like it had been hidden there just for her.

Thank god.

He got in line and was just about to pay when he remembered to check his texts.

There was a text from Mitch, just one word. One heady word.

Condoms.

"Good lord and butter." He ducked out of line to grab those, his cheeks burning a bit. He looked like he was having a great time—rubbers and sugar. All he needed was beer and chips to round the visual out.

The young lady at the check-out rung him up without even a smirk, but he got a wink and a grin when she handed him his bags. "Hopefully you won't need the ice cream."

"Keep your fingers crossed for me." He grabbed his bags and jogged out. Lord have mercy.

Mitch had left the truck running and drove off as soon as he'd climbed back in. "Did you find everything?"

"I did." He started chuckling, the laughter feeling almost...odd.

Mitch chuckled too, sounding kind of adorably embarrassed. "Hope springs eternal."

"That's not all that's springing."

They stared at each other for a second, then they cracked up.

"You are such a nerd, Dan." Mitch reached over and took his hand, then hit the gas, hurrying home to their girl.

"You speak the truth." What? He was going to argue? It was true. He was a giant dork, an artist without the slightest clue what he was doing.

And true or not, Mitch was holding his hand, so he was doing something right. Finally.

He hadn't been letting himself even—how could he? The way Mitch had responded to him in a towel, he'd been ashamed.

Now he was wondering if maybe he should have been smug instead.

"You go ahead in. I'll run Ali home. Or is she part of this ice cream party?" Mitch parked the truck in the driveway.

"We got her ice cream, but she sounds ready to go. I'll put ours in the freezer." He leaned over and kissed Mitch's cheek, because he could.

Mitch rewarded him with a sweet smile. "Sounds good, so send her out. Tell Vicki that Ali's mom wants her home. That usually works well."

"Will do." He headed in, catching up a hysterical, exhausted little girl at the front porch. "Hey, Ali. Mitch is going to drive you home. I know your mom wants you."

"I want my daddy! My daddy should want me!"

Ali looked utterly panicked, and he waved her off.

"Your daddy wanted you and Emory more than

anything." He headed into the front room, to the big, overstuffed chair, carrying her along.

This was his job—loving on these babies, letting her know he was here and staying. Letting her know that this pain was natural and reasonable and right.

"He shouldn't have died then. Ali said her aunt had cancer, and *she* didn't *die*." Vicki crossed her arms with a frown only an angry five-year-old could muster.

"That's not fair. That's not fair at all, because you deserve your daddy." He wasn't going to sugarcoat this shit. It sucked. She deserved to be mad. He was fucking furious.

"Are you done talking to the lawyer guy? You were gone a long time."

"I am done. It took a long time, but I'm here now, and I brought ice cream."

"What did he say?"

He let his head tilt. "The lawyer? That Uncle Mitch and me are going to get to take care of you here in this house."

Vicki gave him a hard look, daring him to lie. "Forever?"

"Forever. I am staying right here with you and Emory." And god help him, he wasn't lying.

She stared at him another second. "And Uncle Mitch too? Forever?"

"I promise I will kick his butt if he tries, but he isn't going. You're his family. We're all family now." Somehow they were going to be. No matter what.

"Pinky." She held up her little hand, pinky raised.

"Pinky swear." He wrapped his finger around hers, holding her gaze. "I will have your back until the end of time."

"Me too. I got you." She gave him a very serious nod and then kissed his cheek.

"Stay and cuddle with me, angel? I'm needing someone

to hold me." He wasn't even trying to distract her. Today had been—big.

"Are you okay, Uncle Dan-O?" She snuggled in hard.

"Yeah. It's just been a big day, you know? My heart feels big in my chest—like I'm trying to feel all the things at once, and I don't know how."

Vicki rubbed his chest. "I feel a lot too." She rested her head on his shoulder. "Does that feel better?"

"It does. You make things easier because you love me so good."

She rested her head on his shoulder and nodded against him. "Uncle Mitch will be home soon." He wasn't sure if she was trying to convince him or herself.

"Uh-huh. He's just taking Ali home. Rest your eyes for me." He closed his eyes, holding her baby body. They could relax a second—Emory was sleeping, Mitch was heading home. All was well.

8

When Mitch got home, he lifted Vicki right out of Daniel's arms and left Daniel out cold in the big chair. She woke up enough to give him a kiss but was too floppy to help much as he got her undressed and into her nightgown. He tucked her in with her babies and turned on the nightlight before he left the room, not feeling the least bit guilty about not having brushed her teeth. His goal wasn't perfection, it was just to do his best and make sure she had everything she needed.

He poked his head in on Emory, who was sound asleep like the little angel he was. Man, if he had to have a baby dropped into his lap, he'd done well.

Mitch wandered downstairs again, finding the ice cream still in the bags and completely melted in the front hall. He scooped it all up and put the pints in the freezer—they'd look weird, but they'd freeze up again just fine. He had another chuckle as he almost put the condoms into the freezer with everything else. That had been a bold text. And Daniel had bought them just as boldly.

He opened a Coke, tossed the box of condoms on the

steps so he wouldn't forget to take it up, and wandered again, this time drawn into the front room to check on Daniel. Daniel absolutely did not need checking on, but he was lovely lying there, face relaxed, totally dead to the world.

He'd done all his second-guessing and dreamed up all the disastrous what-ifs he could think of on the ride back from dropping off Ali. The doubts hadn't lasted long. Daniel's hand had felt too right in his and their kisses had been too heady.

Daniel snored softly, hand searching for something—maybe Vicki, maybe him. Then he relaxed down again with a sigh.

Mitch set his Coke down and pulled a blanket off the back of the couch. He didn't think he should wake Daniel; it seemed like the man had enough trouble sleeping, so he covered Daniel up and tucked the blanket in a little. He dared to give Daniel a light kiss on the forehead before picking his drink up and heading upstairs.

Remembering the rubbers because they might need them one day.

That made him grin, wondering if there would ever be an hour that the kids didn't need them. It seemed doubtful.

Mitch was exhausted anyway. He took a long, hot shower and then climbed into bed, fully expecting to find a movie to watch while he pondered a late dinner, but never even managed to find the remote before he crashed.

The soft sound of his bedroom door opening brought him out of his dream. He opened his eyes, expecting to see Vicki and getting Daniel instead.

"Oh. Hey, man. Everything okay?" He sat up on his elbow, squinting at Daniel. "Is it Vicki? She didn't really get dinner." Jesus Daniel was quiet, and still as a stone. "Dan?"

"I—can I come in? See you?" The words seemed tentative, but they didn't sound unsure.

He nodded but wondered whether Daniel could see that with just a sliver of moonlight in the room. "Yes. Yeah. Come...come here." He swung his legs over the edge of the bed, only just then remembering he hadn't dressed after his shower. Well. That was why Daniel was here, he figured. He took a breath and stood, feeling kind of brave, and waited by the bed for Daniel to come to him.

The best part was the click as Daniel locked the door behind him.

That sound echoed.

Daniel came to him, and he could see the shirt was already gone, and the jeans had been replaced with a soft pair of knit pajama pants.

He should probably say something, but words right now felt awkward and unnecessary. Mitch took Daniel's hand as soon as he could reach it and pulled him closer, offering a kiss he didn't expect Daniel would turn down.

Daniel slid right between his legs, hand cupping the back of his head and kissing him back with way more passion than the surprised kisses from earlier in the day.

Somebody had thought about this.

Mitch moaned into the kiss and ran curious hands over Daniel's skin, fingers learning his shape, his muscle.

There wasn't an ounce of fat on Daniel, and the man's body was hard as a rock, muscles jumping under his hand.

He slid his hands into Daniel's pajamas and pushed them down so they could really touch—really feel. Daniel's skin was on fire, burning like he was, and the sensation made Mitch a little high, made his knees a little weak.

The scent of Daniel was a mixture of Ivory soap, sand, and leather somehow, and he inhaled it deep, filling his lungs. He turned Daniel around, pressing kisses across his soldiers and rocking against a perfect ass.

"Damn, honey." The two words were so husky, rough, and full of need.

"Mm. I'm glad you're here." He slid a hand over Daniel's hip and through soft curls to catch the silky, heavy cock in his fingers.

"Jesus, your hand is warm." Daniel's fingers danced over his arm, his hand, petting his skin.

He kept his hand where it was and moved back around in front of Daniel. "Hot, actually. Like you've made the rest of me." He stroked Daniel's beard and leaned in for another kiss. "Making me ache."

"Good." Daniel drew a line down Mitch's belly, heading for his cock, measuring him tip to root.

Daniel had gentle fingers and a hot palm, and Mitch moaned as his cock stretched and filled against it. The fluid he felt building at the tip of Daniel's prick only made him want even more and he spread it around with his thumb.

Daniel went up on tiptoe and rocked up into his touch. "Can I—I want to stretch out with you. Explore."

"God. Me too." Mitch gave him a soft kiss, then tossed his comforter aside and climbed back into bed.

Daniel came right to him, stretching out alongside him. Those callused hands were on him immediately, stroking his spine.

He sighed at the touch. It had been a while since he'd been with anyone, and even longer since he'd wanted anyone to really touch him—to have *him*, and not to just get off with him. It had been a long, shitty, stressful few months but he could already feel Daniel's hands soothing him, taking him away from all of it. Leaving him hungry.

He let his fingers wander, tracing Daniel's ribs and the

curve of his hip, a muscled thigh and a firm round ass. "I need this," he admitted, as honestly as he knew how. "I just want to lose myself in you. With you."

"I'm right here. I got you." Daniel kissed him again, slow this time, damn near drugging him.

This version of Daniel was unexpected but so welcome, and Mitch would just trust because he knew he could. He returned the kiss and hooked a leg over Daniel's thigh, pinning their hips together.

He felt the heat of Daniel's shaft against him, and it made his heartbeat speed, but the pressure of Daniel's fingers around their cocks was even better.

"Yeah." He slid a hand between them, finding a nipple and rolling the round little nub in his fingers. "Feels good, Dan."

"It does." Dan nipped his ear, thumb sliding over the slit of his cock.

He moaned, not caring if it was shameless. "Fuck, you have good hands." He wanted to be patient. He wanted to make out, fool around, take his time. Daniel was worth all of that, deserved all of it. But his balls had other ideas and his cock too, and he rocked into Dan's hand harder than he'd intended.

"Uh-huh. Edge off. Then we can go again." Dan touched him like he was the hottest bastard alive, like he was totally desired.

"Yeah? I don't mean to be..." *An asshole*. He just needed this connection so fucking bad.

"Shh...we're okay. Right now, this is okay."

Shit, it was more than okay. This was amazing.

He nodded and let himself relax, moving with Daniel, breathing in more of that wild desert musk and kissed Daniel deep enough to make him feel as wanted as he did.

Daniel groaned, fist sliding faster as their desire began to slick the way. This was perfect—hungry, fast, and just what he needed.

He bent one knee, changing the angle just slightly, and that was perfect. "Oh. Oh, fuck, Dan." He pressed his forehead into Daniel's shoulder and sucked in an unsteady breath.

"You're like fire." Daniel thrust against him, driving their cocks into his fist with a low groan.

Fire was right. "Dan...gonna..." His orgasm tore right through him, making him gasp and tremble as it burned away the stress and tension, everything he'd kept walled up for so long.

Dan wasn't far behind him, grunting hard as he came, clenching his teeth.

He rested their foreheads together as they each fought for air, hands clutching at Dan's hip. "Dan..."

"Uh-huh. Whoa. I—Whoa."

Right on. Dan was as coherent as he was.

Once he felt like he'd gotten air, he took a couple of kisses, quick ones, stolen between the need for another breath. "So whoa." Dan was the hottest fucking man he'd ever known and all they'd managed was a hand job.

"Yeah. Wild. We—thanks, man. I wanted you. Bad."

It felt good to hear that, made him feel...like a whole person again. "I needed that. Not just that, but that with you."

Daniel met his eyes, so serious, so still. "Thank you. It's good to hear."

Something about Daniel's stillness gave him permission to breathe. "Hard to believe we didn't get interrupted." He chuckled, fingers gliding gently over Dan's warm skin.

Dan's eyes widened. "Shh...she's going to be demanding her ice cream at two a.m., you know."

"She will. She didn't get dinner. She's going to wake up hungry. You think we can sneak in a shower before she wakes up?"

"I think so. I want to. Saving water is good, right?" Dan winked at him, waggling his eyebrows.

"The shower curtain will hide you if she knocks." He pushed Dan onto his back and stole another kiss before climbing out of bed. Only the master bedroom—Adam's bedroom—had its own bathroom. The rest of the upstairs bedrooms shared one. He snagged his robe. "Grab your pants, Dan-O."

"I'm on it." Daniel sat up, rolling his head on his shoulders. "I'll be right there."

"Hey. You okay?" He tugged his robe on and went back to Daniel.

"I am." Daniel glanced up at him with a wry grin. "Best orgasm in years, and it's in Adam's house."

He held out a hand to haul Daniel up. "It was Adam's house. Now, it's your house. You were handed the deed today. There's something poetic about marking the occasion with an orgasm. Maybe two if we're really lucky."

"Two sounds great. I'm a fan of repeats." Dan squeezed his fingers and stood. "And I have been known to be lucky."

"If I rub your belly will I get lucky too?" Mitch winked and tugged Daniel toward the bedroom door.

Daniel pouched his belly out, teasing. "Try it."

He couldn't resist. He stretched out a hand and rubbed in slow circles, eyes on Daniel's. "You know, I forgot. I'm already lucky."

Daniel chuckled softly and caught his hand against the flat belly, and Mitch got a slow roll, the abs solid and strong.

"I didn't know you would be like this."

"Like what? Goofy? I'm an expert at goofball artist."

"No. Sexy. Confident. Hot as hell." He leaned in and kissed Daniel gently.

Daniel grinned at him, cheeks pinking. "I'll take sexy. In fact, I'll take hot as hell too."

"Right? I'm all over that." Mitch laughed and unlocked the door. They passed the master bedroom on the way to the bathroom. "I wonder if we should...the king bed is just up in the attic."

"I—I don't know. I think we have to? Not today. Not tonight. When we've slept."

"Not today. Good lord. I'm hoping we're too worn out to move tomorrow." Mitch closed the bathroom door behind them. "But we probably should. The weekend, maybe."

"Maybe. Yes." Daniel moved to turn the water on, the steam filling the air in short order. "You like it hot?"

"Yes." That answer was true in any context.

"Good. I do too." Daniel moved into the water; the steam surrounded him.

He climbed in and slid the shower curtain closed, then reached for the shampoo. "It's been a heck of day, huh?"

"God yes. It's been—it's like as if every single hour has been a whole day."

He worked shampoo into Daniel's hair, mostly as an excuse to touch. "Some days better than others." He nodded, grinning. "I learned that to get your attention I have to fake injury."

"You—" Daniel snorted inelegantly. "Shit, I was afraid that I was offending you bad. I didn't even let myself look."

"Offending me? How? I looked. I looked a lot. I looked so much I made myself uncomfortable."

"Maybe I read uncomfortable as offensive. That's a thing. I'm alone a lot."

He worked soapy fingers into Daniel's shoulders, still jonesing for that physical connection. "Maybe we're both exhausted and overwhelmed and burned out. I don't think we even know each other at our best."

"No. No, everything is weird—" Daniel's head fell forward. "Dammit. So good."

He had to smile. Daniel was kind of weird too. But a kind of weird he appreciated. "They're not artist's hands but I'm told they have a little magic in them."

"They're just fine." He must have hit a sore spot, because Daniel gasped and went up on tiptoe.

"Too hard? You're pretty tight." He pressed a couple of kisses to Daniel's shoulders. "And you taste good."

"Mmm...thank you. I appreciate it. You. This. A lot."

He smiled to himself, hearing the incoherence building in Daniel's voice. He wanted so much, but he could feel Daniel fading under his fingers. What the man needed most right now was sleep. Maybe sleep in bed with him at least; maybe they could get away with that.

Mitch turned Daniel and leaned him against the shower wall, then scrubbed up quickly so they could get out. Change the sheets. Snuggle maybe.

"Mmm..." Daniel pulled him close, kissing him, long and lazy.

He really liked how Daniel kissed him, like they had all the time in the world. "I'm trying to get us out of here before you fall asleep standing up."

"Am I sleepy?" Daniel held him close, heavy against him.

"Is that a real question?" He stretched out a hand and shut the water off. "Come back to my room."

"Oh, thank you." Daniel stepped out of the tub and handed him a towel. "Yes, please."

They toweled off and dressed enough that they wouldn't terrify a five-year-old, then he took Daniel's hand. "You want to peek in on Emory? I'll just grab clean sheets."

Daniel gave him a warm smile and disappeared, heading toward the baby's room. Daniel treated Emory like he was porcelain, like he was this delicate thing. And that was fine, but boys were going to want to roughhouse sooner or later, and Emory couldn't stay breakable forever.

Mitch was incapable of hiding his smile as he tugged on pajama pants and pulled the sticky sheets off his bed. He just knew this was the start of something good. A slow start, and that was okay—probably good when kids were involved and all the chaos they were still working out. What was the rush?

He found clean sheets and made the bed while Daniel changed Emory, he could hear the little murmurs and the questions, as if Emory had any answers to give.

Then the sound of Emory's little mobile started playing and soon enough Daniel was at his door. "Hey. He's asleep again."

"Nice work. We have clean sheets." He flipped the covers back, watching the way Daniel stood—the questioning look and slight bend in his shoulders despite having already been invited. "Come on in."

"Thank you." Daniel chuckled softly. "Which side is yours?"

"I like the right. And the left. You?" He took Daniel's hand.

"I have a travel trailer with a pull-out couch. I just fit in the space."

"You have a house now, Dan. This is your house.

Technically, I'm in your guest room." He tugged Daniel down onto the bed with him. "Let's just see where we land."

"Right on." Daniel slid under the covers and held one arm open to him.

Mitch watched him a second, just because he looked so sexy lying there. "I like how you look in my bed." He stretched out in the cool, clean sheets with a sigh.

Daniel leaned in and snuggled with him, easy as you please. "Mmm...hey."

"Hey." He breathed in Daniel's clean scent. "Tomorrow we're going to wake up totally different." They were different now, but they'd be starting something new in the light of day.

"Yes. Tomorrow we start as a family."

He nodded, awed by the idea. "I guess we do. Wow."

"Yeah. Are you scared?" Daniel's eyes were barely visible in the darkness.

"No," he said quickly. "I'm not scared. I'm... I don't know. Bewildered. It's not at all how I imagined things turning out for me. I'm completely fine with that, I'm happy with it all— well, I'm definitely not happy that we lost Adam, but given that we have, I'm happy with what I have now. It's just a lot to reframe in my mind."

"Did you have someone special at all here?" Daniel stroked his arm, touching him slow and easy.

"No. Some close calls, but no one that I would call special." And no one that made him feel the things Daniel did. No one that he couldn't get enough of.

"I'm supposed to say I'm sorry, but I'm not. At all."

"I'm not either. It feels like you're the one I've been waiting for." He kissed Daniel lightly. "Cliche maybe. But it's the truth."

"Maybe you were. Fate is odd." Daniel sighed and stretched. "I don't know. I'm glad you're here with me."

He tucked an arm over Daniel. "Turn your brain off, Dan. You're exhausted." As if he wasn't. But he was determined that Dan would get some sleep.

"I don't know how, but I'll try. Sweet dreams." Daniel kissed his cheek, so sweetly.

"You'll figure it out. I'm here to make sure. Sweet dreams, Daniel." They'd figure it out. They'd figured everything else out so far.

9

Daniel woke up when he heard Vicki start wandering around, flushing the toilet, opening Emory's door and closing it.

He slid out of bed without stealing a glance at Mitch. Had he really been so clueless? More than that, had he really been so willing to just jump into bed?

He had.

He so had.

He didn't even know if he regretted it, or if he should. They were forced together. They had children to raise.

"Hey. Handsome. Come back here and kiss me." Mitch rolled over and stretched out long with a satisfied groan.

How was he supposed to resist a happy, smiling Mitch? "Just a quick one. Miss Vicki is out there wandering around."

"Quick it is, then." Mitch sat up and tugged him down so their lips met somewhere in the middle. "Mmm."

"Oh...you taste right. Good morning."

"Good morning. I just wanted to start our day off together before we get busy with kids. And I have to move things out of my truck and into closets so I can get back to work next week."

"Yeah. We have to make...decisions." And he didn't want to. He wanted to be able to believe Adam was coming back.

"We do. We don't have to make them all today, but we have to at least make a list and..." Mitch sighed. "We have to move forward. The world doesn't stop for these kids."

"I know. In fact, I should make sure Vicki isn't trying to set fires." He was fairly sure that was what he would have done on his own at five.

"Yeah. Go ahead. You get her dressed. I'll check on Emory and go start breakfast." Mitch caught him by the arm and took one more kiss before letting him go. "Okay. Now you can go for real."

Daniel chuckled as he headed out the bedroom door. "Angel girl? Where for art thou, kiddo?"

"Playing with my dollhouse," she called back. "Everybody was sleeping, Uncle Mitch's door was closed, and I couldn't find you."

"I'm here. Are you hungry? Can I come in and play too?" He didn't know what the norm was, but he'd figure it out.

"You can come play. Uncle Mitch makes waffles on Saturdays." She handed him a little doll. "You're the daddy. I'm the mommy."

"Okay. How many babies are there? This is a nice house. I like the wallpaper." He remembered helping Adam put this together, planning for a big Victorian monstrosity in a few years.

"There are four. But one of them cries all the time so he has to stay in bed." She showed him the little baby in a bassinet. "He drives everybody crazy."

"Oh man. Babies are hard. I think they're frustrated, don't you?" He would be frustrated if he was one.

"Frusfrated."

"Uh-huh. That's when your heart wants to do something, and your body can't."

"This is Lulu, she's pretty and smart like me. Oh and this is their cat, Fluffy. Daddy was just going to make dinner." She moved all the little dolls around from room to room, sitting them on couches and making them go up and down the stairs.

"What does the daddy do for work?" He wasn't sure how this playing went, but it was neat to watch her move the little dolls.

"Um. He's...a teacher. He's really smart. And he likes kids." She put little plates out on the table, and tiny mugs beside them.

"Look at the wee cups!" He loved that. He loved that someone's job was creating little plastic cups for a living. "How cool is that?"

"I tried putting water in them once, but they're too small even for a drop!" She beamed at him.

"Wow. Even a drop?" He picked up one of the cups. "Those are wee. I like them very much. Do you think we ought to go help make breakfast?" He thought Mitch could use a hand.

"Okay." She put her dolls down and stood. "Waffles! With syrup."

"Can I have butter too? I love the butter in the little holes." He unfolded himself from the floor and took her hand.

"Yes, silly. Uncle Mitch likes butter too. Emory eats them plain."

"Who wants waffles?" Mitch called from downstairs.

"Me!" Vicki took off, pulling him by the hand.

"Me too!" He scooped Vicki up and carried her over his

shoulder.

Vicki giggled and shrieked happily all the way to the kitchen, where they found Emory in his highchair with some cut-up fruit and a stack of waffles on the counter next to a tray holding butter and warm syrup.

"Nothing like waffles with real Vermont maple syrup," Mitch said, giving him a smile.

"Does it taste different from normal old maple syrup?" It made sense. Different bees made different tasting honey.

"Depends on what you consider normal maple syrup. If you mean fake stuff, then yes." Mitch got out plates and handed him one. "You want to do your own, baby girl?"

"Yep!" Vicki took a plate and helped herself, while Mitch pulled one off the stack and tore it into little chunks for Emory.

Daniel made himself a cup of coffee and sat. "Thank you for breakfast. I appreciate it."

"You're welcome. We need a good start to our day. Guess what I'm—uh. Well, what Uncle Dan-O is doing today, Vick? He's going to register you for kindergarten. You're only a couple of weeks late. I bet you'll be able to start any day now." Mitch winked at him. "I have all the information because I thought—well, you're going to have to go do it. I'm not her guardian."

Well, shit. "Okay."

What did he need to do? Could he add Mitch to a guardian thing? Would that be mean to the kids? To Mitch? To Adam? Why on earth would Adam leave him the kids?

"No. I don't want to." Vicki didn't even sound mad. Just, no.

"We talked about this, remember? School is fun. And it's important. And you'll make friends." Mitch sounded fairly patient, but he could tell they'd had this disagreement before.

"No. Dan-O, tell him."

"I'm pretty sure going to school is the law, angel. You liked your preschool. Why don't you want to go to school?"

She frowned at him. "Daddy *died*!"

"Daddy wanted you in school. We're just late because he was sick, and I was...busy." Mitch gave Emory another hunk of waffle to gum to death.

"No. I won't go. Tell them no, Dan-O."

Well, fuck a doodle god damn doo. "Don't you want to do girl scouts and stuff? Meet other little girls and have birthday parties and new books and school supplies? I used to love shopping for my new backpack every year."

"All my friends have mommies and daddies at their birthday parties! I don't want any more birthdays!" Vicki put her hand under her plate and flipped it, sending waffles and syrup flying.

The plate landed on the floor near Emory, startling him, and he burst into hysterical tears. Mitch's eyes went wide, and he looked at the mess, then at Vicki...then those eyes landed on him.

Okay, man. What would your folks have done?

He stood up, picked her up, and headed upstairs with her. "Fine. No birthdays. No breakfast. You can stay up here until you can act decent."

That was right, right? No screaming. No fighting. Just time out until she could be—whatever the fuck five-year-olds were. Reasonable sounded like a bridge too far. He wasn't sure that was doable.

"I'm hungry and you're mean!" Vicki wiggled and flailed in his arms. "Why are you trying to be my daddy?"

Because that's what Adam wanted. "I'm not. I'm being your Dan-O."

She pouted at him as he put her down. "I don't want to go to school."

"You don't have a choice. It's a law. I think you'll like it, but you have to go one way or the other." It was a law, right? He thought it was. Everyone went to some sort of school.

She sat down on her bed. "I want to stay here with you and Uncle Mitch. Can't you teach me? You're smart."

Smart. Him. Shit. "It's not like you're going to Hogswarts, girlfriend. You're going to the elementary for seven hours a day, five days a week. And you even get recess and lunch."

"What's Hogswarts?" She flopped back on her bed. "Am I decent yet?"

"Do you know Harry Potter? It's a school in a book." He looked at her. "Are you willing to go say sorry to Uncle Mitch? He worked hard on breakfast, and you were sort of mean."

"I just feel very mad a lot." She sighed. "I will say sorry. I like his waffles."

"I feel very mad a lot too, but we'll figure this out. Together. With hugs." God, how was he going to deal with this?

"Hugs make me feel better. Do you want one?" She sat up again and held her little arms open.

"I do. Please." He went to her and hugged her tight. "I love you. We'll make it through. I swear."

"Will you make my lunch for school?"

"Yes. And I will take you and pick you up."

"Wearing a clown nose?"

He tilted his head. "If I can find a clown nose, sure."

She giggled. "You don't need a clown nose, silly."

God, he loved her. "Yes, but my princess, my angel, my

god-girl, my sweet funky chicken! I would find one just at your command!"

"I'm not a chicken!" She slid out of bed. "I command you take me to waffles!"

Did every little girl have mood swings like this? "Yes, but remember to say sorry, okay? Uncle Mitch was nice to you."

"I will, Uncle Dan-O. I promise."

The kitchen was cleaned up and Mitch was wiping down the waffle maker by the time they got back. And Emory, the poster child for lack of mood swings, was still happily munching in his highchair.

"Uncle Mitch?" She looked to Daniel, and he nodded.

Go on, girl.

"Mhm?" Mitch glanced at her, then put his rag down and knelt next to her. "Did you want to say something?"

"I'm sorry I threw the waffles. It was mean." She stayed frozen right where she was, but Mitch held his arms out.

"Thank you. Can I have a hug?"

"Uh-huh!" She dove into Mitch's arms, and he lifted her right off the floor. "I'm sorry. I like your waffles."

"Thank you, baby girl. We're okay now. We're family now, right? We forgive each other." Mitch gave Daniel a nod over her shoulder and mouthed, "Nice work."

"Thanks." Oh, that felt good. That felt really good. He felt like he'd been thrown into the ocean, and Mitch was his only life preserver.

"Uncle Dan-O says he'll make my lunches and pick me up at school and stuff."

"Does that make it better?"

Vicki nodded. "Daddy would have."

"I know, and now instead of Daddy you've got me and Uncle Dan-O and we are not going anywhere."

"Because you're friends?" She let Mitch go and looked between them.

"We are...very good friends." Mitch answered her but was talking to him. "Uncle Dan-O is special to me."

"Me too. Dan-O is my goddaddy." Vicki took a deep breath. "You are too, right? You're mine too."

"I am so yours, Vicki. I'm not your godfather or even a real uncle, but that doesn't matter. You're my family because I want you to be. You and Emory, both." Mitch pulled a plate of waffles out of the microwave. "Still hungry?"

"Uh-huh. Real bad. Thank you." She climbed up in her chair and smoothed out her hair. Sweet baby.

"Dan? Waffles?" Mitch smiled, grabbed the coffee pot and warmed up his coffee for him.

"Are there enough? If not, it's no big." He could go days without more than a granola bar or something.

"There are always enough. I can't make this recipe small." Mitch served up waffles for Vicki and then for him, then pulled a little container of syrup out of the microwave too. "I just put it all in there to keep warm."

"Syrup!" She picked it up, and Mitch let her pour, guiding her hand a little.

He ate happily, trying to understand what life was supposed to look like now. What was normal going to be?

"So, Vicki. Not only are you going to kindergarten soon, but I am going back to work on Monday. The office where... where Daddy and I used to work together? I promised him I would keep the business going, so I have to do that."

"Are you leaving too, Dan-O? To work?" She looked at him, horrified, and he had a moment of pure, unadulterated fury—at god, at Adam, at cancer, and at himself for being so agonized at the thought that he was going to have to give up his art for almost two decades.

"Nope. I'm going to be with you."

"We haven't figured it all out yet, baby girl. But for right now, Uncle Dan-O will be home with you and your brother." Mitch touched his shoulder. "There are a lot of things we still have to decide."

"Regardless, we got y'all, okay? All the way. I swear." He found her a smile, and he drank his coffee, trying to get the waffles down.

Mitch's hand slid down his back and made a small circle. Vicki watched them both a second and then nodded. "Okay. I believe you."

Emory banged both hands on his tray and Mitch left him, hurrying across the kitchen. "I know buddy, you've been stuck in that chair forever. Such a good boy. You have breakfast all over you. Yay!"

The tiny, sunny smile lit up the kitchen, and he recognized it immediately because it looked just like Adam's smile.

Why did you have to get cancer, you asshole? Why couldn't you do something easy? Why didn't you get shingles or crabs or ass boils? Why the fuck did you have to die?

Emory's laugh filled the air, like the baby was teasing him, telling him to grow the fuck up.

Mitch came to him, one hand resting on his shoulder again. "You want to hang here with Miss Waffle-eater, or take Sir Poops A lot for a change?"

"Poops a lot!" Vicki laughed, and that made Emory giggle again.

He was a little scared of hurting the baby, but he knew he had to do it. He had to.

"It's not about perfect, remember." Mitch handed Emory over. "You did fine the last time."

"Hey, little buddy." He took the baby, making faces at

Emory, who immediately began to sob. "Oh, come on. I'm not mean."

"Relax. Talk to him in a stupid voice. He'll be fine once he can't see me anymore. You've got this." Mitch patted his butt, scooting him toward the kitchen door.

"Yeah. You better stop. I know I'm not your Uncle Mitch, but I'm okay. I swear." He hoped.

He bounced the baby gently, trying to be careful with his little body.

Emory got quieter as they left the kitchen and was studying him curiously by the time they got to the top of the stairs. That was an improvement, right?

"So, do you want to play? Do you like those weird dangly tent things for babies? I got you one when you showed up. Did you know you were early? You scared your dad half to death."

Emory reached for his beard and got a good grip on it, giggling as he tugged. The kid had no idea he'd been early. He didn't even know what early meant yet.

"I'm serious. You've been trouble since the start." He pushed into Emory's hands, and the baby cackled.

Those wide blue eyes watching him as he changed Emory and cleaned him up, finding bits of waffle in the baby's hair, in his onesie, even in his diaper.

"You are a mess, aren't you? I appreciate that in a person. I am also a mess, when you get right down to it." He wiped the little one down, de-waffling him.

This was going better than he'd expected. He tried to pretend like he hadn't noticed. He didn't want to jinx anything.

Emory blew raspberries at him, the baby watching him closely.

"So, what do I do with you. I suppose we'll be together a lot when Vicki's at school, so we have to figure it out."

Emory kicked his feet and gurgled as Daniel picked him back up. He was a good baby. Sweet and easy. Maybe this was going to be okay.

"I miss him, you know?" he whispered. "He was like my brother. He was the only person who believed in me."

"Mm-mm-mm." Emory hummed, then lurched forward and gave him a wet, open-mouthed baby kiss on his chin.

He snorted, then started to laugh, just ridiculously tickled at this goofy, neat little boy.

"Sounds like someone's happy. I told you that you'd do fine." Mitch kissed his cheek and then blinked at him, looking as startled as he was.

"He gave me a kiss, I think. It was gooey." But adorable and funny and it made him laugh. "Baby spit as moisturizer."

Mitch laughed. "Gooey sounds about right."

Vicki skipped over and kissed his other cheek. "Now we've all kissed you."

"How about that?" Mitch winked at him.

"Perfect. That's what I needed. All the family."

"Okay, Miss Vicki, you need to brush your teeth, make your bed and get dressed. Go on and call me if you need help, okay?"

Mitch watched her sprint off and then handed him his coffee. "Want to stick him in his play yard and then we can talk...or whatever. I think we have things to talk about?"

"Sure. We have everything to talk about, right?" Like everything from why and when. Less where. Lots of how.

Mitch nodded and topped off their coffee cups one more time. "Let's go sit. Maybe we can get Vicki involved with a movie for a little while. I'll promise her a hike out to the pond. It's nice out there this time of year. You've been there with Adam I assume."

"I have. I can't believe how it'll be snowy soon. It's just been a quick summer." At least for him, it had been. It had zipped by.

"I don't think I saw summer. And talk of fall reminds me, are you cool with driving and picking up Vicki? I'm going to try to leave the office early and work here in the afternoons for a while, but I can't promise I'll be reliable with my schedule."

"Sure. I need—the car is a rental. I have to take it back." His whole life was back in New Mexico, and he needed to go fetch it.

"Well, there's Adam's truck. It's in the garage. We can move the car seats back from mine or...maybe we should get a second one?"

"Maybe. My truck and trailer are back home, but that's not family-friendly either. We might be better off getting another dad-mobile. Uncle-mobile? Dan-mobile?"

"We can do that. Sell the truck and buy something else. Where is your trailer? What does back home mean?"

"Northern New Mexico. I've got it in a long-term storage place, along with my pickup." At some point he needed his things, his supplies, his pillow.

"You know, I don't know anything about what you did— do—how you do your art. Or...sell it. All that stuff."

"I have an agent in Santa Fe. I deliver the canvases or mail them, depending on where I'm parked at the time." He didn't have a computer or a TV. He had a phone and a bunch of books and a great job.

"Well, I guess you're parked here for a while. Will you be able to paint here?" Mitch seemed genuinely interested. Concerned.

"I don't know. I guess I'll have to." He couldn't think about that too much, not really. It scared him.

"You will. We'll...figure that out. I guess we better...okay. So, to address the elephant in the room first, I think I should move in. For good. Even if this...well, I think regardless of what happens between you and me, the kids need both of us." Mitch tilted his head and leaned a little closer. "Right?"

"Yes. We are a family. If you're willing, I am." He hadn't chosen this, but Adam had, and he'd always trusted in Adam to show him where to go.

Mitch smiled. "I'm more than willing. I'm looking forward to it, because I think things are going to be good. Really good."

He hoped so. He really did. He felt like he was wandering in the wilderness, which was ironic given he was closer to a town right now than he usually ever was.

"Okay, so that's settled. I'll... I guess I'll see if I can get out of my lease. That's...so weird. What's next?"

"I—what do we do about bedrooms? I mean, what's right?" Were they supposed to just leave the big master like a shrine? Was that creepy? Disrespectful? He didn't know what was normal.

"What we said last night? Or was that a weird in the moment thing? The bed is easy to move back in or—or we could get a new one. Our own. It's the nicest bedroom in the house and I'm so ready not to share a shower with baby toys."

"Will that hurt Vicki's feelings?" Because he would like a little private space too. He was used to spending weeks alone, and this was all so new. "I'd like to move to the big room with you."

"I'd like that too if it's not too fast for you. I know I surprised you with all of this. And about Vicki, that's a good question. I don't know. I guess we could sort of...move in slowly. Do you think she'll be okay with us? Together?"

"She doesn't know anything else. Maybe it's a comfort?" He didn't know. Adam had been the first gay man he'd known who got married, had babies. Everyone he'd known in college were...college-aged.

"Could be. If we just make it normal?" Mitch laughed. "We really are making this shit up as we go along, huh?"

"Making what shit up?" Vicki came skipping in with a hairbrush and handed it to him.

"Everything, you know? We're having to make plans." He took the hairbrush and made turn around motions.

Mitch shook his head. "I shouldn't use words like that, and neither should you, okay?"

Vicki turned for him and looked at Mitch. "Daddy did *all* the time."

"Yep. He did. But he didn't like you to, so please don't. Okay?"

"Okay—ow! Uncle Dan-O!"

"Oops. Sorry, angel. You've got a vicious little tangle back here. Did an imp chew on your hair in the night?" He eased up and brushed easier.

"No." She rolled her eyes. "There's no such thing as imps."

"Since when are you the expert?"

"Uncle Mitch! They're just in stories."

"Do you think so?" Daniel shrugged. "I sort of think that there might be imps. Especially up in the mountains."

"Okay, but don't tell that to the imp who ate the last chocolate chip cookie yesterday." Mitch teased.

"That was m—"

Mitch raised an eyebrow. "Hm?"

"The cookie imp!"

"That mean old cookie imp!" Daniel was more than willing to play along. He loved the idea of magic, of wonder.

"Is your hair all done, baby girl? I'm going to put on a movie for you. Uncle Dan-O and I have stuff to talk about, okay?"

"*Frozen*."

"Again?"

She looked at him confused.

"I mean, sure. You love *Frozen*. Right." Mitch picked up the remote and had it playing in no time.

Daniel sat there, quietly, thinking about how Adam used to belt out "Let it Go," and make Vicki cackle.

"I hate using the TV as a babysitter but sometimes, you have to, you know?" Mitch came and sat with him again, closer this time. "So I think we were acknowledging that we have no idea what we're doing..." Mitch leaned an elbow on the couch, head resting in his hand.

"Right. We're flying along like we know what we're doing, and I have to say, you're faking it beautifully." Mitch seemed like he was handling it way better.

"Well, to be fair, I've been faking it for a month or so on my own already. But Adam was here making decisions, you know? I just did things. I wasn't trying to live real life."

Daniel nodded, but he understood, on a bone-deep level. He wasn't particularly good at the whole real-life thing. It was...too structured.

"This week is going to be tough, I think. Are you okay being on your own with the kids? I'll have to leave about eight fifteen to be at work by nine, and then I'm thinking I'll work until maybe one and then try to come home and finish out the day here. Once Vicki is in school it'll be a little easier on you, but until then... I think you should go register her on Monday afternoon and ask to start her ASAP, you know?"

"Okay. I'll manage. Worst case scenario, I'll leash them both to the front porch." He was joking, mostly. He had to figure out where the school was, how to register someone to do that—surely you could do it over the phone, right?

"I'll make sure to be home around lunch so I can watch Emory." Mitch sipped his coffee.

Okay, maybe not over the phone. Damn.

"Hey. Don't panic, I have all the paperwork done. It should be cake."

"No problem. I got this." He was fucked. Utterly fucked. No one even trusted him to keep a dog alive, much less a small person. Worse, *two* small people!

"You do. Remember nobody needs perfect. We just need to get by. Okay?" Mitch leaned close. Really close. "Okay?"

"Okay." He wasn't sure whether or not it was reasonable to admit how scared he was.

Mitch kissed him lightly, gently, just a moment's connection. "Okay. So what else?"

"Uh—food allergies? I cook on the grill a lot." Was there a list of what all needed doing? "I live in a travel trailer, so I know about repairs and grills and emergencies."

"No allergies. And good, because I'm not as handy as I should be. You want to go see if we can get that bed out of the attic?"

"Yeah. She's basically hypnotized by Elsa. The hospital bed is gone, right?" This was better. Moving shit was in his wheelhouse. This he understood.

"It's gone. All the med crap is gone. I even cleaned out that kitchen cabinet a couple of nights ago when I couldn't sleep and sealed all the meds in coffee grounds and trashed them. It was bothering me that they were still there. Is that weird?" Mitch got up and peered into the play crib. "He's asleep too. Good timing."

"Not weird at all. I'd be wigged out with all that stuff in the house." He was a little more of an herbal remedy type of guy, to be perfectly honest. Green was good.

"Okay let's do this. I need to *do* something, you know? Not just talk about it." Mitch glanced at Vicki, who was glued to the TV, then headed upstairs.

"I like how you and I are on the same wavelength. It feels good." In fact, it made him feel functional.

"It does. We're going to make a good team. I know it." Mitch pulled down the attic steps. "This is not going to be fun. It was a pain in the ass getting it up here. You want to stay on the ladder, and I'll hand pieces down?"

"Yeah, I'm taller. That seems right." He stopped Mitch before he went up and kissed the man hard, trying to say thank you for everything.

Mitch blinked, startled, but returned his kiss, tucking an arm behind his back.

It was the best he had—the only real way to say what his heart felt.

When the kiss ended, Mitch looked into his eyes and nodded, the look and the nod both carrying a weight he recognized. Then Mitch took a deep breath and started climbing the ladder to the attic. "Bed."

10

Pulling on his suit and driving away from the house was the hardest thing Mitch had done since the morning he'd had to call 911 to report that Adam had died. That was really saying something because he'd done a lot of hard things since moving into the house in the first place, both before and after Adam's death.

But that ache in his chest and dread in the pit of his stomach were offset by the warm welcome at the office and the joy of welcome back cards, and the "new dad" laundry basket that had been left on his desk by his coworkers with useful items such as diapers, earplugs, a stress ball, caffeine mints, restaurant gift cards, a coupon for a full body massage, and a bottle of Jack Daniels.

God, he'd missed his job. He loved the kids, and something wonderful was building with Daniel, but he needed his work. He'd forgotten how much.

"Hey, boss. How goes it?" His PA was a cheery young man with the organizational skills of a techie Martha Stewart. "You glad to be back?"

Just the question made him smile. "I am. For some

reason, I missed you all. Thanks for having my back for the last month."

Walt bowed dramatically, then came over and hugged him. "We're all sorry. We loved him too."

"I know." He returned the hug, appreciating that Walt wasn't avoiding the elephant in the room. "He was careful to leave the firm in a good place legally speaking, which took some effort on his part, because he loved all of you too. I'm very ready to get back to work. Do you have some time tomorrow to catch me up?"

"You know it. I've been handling a lot of the emails, and I did schedule an appointment for the Hasker account at the end of the week. They want a new campaign for their new line."

"Oh, great. That sounds like something I can jump right into. Cool. Can you forward me their request?"

Walt grabbed his tablet, and Mitch's phone beeped in a few seconds. "Done."

"Thanks. I'll read it over tonight after we get the kids in bed. I left Dan home with them by himself for the first time. I figure he's going to need a sanity break." He hadn't gotten a call that anyone had died yet, so he figured that was a win. "I'm going to head out soon."

"Sure, of course. If you need babysitters... I'm willing, and so is Sue. How do you like the kids' godfather?"

He tried to keep his smile from looking as smug as he felt.

He's smoking, and I'm planning on seducing him right after the kids go to bed tonight.

"I like him a lot. And he loves the kids. But two little ones are a big responsibility, and he has his work too, so it looks like I'll be moving out to the house for good. We're working out a schedule."

And we just finished putting the bed back together. I can't wait to use it tonight.

"Excellent. I—If I can help..." Will shrugged and looked a little worried. "I know this is weird. Are—are you intending on bringing in another partner?"

His stomach clenched. He hadn't been ready for that question, even though he probably should have been. He took a breath before he answered. "Not any time soon. But as long as you've asked—how does everyone feel about it? Have you been overwhelmed? Should I plan a discussion?"

That was a good answer, he thought. He'd been leaning on the younger associates and his staff hard the last month or so.

"I think we're busy but not overwhelmed. Grieving, but getting back to work." Walt inhaled deep, then let the breath out. "That sounds mean to say."

He shook his head. "It's not mean. It's just right. Adam loved this place and all of you, and he intended for us to continue and to grow without him. I look at it as honoring what he helped build." It took every ounce of self-control he had not to let his emotions win. It was his business now, and people were looking to him for leadership.

"Well, holler if you need me. I'll be right around the corner."

"Thank you, Walt." He looked at his watch. He needed to get going, so Dan could get to registration before it closed. He stood and closed his laptop, packed it up and called Dan on his way out the door.

"'Lo?" Dan sounded out of breath and frustrated. "Can I call you back? I'm lost."

"Lost? I'm on my way home." Was he running late? Shit.

"It's okay. We went to the park and to buy school supplies. I'm trying to figure out where I am."

"Um. Are you in town or in the middle of nowhere?" Vermont was always either one or the other.

"In town. I think the outskirts. Shit. I'll be there soonish."

"Okay. Pull up directions on your phone. You have the address, right? I'll meet you at home." Outskirts of town meant twenty minutes at least.

"Okay. She's in school. She has a backpack and crayons and such. I bought grapes and apples and turkey. She starts tomorrow. See you soon! Bye."

Click.

Huh.

And all he did was go to work. So when he got home, he started planning dinner and threw some chicken into a bag to marinate for a while before running upstairs to get out of his suit. Emory would definitely spit up on his tie.

"We are home!" Vicki hollered at the top of her lungs. "I am a king-er-garter! I have a ladybug pack-pack and a ring pop because I am the *best*!"

Oh, god. How fucking cute was that? He put aside the veggies he'd been chopping for dinner and hurried out to the living room, looking for her, and for Dan. "Where is my best girl?"

"Uncle Mitch!" She came running, feet slapping on the floor, sounding like a herd of elephants. "I meeted my teacher. She's so pretty, and she likes horses, and she says that we get to color and play on the playground, and that everyone wants to meet me! And there's a swing set and a jumble gym! And I gotted brand-new colors and pencils and a new dress for my FIRST DAY!"

He scooped her up and hugged her hard. "So exciting! I can't wait to see you in your dress." Mitch felt so proud of her, going from a hard no to looking forward to her first day.

And he was proud of Dan too, because shopping with both kids wasn't easy, he knew from experience. "Where's Dan-O? Did you have lunch yet?"

"Dan-O has the poopy baby. He got us burgers and fries and they're on the table with all the shoppings." She gave him a sticky kiss. "Wanna see my pack-pack?"

Oh. He should take over for poor Dan-O, but Vicki needed him first. "I do. Show me everything." He followed her so she could show off her loot.

"It's got spots because Dan-O says I can wish on them, and I like red. My dress and shoes are red too." He got another hug as she opened her backpack. "And? Ladybug barrettes. I will be fab-u-lous."

He laughed. "You will be. I'm so happy for you. You're going to rock this kindergarten thing." Ladybug everything. How adorable.

He wished Adam were here to see this.

"So you liked your teacher. That's great. What do you want for your first day of school breakfast?"

He hadn't heard a peep out of Emory, and he wondered if Dan had managed to get him down for a nap.

"I want cimmen toasts and daddy eggs."

So cinnamon toast and scrambled hard. Excellent.

"You got it. I love cinnamon toast." He helped her pack her "pack-pack" back up again. "Why don't you take everything to your room, baby? I'm going to check on Dan-O."

"Okay! The baby pooped everywhere!"

He headed upstairs, frowning at the sound of the shower running.

Everywhere must really have meant *everywhere*. He knocked on the bathroom door before he poked his head in. "Hey, Dan. All good? Do I need to clean up the truck?"

Dan was leaning in the shower, Emory on his chest sound asleep, the water falling on them. "Seemed like the easiest way to clean him and help him relax. He was a mess."

"Oh, look at you guys. Hang on." He grabbed a towel and reached for Emory, taking him from Dan and wrapping him up quickly to keep him sleepy and warm. "I got him," he said, though he'd have much rather climbed into the shower with Dan. "You take your time."

"Just let me wash my hair, and I'll be out. Lunch is on the table, man."

"Awesome. I have dinner marinating." They'd managed to walk right around each other, which just reminded him how big Adam's house was.

He got a diaper on Emory, slipped him into a onesie, and put his drowsy butt into the crib. He wasn't sure what he'd have done if Emory wasn't one of the quiet ones. He could pretty much count on the baby sleeping for a couple of hours.

He poked his head into Vicki's room and held a hand out to her. "Hey, let's go eat burgers."

"Do you think Daddy likes my pack-pack?" She came to him. "I think he does. Me and Dan-O told him all about our day on the way home in the car."

"I am sure he does. Who doesn't like ladybugs?" He led her downstairs for lunch, trying not to let his heart break for the second time today. Maybe third time. Who was counting? "It was so important to him that you go to school. He talked about it with me a lot. So I know he's super proud of you."

"Yeah. Dan-O said so too. He said Daddy was the smartest guy he ever knew, and that he saved Dan-O's life. Did you know that?"

"I do." Well, Dan had mentioned it back before the funeral, before everything changed, long before he'd wanted to ask Dan any personal questions. He knew about it, but he didn't know the details. "I'm not surprised, your daddy was an amazing person." Mitch lifted her up and sat her in a chair. "Which burger is yours?"

"The chicken nugget one."

Of course. What a silly question.

"Right. Good call." He opened up her container, put some fries in the other side and went to the fridge for the ketchup.

"Hey, guys. I'm doing laundry. Anyone need anything washed?" Dan rolled his eyes on the way by.

"I think we're good. You look pretty well loaded down, there, buddy." He didn't laugh. He wanted to, but he didn't.

"Yep. I only brought a pairs of jean, so..." Dan started a load of laundry, whistling as he did.

"Man. Next time we're taking *you* shopping." Two pairs of jeans? Dan really had no idea he'd be staying beyond the funeral. "Maybe we need to think about getting your stuff."

"I need to go fetch it. I don't know how to manage that, yet."

"I know. We'll talk about it." Soon, hopefully. They needed to get the kids and the routine settled first. And sort themselves out. He wandered over and stood hip to hip with Daniel at the washer, inhaling the scent of freshly showered man. "I am so impressed with everything you did this morning. Shopping and school, both kids in the car. Lunch. You're a rock star."

"I needed to swallow the frog, you know? Worrying didn't get it done."

"Nope. You're right about that, and these kids are a constant reminder that people are counting on you to get it done." He glanced over his shoulder and saw that Vicki was occupied with her lunch, so he snuck a quick handful of Daniel's backside. "I am making dinner for you...and you're dessert."

"You are? I am? Oh, I'd like that." Daniel seemed to relax, then offered him a wild, honest grin. "I'd like that very much. I'm all squeaky clean and tasty."

"I am. The way to a man's heart, and all of that." He winked, soaking in another second of that smile before he went to check on Vicki. "Did you eat my burger too, baby girl? I know you..."

"Nope. I eated some of Dan-O's rings. They're *good*."

"Onion rings are a brilliant invention." He reached over Vicki and took one too. "Mmm. We're eating your onion rings, Dan-O."

"That's why I bought two orders. I understand the call of the onion ring." Dan-O chuckled and stole one for himself. "Did you tell your Uncle Mitch about our day?"

"I showed him my dress and my pack-pack." She nodded, head bobbing. "And I told him Daddy knows all about it, and that Emory pooped ev-er-y-where. Ew."

"Not everywhere. Your dress was clean," he joked, gently poking her in the ribs.

"Well, almost everywhere. Last one!" She shoved a nugget in her mouth, whole.

Dan snorted, sat, and grabbed his burger. "Nicely done. Jesus, I'm tired."

"I bet. You just eat. You want a Coke? Some coffee?" Dan had to be tired. What he'd done today wasn't groundbreaking, or even unusual; parents did that stuff all the time. But Dan hadn't been a parent two weeks ago. He hadn't even considered it. He dove right into the deep end without knowing how to swim—just knowing he was going to have to learn fast.

Kind of like what he'd done two months ago. Only he hadn't been a loner first.

"No. No, sit. I'm good. Just being lazy for a second." Dan handed Vicki an onion ring and sat back, just breathing.

Mitch sat and dug into his burger, stomach rumbling as he chewed the first bite. He hadn't noticed he was so hungry, but he was grateful for lunch now. "How about you, little girl? You ready for some downtime? Maybe read for a while, play with your dollhouse? Lie down even?"

Vicki had mentally outgrown naps, even the word was forbidden. But that didn't mean she didn't need them from time to time. You just had to be tricky about it.

"I think I want to color for a little while in my room, okay? I want to make a picture for my teacher."

"Oh, perfect. She will love that." Such a sweet girl. "Do you know where all your coloring stuff is? If not, I can come up and get you started in a minute."

"I know, Uncle Mitch. I know. And colors only go on paper and color books." She rolled her eyes dramatically.

"When I get the art room set up, you can color in there, angel." Dan finally unwrapped his burger.

Maybe. Maybe Dan didn't understand yet about the benefits of coloring on her bed.

"Good girl. You can go up whenever you're ready. And please don't wake your brother, okay?"

"Okay!"

Mitch was beginning to understand that Daniel had been alone so long that he was going to have to relearn all sorts of clues again.

Like when a man was hitting on you.

He glanced at Dan, then chuckled and shook his head at his thoughts.

Dan grinned at him. "Share the joke?"

"It's nothing, really. I had a weird day too, and you're just...kind of wonderful. Thank you for lunch."

"You're welcome. Can I kiss you?" Just like that. *Can I kiss you.*

He picked up his Coke and took a sip, then smiled and slid off his stool, watching Dan as he moved closer. "Yeah. You can."

"Cool." Dan wiped his lips, stood up, and brought them closer together. The kiss was soft, but sure. Confident. Blistering.

"Mm." He relaxed right into it, letting Dan have a taste and meeting Dan's hungry tongue with his own. He wasn't worried about Vicki walking in on a kiss, not even this one, so he let himself indulge.

Dan groaned, one hand coming to cup the back of his head and tilt his head so the kiss could deepen. He hooked his fingers into Dan's belt loops and pulled their hips together, feeling like he just couldn't get close enough.

The sound that pushed into his lips made his eyes cross. That was what he needed, proof that Dan needed him.

His cock pressed against his fly, and he knew Dan could feel it. Maybe Vicki would crash. Maybe they didn't have to wait for dessert. He wasn't sure his balls could take it. "Dan. Fuck."

"Mmhmm...is it her bedtime yet?" Dan grabbed his ass.

"No, damn it. I'm hopeful she'll fall asleep, but it's not a sure thing. And we'd have to be quick." He wanted more than quick, they'd done that, and it just made him need to take his time with Daniel even more.

"We got time later. I mean, if that's cool. I think it would be cool."

"I told you, you're dessert." He took another quick kiss and stepped away, chuckling. "We just need to keep some space between us for a few hours."

"No fair." Dan brushed against him, fingers teasing his cock. Not so good at impulse control. Good to know.

He swallowed and took another step back, giving Dan's hand a playful slap. "Tell me about your day. I meant it when I said I was impressed. To be honest, I was kind of afraid I'd come home, and you'd be drooling with Emory on the floor."

"He was pretty okay. I haven't spent a lot of time in a big town in a while, so I got turned around, but Vick and I figured it out. The school folks were super nice." Dan leaned back against the counter. "I put you on as the person who can pick up Vicki too."

"Thank you. That was a good idea in case you're stuck." Big town. Burlington was pretty small, but he could see how it might seem big to someone that hung out in the middle of nowhere most of the time. "We'll get a routine going soon I think." They'd better. It was a survival tactic.

"Yeah. Yeah, we'll figure it. I met the teacher—she's sweet and young. The school seems decent. Vicki loved picking stuff out for her list."

"She was so proud of everything. It's just nice to see her happy and looking forward to something. Thanks for doing that." He realized suddenly that he was actually a little sad that he'd missed it. But there would be lots of school stuff he'd make sure to be there for. And this was good. Dan needed a win. He needed some confidence.

"I'm hoping you would pick her up with me—or without me—tomorrow? To hear about her day?"

He smiled. Damn, Daniel was perceptive. "Let's go together. I'll leave work early and meet you there. Maybe we can all go to lunch after, or ice cream or something." School was halfway between work and home.

"Sounds perfect. Mr. Emory and me have to do...things."

"Mm. Things. Like, eat and drink and poop, and read books and play in the play yard for a while so Uncle Dan-O can paint maybe."

"Maybe. We'll have to see. Do—is there like a cleaning schedule or something?"

"There's a service. I hired them because I just couldn't manage everything. The schedule is on the fridge. But like, laundry and stuff I've just been doing when we're desperate." Not on purpose, he would just open a drawer one morning and, oops. No undies.

"Oh, cool. I wasn't sure. I have to go to a laundromat usually, but I want to make it okay for the kids. Cleaning service is good. Do I have to be here? Be gone?"

"I've always been here because I couldn't leave Adam alone. They were fine with it. They cleaned everything right around us. I don't think it matters." They'd been kind actually, friendly.

He was kind of dreading their next visit because Adam wouldn't be in his room.

They would be.

"Okay." Dan went to the fridge and took a picture of the schedule with his phone. "Okay, cool. I can handle that. No problem."

"Folks at work seem cool with me working half days for now. Someone did ask me if I was going to bring in another partner. I didn't know what to say. Adam and I had enough work for the two of us before he got sick, and since then they've been doing most of the work entirely without either of us. I think they're feeling pretty stretched." Mitch was going to have to consider bringing someone new in; he knew that. Especially if he was going to continue to have to be flexible. "It was a strange day."

"I bet. I'd offer to help, but I can't." That was clear and sure—possibly even definite.

He blinked at Dan, then started to laugh. "I love how you just got yourself out of that by playing dumb."

"Not even a little. That's something Adam taught me."

That was interesting. "What did he teach you?"

"I took an advertising class with him. I did one assignment, and he called me into his office to tell me I was never going to be a commercial artist. By the end of the week, I'd quit school."

"Wow. That seems kind of...discouraging. I don't know if I'd want someone to tell me that if that was what I wanted to do. Gutsy." Now that Dan was telling him this though, he remembered a conversation with Adam about Dan and how talented he was.

"I needed someone to tell me to stop being scared. I was trying to do what the smart thing was instead of my right thing."

"And I guess it was a good decision? You've been happy doing your right thing?"

"I was. I'm not an office person. I don't do well with schedules and rules and ties and all. I don't even like wearing shoes."

He laughed. "Well, this dad gig should be right up your alley then."

"Yeah. I guess it better be, or we'll all be screwed." Dan stopped, then chuckled softly. "And not in the fun, spanky way."

Mitch's chuckle was low and warm. "No. Though I don't know if I'm a spanky kind of guy."

"Yeah, well, last punch that got thrown at me didn't end well for the throwee. At all." Dan rolled his eyes. "Although, really, I'm not a fighter. I just want to make art."

"I know. We'll make it happen. Somehow. There will be time." They'd have to make it because these kids were here twenty-four-seven and so was Dan. But they couldn't solve everything today. Maybe not even this week.

Dan shrugged. "It'll just take time. I know that. Eventually everything will settle. First things first—getting through the afternoon without anyone exploding."

"So far so good. Are you done eating?" He started cleaning up. "If you want to take some down time, you should." He could hold down the fort. Dan had already done the hard part.

"I think I'm going to take a walk. Be in the sunshine."

Like she'd been called, Vicki popped up. "Can I come? I like to walk. I'll show you where things are."

Daniel smiled at Vicki and held out one hand. "You can. You want to come, Mitch? I'll carry the poop machine."

"Sure. Yes. We can hike out to the pond. We have this neat backpack thing for the baby. Let me find it. You think he's awake?"

"Probably not, but he can sleep on the walk. I think that's so cool, the idea of going on a walk sound asleep."

So much for Daniel's break. Then again a walk in the sunshine wasn't the worst idea. Vicki would wear herself out and sleep well. That would be handy.

"You need good walking shoes, baby girl. Go get your sneakers on."

Vicki rolled her eyes and melted, swinging her arms as she walked away. "Sneakers are so boring!"

"Blisters hurt, though. And they're icky." Daniel grinned and wiggled his toes in his rope sandals. "I hate the wet part of broken blisters."

Mitch found the baby carrier in the closet. "If he's asleep you'll want to carry him in front. I think I know how this thing works…"

He had no fucking idea. But how hard could it be?

"Okay. Is it like the ones they make for dogs?" Daniel looked and got it slipped on like it was nothing. "Pretty much, yeah."

"They make them for dogs?" He blinked at Dan. "Well okay then, show off. Let's get the baby."

They got Emory into the carrier and went off on their walk, with Vicki leading the way just like she said she wanted to.

"I have a swing here. Daddy hung it up. It's strong enough for grownups. He told me so."

"Yeah? I'll have to go try it out." Daniel tugged at the rope, testing it. "He did a good job."

Adam had hung it last spring before his diagnosis. Mitch remembered because Adam had had a cookout in May, one of the last events he was able to attend, and all the kids were using the swing. "I'm sure it's fine, since it's only been up there since spring. You think we should take it down for the winter?"

"I want to swing in the snow!" Vicki hopped right on it and Mitch gave her a push.

"I guess that would be okay. It's chains, not rope, so that would be okay I think." Maybe. Maybe he needed to do some research.

"It's fun!" Vicki's laugh filled the air, and when Mitch glanced over at Dan, tears were on the man's cheeks.

"Hang on, baby girl. Big push." He gave her a good

shove, hoping that would hold her for a minute, and took Dan's hand. He wasn't sure what to say. He wasn't sure anything he said would help. "This is fucking hard, huh?"

"It is. He should be here. They both should be. These are their babies, and they're missing this. This joy belongs to them, not us."

He nodded. Dan was right, but that ship had sailed. Maybe he was too practical, but he couldn't sit in that place —in the should have been—it wasn't helping anyone. These kids needed them to move forward.

"Adam gave this to you. He wanted you to have it, and more importantly he wanted them to have you. The best thing you can do for these kids now, and for Adam, is honor that. This joy is yours now. Ours, since you've allowed me. They're not here, we are. We can't let it go to waste."

"No. No, I guess not." Dan nodded and hugged Emory, the little boy zonked out. "You'd better push that baby girl. She's slowing down."

He squeezed Dan's hand and gave him a nod. "I'd better." He jogged back over to Vicki. "Do you want to keep swinging or take the path through the woods to show Dan-O the gazebo by the pond?"

"Oh! The water! Do you remember the water?"

Dan chuckled and nodded. "A little. I bet you can show me new things about it."

"There are lights now. Sun-lights?" She squinted at Mitch. "Sunor?"

"Solar." Mitch nodded.

"Yes. And you can see at night now. It's so cool. And in the snow we can skate." Vicki took off down the path.

"Whoa, stay where we can see you, Vicki! Remember, bears."

Vicki came right back. "Bears," she repeated solemnly.

"Bears." Daniel nodded. "I have bears where—well, where my trailer is. They get into the trash and make dogs bark."

"They're pretty happy staying away, but small people like Vicki might not be as safe as bigger people, right?"

"Right. And if they're on the path we might scare them."

There were definitely bears that moved through the back acreage. He and Adam had seen them a few times. They liked the pond.

"Where is your trailer, Dan-O? Are you bringing it here? Because you live here now right?" Vicki walked ahead of them, tossing questions over her shoulder.

"I am. It's in the mountains. I'll have to figure it out, but I have to do something with it."

Dan was like a magnet as Mitch walked beside him, and his fingers kept itching to touch, hold hands, anything. It wasn't a bad thing that they'd waited this long—or been forced to wait this long—it gave them time to be more sure of each other. But they'd waited long enough, now. Mitch couldn't help feeling impatient.

"Can I go with you to the mountains to get your trailer, Dan-O? Me and Emory and Uncle Mitch?"

"I don't see why not, but we have to figure out what is what. I don't know what to do right now."

"Oh. Okay." Vicki skipped over to Dan, hugged him, then skipped away again.

"I feel badly that all your things are...not here. Your art supplies and clothes and such. It must be making you crazy."

"Not yet. I used to come up for a few weeks at a time, so I'm okay now. I will have to think about what to do."

Dan had said that a few times now—that he would have to think about it—like the subject was something he wanted to discuss. Mitch let it go. Maybe it was too much right now. Or maybe there was something bigger going on, settling down when he'd been free to roam, obligations he'd never had before. Who knew?

But Mitch was here for it, whatever it was, whenever Dan did decide he could open up. All he knew was that he and Dan were so different. Dan felt everything more deeply, held onto things longer, and sat in the moment better than he did.

They walked along the path until it emptied out onto a sandy area that led down to the edge of the pond. Off to the right was the gazebo and Vicki ran to it and spun in circles in the middle of it. "Isn't it pretty?"

"It is! Look at this. It's so cool, angel." Daniel smiled and stepped onto the floor. "Oh, it makes great noises. It sings!"

"It does?"

"Sure. Listen." Dan stepped here and there, making the wood creak and groan in a weird-assed song. Vicki listened, then her eyes lit up.

"I hear it!"

He watched them stepping around the gazebo in a strange dance, making the gazebo "sing". Mitch would never in a million years have thought to call all that creaking a song. He would be looking for the weak spots and calling a contractor. In fact, he was considering that right now.

The more he watched Dan with Vicki, the more he began to see why Adam chose Dan as guardian. Dan was creative and young at heart. He was very like a kid himself.

Mitch wasn't any of those things really.

"Uncle Mitch! Uncle Mitch, come play with us!" Vicki beamed over at him. "We're making wood music!"

Wood music. Jesus. It was—It was insane and charming, weird and wonderful, all at once.

He stepped into the gazebo warily. "Be careful you guys, you don't want to go through the floor."

"Floors don't break, Uncle Mitch," Vicki said with an eye roll and all the conviction of a five-year-old that knows everything.

"They're not giving. They just sing, man. I swear. Wood's got soul, and it's easier to hear than stone." Dan led them off the gazebo though. "Show me the water, angel girl."

"What do you mean 'hear stone'?"

"Over here, Dan-O!" Vicki skipped off to the water's edge, but stayed safely on the sand.

"Stones talk too. It's just deeper, like bones, you know?"

Nope. He had no idea. He shook his head, chuckling softly. "I have no idea what you're talking about, Dan. But I bet Adam did."

Daniel shrugged and pinked. "If he didn't, he listened and faked it and wrote it up to flights of fancy. Really, most of the time you just have to nod and pretend that I make sense. I'm basically harmless."

"I could do that. I can listen. But I'd rather try to understand." He stepped in behind Dan and stood very close and nuzzled behind one ear.

It was visible, when Dan relaxed and eased back, leaning into him. "Hey. That's tingly."

"Annoying tingly like your foot's asleep, or hot tingly like electrical current?" Mitch was teasing, but he thought he'd like the answer.

"Nothing is asleep. Electric, hell yes." Dan smiled for him, warm and easy.

"Mm. I hope so."

"Are you kissing Dan-O?" At some point Vicki had wandered back and was standing less than a foot away, watching them.

"I was...blowing in his ear. Because it tickles." Should he just have said yes?

"Does it tickle?"

Dan nodded. "A little bit. Is it okay with you if I kiss your Uncle Mitch?"

Vicki looked at Dan curiously. "Well, do you love him?"

"I do. He's our family." Dan didn't even flinch. "We're going to raise you and Emory together."

It was official. Dan was ten times better at this kids thing than he was. Love was complicated, but Dan made it simple enough to understand. Even simple enough for him.

"Well, then you should kiss him. You're supposed to kiss people you love." She hugged Dan's leg. "We're a good family."

"We are a good family. I love you, angel girl."

"I love you too, Dan-O. Want to go see my favorite tree?"

"Yes! Show me."

Vicki led the way again. "I can climb it. It has lots of strong branches."

Mitch took Dan's hand and held it with more confidence than earlier. "So kiss me, then."

Dan turned and kissed him, not playing tonsil hockey, but not this chaste thing either. It was a kiss.

He hummed and returned it happily, feeling that electric tingle that Dan was talking about earlier. Emory wiggled between them, and he ended up cutting it off with a fond laugh. "If it weren't for these babies..."

"He's a little weird, but we'll make it so that he can develop his super weirdosity."

"I get him. I was weird—am weird. There are coping skills." He winked at Dan.

"Look at me!" Vicki shouted from her perch up in her

favorite tree. She was right, the branches were sturdy, but it still made Mitch a little nervous.

"Is she okay up that high, Dan?"

"I hope so." Daniel looked up. "We should talk about a treehouse. Or maybe a playhouse in the backyard, huh?"

"Oh, good idea. I'm not sure I know how to build a treehouse, but I'm game." He looked up at Vicki. "Come on down, baby girl. Emory's waking up and he's going to be hungry."

"Okay, Uncle Mitch." She sounded disappointed but made her way out of the tree without arguing.

"You are like a little tree monkey. Ooo-oo-oo!" Daniel grabbed her and spun her around.

Poor Emory. He just never complained. "Don't come crying to me when you throw your back out, Dan-O."

"I've got this. I swear." Dan winked at Vicki. "Tell him I'm a stud, angel girl."

"Dan-O is a stud, Uncle Mitch!" Vicki giggled, feet kicking.

Yeah, he knew. He wanted that stud in his bed, and soon. He went for a kid-friendly tone but adult-friendly innuendo. "I don't need Vic to tell me that, Dan-O. I already know."

"Mitch and Dan-O sitting in a tree..." Her little song filled the air.

Dan snorted. "That was you, my little monkey!"

"I'm not a monkey!" Vicki wriggled to be let down and ran back toward the path.

Mitch took Dan's hand firmly in his. "I'm not really into kissing in trees."

"No? I prefer horizontal, myself." Daniel pinked as he said the words, but that grin wasn't worried.

That blush made him happy. "Hm. I'm not sure I know

what you mean. You'll have to show me later. I want to know everything."

"I think that's a good idea." Daniel's grin grew like a flower blossoming. "An incredible idea."

"You guys are so slow!" Vicki complained, calling back down the path.

"Are we slow?" He kissed Dan's cheek.

"We're old, and I'm carrying a heavy baby!" Dan called back to her, making Vicki laugh.

He watched Dan, thinking this little afternoon stroll with the kids kind of life could be enough for him. But he couldn't help but worry whether it would be enough for Dan.

"Old? Speak for yourself, Uncle Dan-O."

"Ancient. Absolutely decrepit." Daniel managed to keep a straight face.

"You're going to get yourself in trouble, mister." He gave Dan's ass a playful swat.

"Am I, Uncle of Oldness? Mitcethusela?"

Vicki was back on the swing when they stepped off the path and into the backyard again.

"Seriously, if you weren't carrying a baby right now I would tickle you until you passed out."

"Ah, my amazing little man." Dan kissed the baby's head, barely managing it with the wild laughter that was bouncing Emory. "You saved me."

He jogged over to give Vicki a push. "I have to start dinner soon, baby, and Dan-O has laundry and boring stuff. Do you want to listen to some music in the kitchen with me or watch a movie or something?" The mundane part of parenting. What to do with the kiddos while you get stuff done.

"I want to play with my babies, okay? They need to have their bottles and then we can play with our Legos."

"Sounds like a plan, angel girl." Dan watched her with an admiring smile.

"Come on, let's go in. I think it's going to rain." He stopped Vicki's swing. "See that cloud?"

"Which one? Where?" Her eyes were wide as she scanned the sky.

"The dark one right there. It looks like uh...kind of like a bear, maybe? Yeah. Sort of like a bear. See it?"

"Oh...is it a sad bear? Is it going to cry on us?"

Oh. Sad they didn't need. "No. Nope. It's a naughty bear, and it's going to pee on you."

Well, it sounded funny in his head.

Dan cracked up. "Let's hurry! No cloud pee for me!"

"Ew!" Vicki shrieked and ran for the back door. "No cloud pee!"

"I'm going to be sorry I said that, aren't I?" He shook his head and followed her.

"I think it was amazing! Good job." Daniel grabbed him and kissed him hard. "It's about to rain. Go!"

The kiss made him a little dizzy and he blinked at Daniel for a second before remembering to move. "Right. Inside. Going."

"Come on, baby boy! In the house!"

Emory's laugh was joyous—this wild, honest noise that shocked him. Listen to that.

Suddenly he understood better what Daniel was feeling when Vicki was swinging earlier; he could feel it deeply himself now. That laughter was something Adam would never know again, and that was sad. But his children knew it, and would know it with them, and that was something to be grateful for.

He closed the door behind Dan and the rain started—huge drops pelting the sliding glass door. "Wow. We just made it. That rain cloud came out of nowhere, huh?"

"Yeah." Daniel watched with a smile. "It's so much different here. In the desert, the rain is like a sucker punch."

"Oh yeah?" He squinted at the sky. "I bet this goes on for hours. I think it's supposed to rain all night."

"Yeah. It's something else. A whole new world." Daniel smiled and Mitch wasn't sure whether it was peaceful or bittersweet or happy.

Probably a little of all of that at once.

"Have you never sat and listened to the rain come down for hours? It's so relaxing. We can open the window later, you'll see." In bed. He'd open the window so they could listen to the rain together.

"Sounds like a plan. I'm in." Daniel pulled Emory out of his carrier. "So, tiny human, do you want to play on your mat or your swing or what?"

Then he waited, like Emory would answer.

Emory flopped forward and sucked on Dan's chin.

"Hungry. Told you." Mitch giggled and went to the fridge for some fruit.

"Babies need food to grow, right?" Daniel followed along. "Can I give him another bottle?"

"Yes. He is a bottle fiend. Start him there and then I'll see what I can cut up for him. You want to plop him in his chair?"

"Plop him. Do you hear how he talks about you? Not place you carefully..." Dan was laughing, teasing Emory and making the baby chuckle.

"P-lop." He wandered out of the kitchen to check on Vicki. "Vic? You good, baby girl?"

"Shh! I'm giving my babies bottles, and they're trying to

go to sleep!" Vicki shouted back, three times as loud as he'd been.

"Oh. Sorry." He snorted. "Dan, we did this all backward. We have kids and we haven't even fu—you know. Yet."

Dan chuckled softly. "Right? We've got a house, kids, a whole relationship, and we've been...almost monk-like."

"I am not a monk. I don't want to be a monk. I'm looking forward to breaking our monk streak and maybe the bed along with it. And then—" Mitch pulled some strawberries out of the fridge and set them on the counter, passing behind Dan much closer than needed. "Then I want to snuggle, and pillow talk, and get to know you better."

Dan caught his gaze. "I would love that. Very much. All of it. The bed, the pillow, the snuggling."

That made him smile and made him feel like he knew Dan pretty damn well already.

Emory shrieked and pounded his hands on his tray, and Mitch leapt into action. "Right. We were feeding the alien baby." He found a knife and started slicing up some strawberries. "Maybe I should make him some eggs."

"Does he eat real food like eggs? They don't need a lot of teeth, I guess." Dan chuckled and shook his head. "They make baby cookies, right? Like for teeth?"

"Cookies to chew on you mean? I think so, yes. But I have to tell you, I have the five-year-old gig down cold, but this baby thing is a trip down Google Lane every other day." Emory was still getting most of what he needed from bottles, but he liked anything he could pick up and gum to death too. Eggs were a favorite mushy snack.

"Right? I mean, I knew Vicki when she was a baby, but in that benevolent uncle way. Not in the she pooped on me way." Dan rolled his eyes dramatically. "Emmers and I have shared a moment."

"You have. Very profound. It's a shame he won't remember it." He put the strawberries on Emory's tray and backed up a couple of feet. "I've shared a few moments too. A couple of my T-shirts have been forever changed by the experience."

Emory slammed his hands into the strawberries. Bang. Bang. Then one went flying, and he'd be damned if Dan didn't swoop down and catch it in his mouth.

"Ha! Show off. You've got this well in hand, so I'm starting your dinner." The chicken had been marinating since before their walk.

"What's supper? Are you making something amazing?"

"Just some roasted chicken. Do you like asparagus? Vicki loves it, and we have some I need to cook."

"Sure. Vicki loves it? That's cool. I like that." Dan shook his head. "I've never cooked a real chicken. I would freak out."

"What? What do you cook? These are just parts, not really a whole chicken." Vicki was a veggie kid; she ate all kinds of things most kids didn't even want to try.

"I eat turkey sandwiches, tamales, instant oatmeal, soup. I eat a lot of soup." Daniel shrugged and grinned. "I work a lot, and there's no reason to cook for just me, is there?"

"You're worth cooking for, Dan. Just you." He winked and pulled out a sheet pan so he could arrange the chicken and get it in the oven.

"Ha." Daniel went over and fed Emory a bit of strawberry. "You are the droolingest thing."

"I read that excessive drooling means teeth. Hopefully he stays a happy, chompy baby because the whole teething sounds like a nightmare." He pulled out a bag of baby potatoes and started cutting them in half. "Of course,

Google can turn anything into a nightmare so maybe it's not as bad as it sounds."

"Well, we just deal with it, I guess? I can always give him Otter Pops."

"What's an Otter Pop? Like a popsicle?"

"What's an Otter Pop? Oh god. I have to go to the store and buy a box." Dan staggered around like a clown. "Seriously, they're the ice-pop dealios in the tube? The ones you suck?"

"Oh! I remember those. Messy, sticky things we were only allowed to eat outside." He tossed the potatoes with olive oil and garlic and whatever else his fingers landed on, then tossed them on the pan with the chicken and popped it in the oven.

"Amazing, sweet icy chunks of joy, I think you mean." Daniel watched him, obviously fascinated. "Can you cook those together?"

"Oh. Yeah. Neat trick, huh? One of the associates at work taught me this one. She has a handful of kids so easy is her go-to. I could throw the asparagus on there in a bit too, but Miss Vicki likes them steamed. I don't think Adam did kid food much."

"He didn't understand the joy in chicken nuggets and fried bologna sandwiches."

"Oof. I don't think I understand fried bologna either." He laughed. God, that sounded vile. "But mac and cheese, peanut butter and jelly, pasta with butter, English muffin pizzas... I've introduced Vic to all kinds of things. Adam used to ask what I was making, and he'd roll his eyes."

"Fried bologna is the perfect summer sandwich, I'll have you know." Daniel wandered past, goosed him, and grabbed a Coke. "Want one? And tell me you eat tacos."

"Sure. And only heathens don't eat tacos." He'd been known to eat several in a sitting.

"Tacos are my one of my all-time favorite things." Daniel handed him a Coke, then headed back to peek at the rain. "I've never seen it flood here. Does it?"

He shook his head. "No, not up here. Some of the valleys like Waitsfield will flood if we get serious rainfall or something, but we're pretty high up here." He gave Dan a sideways look. "It's freaking you out that it's still raining, isn't it?"

"Freaking is a strong word. It's just weird, that's all."

Huh. Dan was totally freaking.

"It's just water. Open the sliding door and listen for a minute. It's soothing. Really." Chilly, so hopefully Dan didn't open it for long, but he loved the sound of a fall rain.

"I remember in Austin, I used to play in the rain all the time. It was wild. Strangely exciting."

"It's lovely. In small doses." He set up the asparagus steamer on the stove.

"Yeah, I guess. I remember the first time I saw real snow in Chama. I thought I'd die."

"You'll see good snowfall here too. Do you ski? We get lots of tourists up here during ski season." He didn't mind them; they made the place lively. Though the slopes could get pretty crowded.

"I don't. I mean, Adam tried to teach me once, but I'm not real coordinated. I make a mean snowman, though."

"That is a worthwhile skill with kids in the house. We're going to have to figure out how to plow this driveway. Adam has a plow that hooks onto his truck. That will be an adventure, assuming we live through it." He'd done a lot of snow-related chores—shoveling, clearing the roof, but he'd never handled a snowplow.

"It can't be a lot harder than driving the fifth wheel. I bet I can figure it out." Daniel shook his head. "I need to start making notes, I guess. One. Take child to school. Two. Figure out plowing with baby. Three. Pick child up."

"Oh no. If you're plowing then the snow is too deep for me to get to work. I'll be here to watch the baby. Your list needs to be about how we can't ever be so low on diapers that we won't make it through a two-day snowstorm."

"Right. Fill the basement with diapers, wipes, and chicken nuggets." Daniel chuckled. "I might have to get a bonus freezer."

"If you get a bonus freezer we can fill it up with chicken nuggets and adult popsicles." He dropped the asparagus into the steamer.

"And ice cream. Ice cream is important."

"Mint chocolate chip. This small talk is nice, but I wish I could just take you to bed now." Vicki needed dinner. Both kids needed baths. Their night was so not their own yet.

"Yeah. I hear you, but if wishes were fishes we'd all swim away." Dan chuckled softly. "Parents do this all the time, right? Figure out how to get off with their partner?"

"Oh, sure. Usually they have a pretty good track record before the kids end up in the mix though. And I have to believe there are plenty of times like this too." Too many, probably. "I'm impatient."

Daniel opened his mouth, and then Vicki screamed.

"BUG! BUG! HELP!"

Uncle Mitch to the rescue. Some things superseded sex.

11

It was still raining.

Daniel slipped outside while Mitch was in the bathroom and sat on the porch, just watching the rain.

It looked a little like tears, sliding off the gutter.

The kids were asleep, Vicki holding her backpack, Emory on his belly, butt in the air. Mitch had cooked. He'd done dishes. At some point, he would stop feeling like he was living someone else's life, right? Eventually he would stop experiencing the world from behind this odd fog?

Daniel wasn't sure why Mitch was into him. He hoped it wasn't because Mitch was scared of losing the kids. There was no way he'd keep those babies from someone that loved them. That wasn't how love worked. Love wasn't possessive. Love grew.

"There you are. Still raining, huh? It's chilly out here." Mitch's warm hands landed heavily on his shoulders. "You okay?"

"I am. Just sitting, you know? Staring into the darkness, I guess."

Mitch's fingers worked into his muscle, kneading gently. "You don't seem like the type to just stare."

"No? I guess..." He sighed and let his head fall forward. "That feels fucking amazing. Can we go upstairs soon and be behind locked doors?"

"Vicki's lunch is made for her first day of school, and the dishwasher is running, so I think we can escape right now." Mitch bent to kiss the side of his neck. "Finally."

He nodded. It had been the longest fucking day in the history of days somehow, and he'd been at the funeral. "Let's go."

The rain wasn't going anywhere.

Mitch held the door for him, and they went back inside where it was warmer, and the rain was quieter. "The last time I was this deliberate about sex I had decided to pick someone up at a club in Boston." Mitch laughed. "Is it still sexy if it's planned? I've wanted you all damn day."

"Do you want me as much, even though we planned?" He stepped right into Mitch's space, letting himself release his worry and rushing thoughts to focus on touching.

"I do." Mitch inhaled sharply as he got close, and his hands caught Dan's biceps like he was steadying himself. "Oh. Hi." Mitch's breath sped up, and Dan was surprised by the quick hard kiss. "Yeah, I very much do want you."

"Then I give no shits that we planned this. Absolutely none." Daniel took Mitch's hand and led him upstairs, feeling more than a little bit studly.

"I'm suddenly a big fan of plans." Mitch squeezed his fingers and followed close behind. When they got to the bedroom, Mitch closed the door quietly and turned the lock.

Dan turned to Mitch and moved in close, plastering to

the solid line of his spine. Mitch was warm against him, and there was electricity sparking between them. "Hey."

"Mmm." Mitch's chest rose under his hands and Mitch caught one and slid it up under his shirt where it rested against firm abs.

He loved the way the rippled, fuzzy belly felt under his fingertips. More than that, the roll and jerk of Mitch's abs, the proof of how much effect he was having.

Mitch turned in his arms, slid fingers into his hair and kissed him hard enough to back him into the door.

It was like Mitch had flipped a switch inside him, and he groaned, his toes curling as he rocked up hard against his lover. This was what he needed, the distraction and the hunger and the fire.

Mitch seemed to like that and rocked back, moaning against his lips. "Dan. You feel so good."

He did. He felt better than good. He felt like he was flying. Dan reached around and grabbed Mitch's ass, dragging them together.

Mitch nipped at his jaw and down his neck, then tugged the collar of his t-shirt aside to add a couple of biting kisses to his collarbone. He lifted his chin, offering all his throat. There were so many hot spots, gathered right there, that he couldn't bear it.

Mitch's t-shirt disappeared, then Mitch was pushing his up and off too. "I need more of you."

"You can have all of me, if you want. I'm willing." And basically able.

Mitch leaned back enough that Daniel could see him better. The smile was sweet, but those eyes were still full of heat. "I want."

He groaned, because that flash of passion made him feel twenty thousand feet tall. "I do too."

Mitch started exploring him, hands moving over his belly and ribs, across his chest and over his shoulders. A hand slipped into his and Mitch pulled him toward the bed and when they got there, Daniel got another kiss, a long one, like there was nowhere else Mitch wanted to be.

Everything Mitch was doing was focused on him, all about him.

They settled on the edge of the bed, facing each other. It was easy to touch this way, easy to share one drugging kiss after another.

His hand found Mitch's thigh, sliding up as they devoured each other.

Mitch covered his hand and guided it higher, tucking it tight against his fly with a deep moan. "All fucking day," Mitch whispered against his ear and followed it with a line of kisses along his jaw.

"I want to suck you off..." Daniel bit his bottom lip, then he started to work Mitch's fly open. "I'll warn you—I'm pretty oral."

"Warned. Happily warned. No complaints here." Mitch lifted his hips to make it easier on him. "This is something you actually have to warn people about?"

"Uh...not usually. Sometimes. You know, some guys aren't into kissing. Some guys just want to fuck. I like a little bit of suction." Daniel started to chuckle. Jesus, he sounded like a dork. "What I mean is, I am totally into sucking. Get ready."

"Get ready? Do I need to sign a waiver? I want you, Dan. Kissing, sucking, fucking, all of it." Mitch seemed plenty interested and wiggled his jeans out of the way.

Daniel cracked up, helping Mitch strip off. His palms dragged over lightly fuzzy thighs, and he kissed the exposed skin as he found it.

Mitch's skin was blushing everywhere, even his thighs, and Mitch's fingers scritched through his hair. "I'm ready, no lie. Bring it on."

Daniel chuckled, tongue sliding along Mitch's shaft, from the base all the way up to the tip. He lingered there, tasting, drawing out one salty drop after another.

Mitch hummed, fingers exploring his hair, his ears, his chin. "It's been a while, Dan, and that feels so good."

He imagined it would feel good one way or the other, but he appreciated it, balls to bones. He focused, sucking good and hard, working Mitch as best he could.

"Yeah." Mitch groaned and let him go, stretching and leaning back on his elbows. He could feel Mitch's eyes on him, watching him move.

He needed this more than he'd needed anything—to relax and breathe, to suck and swallow and make Mitch moan. Oh fuck yes. He was right there, needing this.

Mitch wasn't shy about letting him know it was good, either. He took a deep but shaky breath and the sound he made was tight and urgent.

"Fuck, Dan." One leg slid up and Mitch perched a foot on the edge of the bed. His hips rolled, his back arched... all sorts of pretty poses that proved that Daniel was wanted.

Daniel slicked his finger and slipped it back behind Mitch's balls, teasing the tight hole as he began to deep throat.

"Jesus..." Mitch's cry was muffled and Daniel glanced up to see that he'd stuffed a fist into his mouth. Good man, because they didn't want to wake the kids now. Mitch dropped his knee out to one side, opening for him, offering, totally his in that moment.

Fuck, that was—He stopped searching for words,

focusing on sending this beautiful man over the edge and making him wild.

"Dan..." Mitch's voice was a rough whisper. "You're going to make me—I'm gonna—fuck, Dan."

"Mmhmm..." Fuck Dan didn't sound like the world's worst thing ever. He was willing to pitch and catch.

Mitch shivered and curled up, hands wrapping around Dan's nape as he shot. He didn't say much, but he let out the best sounds, groans and soft grunts, shallow pants and a low moan.

When he quirked his finger, Mitch swallowed a cry, his body clamping down on his touch. He repeated the action as he moaned and went down, stroking and swallowing and sucking hard.

"Dan..." Mitch collapsed flat on his back, chest heaving with gasping breaths. The pulsing and shivering subsided finally and Mitch settled into breathless pants, though the grasp on his finger was still very real.

He couldn't resist stroking again, just to keep the everything going, keep them on the ride.

Mitch gasped and tried to curl up off the bed again but didn't get any farther than his shoulder before falling back again. "Jesus fuck, Dan."

He kissed the tip of Mitch's cock, his belly. "Good?"

Daniel was betting on better than good.

"Huh?" Mitch reached for him and coaxed him up onto the bed. "Good? No. No...uh. A bigger word. Jesus. I can't think."

Excellent. Incoherence was a fabulous goal.

Incoherence, first, then orgasm.

Mitch puffed out a breath, and chuckled softly. "You do need a warning label; you were right."

"See? I told you." He winked over, but he needed more. He rocked closer, rubbing against Mitch's leg.

Mitch pulled him in for a kiss, then whispered to him. "How do you want it?" A hand wrapped around his shaft, thumb circling the head of his needy prick.

"Fuck yeah." Right now he just wanted it. Anything. "Touch me. Everywhere."

"Everywhere." Mitch gave him one more quick kiss and then went right after a nipple, sucking it up between teeth that pinched him just lightly. That hand slid lower to cup and tug on his balls.

His legs popped open like there was a button behind his sac. Bingo.

Mitch hummed low and sucked a little harder as those fingers explored, sliding along sensitive skin. He pulled his knee up, letting himself spread wide. He didn't have any reason to hide, and he needed this touch.

"I can't promise fireworks," Mitch said, moving lower on him, lips gliding over his ribs and abs. "But maybe a couple of shooting stars."

"I got faith, man. I have total faith." He loved stars.

"I'm just glad I can speak again." Mitch's laugh vibrated against his hip and then a hot tongue drew a line from his balls to the tip of his cock. It slid across his slit and then pressed in, stretching the opening just a little.

"Fuck." His teeth clicked together, his hips rocking up in an uncontrollable motion.

"Next time." Mitch caught his shaft in a tight fist and covered the head with his lips, then slowly took his length into a hungry mouth.

His belly clenched, and he curled over Mitch's head. It was as if he was flooded with heat, like he'd been dipped in a pot of water. The sensation was fierce enough to make his thighs shake.

The sound of Mitch breathing deeply through his nose mixed with his own breathing filled the room, and the suction and heat never let up. Mitch was focused, fingers still fondling his balls and sliding along the sensitive skin behind them, teasing at the edge of his hole.

That was all she wrote. Daniel came so hard it damn near hurt, his bones rattling as his balls emptied. Mitch swallowed and sucked him through it, keeping up the little teases and strokes.

The best he could do was blink and stare at the patterns in the ceiling.

Then Mitch was crawling over him, and he stared up into blue eyes instead. "Good?" Mitch grinned and nipped at his chin.

"Fuck yeah." Daniel couldn't stop grinning. "C'mere." He grabbed Mitch and wrapped around him, happy as a pig in shit. "Hey."

"Mm. Hey." Mitch leaned on him, draping an arm over his middle. "You're amazing, and that was amazing, and I feel fucking amazing." Mitch chuckled. My brain's still a little shorted out."

"Excellent. I'm into it. You. This." Right. Shorted out. Go team.

"Are you?" Mitch drew a circle with light fingers on his side. "Because that's starting to matter to me. A lot."

"Yeah?" He appreciated the patience, because he knew he was slower, that he wasn't as used to people as Mitch was. He felt like he was a babe in the woods, but Mitch was right there—this gay shining light. "I really am."

"Me too, Dan." Mitch pushed up on one elbow, smiling at him. "I'm very into you."

He didn't know what to do, so he smiled back and cupped Mitch's jaw. "I'm going to try hard to do this right."

"Yeah, I hear that. Me too." Mitch kissed him, just slow and sweet, lazy, like they had forever.

Which they both knew they didn't.

He'd bet it wouldn't be an hour before another attack of the poop monster.

12

Having small local clients was amazing, and Mitch loved it most of the time. But the thing about small clients was that stuff came up. A lot. He had to be flexible because a lot of his clients were boots on the ground types—managing their businesses themselves, dealing with day-to-day issues—patience was important in his line of work.

But today, Mitch was running very low on patience after four hours of interrupted sleep. Emory's teeth were making it hard for him to settle, and all the teething had given him wicked diaper rash. And at five, Vicki wasn't good at not being the center of their attention. She'd played the I can't sleep card and ended up between them in bed.

No matter how he tried to sleep, he had heels in his kidneys or elbows in his chest. At one point he woke up and there were feet on his pillow.

So when his third meeting of the day was cancelled and rescheduled he only barely managed not to throw his phone across his office. He was done. Fried. He'd prepared for three meetings that hadn't happened, and he was ready to set his desk on fire.

T-fucking-GI-fucking-Friday. He needed a drink.

He could grab a Jack and Coke before he headed home, he supposed. Maybe bring food home.

Mitch liked that idea, and he dialed home, yanking the phone from his ear as a wild screaming answered him.

"NONONONONONONONONO!"

Holy shit.

Nope.

He hung up the phone. He'd give that a second to cool down and try again.

Maybe he should go get that drink. Keep it short, like fifteen-twenty minutes. It wasn't like Dan would even know.

That would be a dick move though, right? When he knew Dan was probably losing his mind at home? Mitch was exhausted, and he was frustrated, but he wasn't a dick.

Jesus, he missed the days he could just go chill on a Friday from hell. Play his guitar, have a beer.

Not parent.

He stood up and tossed his laptop and a bunch of other crap he might need for the weekend into his bag, shrugged into his coat, and headed out. He'd call Dan back from his truck.

His phone rang before he got out of the building. Dan sounded preternaturally calm. "Hey, what did you need?"

Did you gag her? Toss her in the pond? Tie her up with the rope swing?

He took a deep breath, trying to give that calm right back. "Just letting you know I'm on my way home. Do you need me to pick up anything?"

"Body bag. Duct tape. A bottle of Cuervo."

Ah. Okay. That made...sense.

"On it." He didn't need to stop for Cuervo, it was in the cabinet over the fridge. "I'll be there soon. Maybe we can get them in bed early." Who was he kidding? It sounded good though.

"Vicki is in her bedroom. She can stay there for a bit. She hit Emory hard and bruised him."

Whoa, a bruise? "Dare I ask what happened? Or should that wait until I get home?" He hit the gas, hoping to get there a little faster.

"He grabbed her hair, and she pinched the shit out of his arm. Just sibling shit, but loud and—" Daniel's voice cut off, and a litany of, "I hate you!" sounded. "Let me let you go, man. See you when you get home."

Click.

"Damn." Mitch sighed. Hell hath no fury like a little girl who'd lost everyone in the world that she loved. And Vicki had a right to be pissed.

There was a line, though, and it sounded like she'd about hit it. He worried all the way home, the bullshit of his own day mostly just a stabbing pain behind his left eye now. It wasn't pleasant, but it wasn't a little girl shouting "I hate you" either.

Mitch pulled into the driveway almost surprised to find the house wasn't on fire. He parked and grabbed his bag, forcing himself to take a breath and count to ten before opening the front door.

Daniel was sitting in the middle of the floor with his earphones on, eyes closed. Emory was playing in his playpen, and Vicki was...sitting in the corner, looking a little shellshocked.

Okay. So, this was either a "wait until your Uncle Mitch gets home" situation, a tentative truce, or a stand-off.

He walked up behind Daniel, heavy on his feet so Dan would know he was coming, and laid a hand on Dan's shoulder.

Daniel looked up, the tears just held back. "Hey, you. We were having a time out to refocus our energy."

Fuck. He was ready for just about anything but Dan in tears broke his heart, and he had a hard time holding back his own.

"Okay. I'm going to change, and then...then I don't know. I'm going to change and think about it." He bent and kissed the top of Dan's head. "Vicki. You stay put, and I'll be right back. Dan, do you want to come up with me?"

"Sure. You cool there, angel?"

She nodded. "Can I lay on the sofa, please? My heart hurts."

"Sure. Just go breathe for a few. We're just going upstairs. We're right here."

Her heart hurts. God, didn't they all?

He gave Dan a hand up and caught him around the waist to steady him as they headed for the stairs. He thought about what he should say but decided it might be better to let Dan talk when he was ready.

Dan sat on the end of the bed for a long time, then he sighed, just letting it all out. "So that sucked."

"Yeah, I got that impression," he said carefully, hanging up his tie and kicking off his dress shoes. "Are you okay?"

"Fine. I was a little overwhelmed. So I decided I was better off just removing my infuriated ass from the situation for a second." Daniel shot him a worried look. "That's okay, right?"

"I think it's fucking brilliant." His shirt went into the laundry and his dress pants back on the hanger. They could go one more day. He stopped and kissed Dan's cheek on his way to find sweats. Maybe a glance at his ass in his briefs would cheer Dan up a little. "This has been a long week, huh?"

Dan stretched up tall, his back popping. "It's been a long couple of weeks, but she was due for a meltdown. I can't let her hurt Emmers, though."

"No. So tell me what happened? This was just a meltdown? Or a specific sort of meltdown?" He wandered over and found sweats and a soft t-shirt and pulled them on.

"She didn't have a great day at school. Some older kid made fun of her because of god knows what? Maybe the kid was just mean. She wasn't clear. Then she spilled her snack. Then we smacked our heads together when we tried to clean it up." Daniel chuckled, the sound wry. "And of course, her brother pulled her hair, and *she* got in trouble for hurting him."

"Mm. Wow." He went back for a hug, tucking his arms tightly around Dan's middle. Even stressed and frustrated, Dan smelled so good. He tucked his nose against Dan's neck and breathed in.

"Hey. How are you? Happy Friday?" Dan held him close.

"Happy it's over. Some Advil ought to fix me up." He still had a gnome stabbing him in the forehead.

"Ah. There's some in the bathroom medicine cabinet." Dan stood and pulled away a little. "There's all sorts of stuff in that cabinet. It's like a Tardis."

He headed for the bathroom. "Yeah, no kidding. You should have seen it with all of Adam's meds in it. It was like a pharmacy." He made a face as soon as he'd said it, it had just rolled right past his Dan-is-already-a-wreck filter. Damn.

He found the Advil and shook two into his palm. Then he added one more for good measure and swallowed them all with a tiny paper cup of water.

Daniel was waiting for him by the bedroom door. "You want to lay down a minute or something?"

"No." He squeezed Dan's fingers. "Not without you. Let's go have a shot of something and then be parents."

"After, can we order pizza and have another shot?" Dan was trying, Mitch could tell.

"Yeah. That sounds like a plan. It's a shame we can't give Vicki a shot of something and send her to bed." He tried out a smile for Dan, it felt kind of lame, but he managed it.

"Right? She's cried enough she's going to have a vicious headache, I'm betting. Is there...baby aspirin?"

"Baby aspirin is only for adults these days. Go figure. We have children's Tylenol though, and she takes it like a trouper." He followed Dan down the stairs. Pizza was actually starting to sound pretty good.

"Ah. My mom wasn't into us having headaches, so I wasn't sure."

Okay...wow. What parent was into their kid having a headache? "I wasn't trying to start an argument. Sorry." He thought they'd been doing pretty well, considering.

"An argument? With who?" Dan looked totally confused, then he blinked. "Me? No. No, I was being sarcastic. You didn't tell my mom you had a headache. She wasn't... maternal."

"Oh boy. I need that shot. I guess I'm I wound up." He glanced over at Vicki who was lying still on the couch and wondered if she'd fallen asleep. Emory waved a squishy block at them as they walked by and went back to chewing on it. "So, you raised yourself?"

"Yeah. I left home at fifteen. We'd learned everything we could together."

"So...no dad I guess?" He smoothed a hand over Dan's back. "Sorry, we don't have to talk about this now. It's crap timing." He reached above the fridge and opened the cabinet. "Cuervo?"

"Yeah. That'll work, thanks." Daniel pulled a lime out of the weird little basket that was filled with citrus now.

The basket full of citrus. The shelf of hot sauces and spicy shit. The case of Dr Pepper. He knew what the kitchen was like with Adam in it. So anything new was evidence that Dan lived here now, and all of it made him smile.

He pulled down the Cuervo and found a couple of shot glasses while Dan sliced the lime. He filled them and set the bottle down. "One for you. One for me."

"Where's the salt shaker? I need this today." Dan grabbed the shaker and licked his hand, salting it before grabbing the lime wedge and the shot.

"Hang on, wait for me." He licked, salted and looped his arm through Dan's. "Ready?"

"God yes."

The burn was perfect, and he let himself feel it, all the way down. That woke him right up.

He set his glass down, nodding. "Yeah. That's what the doctor ordered."

"Yeah." Dan closed his eyes for half a second before he grinned. "I needed a reminder that I was still a grown-up."

"I am more than happy to remind you how grown-up you are, any time." He slid a hand over Dan's ass and gave it a squeeze before putting the top back on the Cuervo and stashing it back over the fridge.

"Is that a promise? I could so take you up on it." Dan inhaled deep, slowly blew the breath out.

"I promise. As long as we can get a little alone time, and we don't just pass out." Mitch laughed. Passing out was a real possibility.

"Well, that's vaguely adultish, right?" Dan's pretty eyes rolled, the look dramatic and goofy enough to make him laugh.

He snorted. "More vague than I'd like, but yes. Here. To hold you over." Mitch caught Dan by the nape and tugged him in for a kiss. He'd meant it to be quick and fun, but it turned deeper quickly. He just never had enough of Dan.

Dan whimpered softly, one hand lifting to cup his jaw, opening up and letting him in. Tequila tasted good in Dan's lips.

He leaned, pressing Dan against the counter and sliding their tongues together. They needed to check on the kids, but his day felt so much better now and he just needed another second.

"Mmm..." Dan hooked one leg around his thigh, tugging them together.

He caught Dan's thigh and slid his hand along it. "We better..." Damn, he was more breathless than he'd expected. "Kids."

"Uh-huh. I know." Dan nipped his bottom lip, making it sting.

He hissed and licked at his lip, pressing closer to make sure Dan knew how much that made him ache.

Dan nodded like he'd said something, the low moan vibrating between them.

"Fuck." He hated being a grown-up. He put a hand on Dan's chest and pushed back, sucking in a deep breath. "Bedroom quick or wait until later." If the kids were napping...

Dan's chest worked like a bellows as he fought to calm himself. "I'm not willing to wait for long."

Mitch nodded and walked away. Like, *away*, all the way across the room. He was wound up from work, wound up worrying about Dan and the kids, wound up by Dan himself and that incredible kiss. Unwinding was going to take a minute. "Me too." Willing. Able was obviously another issue.

Daniel went to Vicki. "Want to play outside before it gets dark? It's good for you to run around like a hooligan."

She eyeballed him from behind a blanket on the couch. "You're not mad?"

"My feelings are hurt." Daniel didn't bitch, just stared her down.

Mitch watched from the kitchen doorway. For someone who didn't have a parent that parented him, Dan was pretty damn good at this. Vicki pursed her lips and frowned, then glanced up at Dan again.

"I'm sorry I yelled and said mean things." Her expression went from worried to hopeful. Mitch could read her like a book.

"Me too, but I'm more sorry that you hurt Emory. You're bigger than him, you know?" Dan sighed softly. "I know you and me can do better, okay? Together?"

"Okay. Yes. Can I have a hug?" Vicki lowered her blanket slowly like it had been armor she was protecting herself with. And just when all was starting to feel right in the house again, Emory's butt made a rude noise.

Vicki's eyes went wide. Mitch whipped around and scooped Emory up before it became a full blowout. "Got him!"

He heard Vicki's giggle as he dashed up the stairs.

Emory's laughter was loud and merry. He wasn't worried at all about having a poop-splosion, was he?

"Of course you're not worried. You think it's fun making me scramble and make weird faces." He set Emory down on the changing table and made quick work of removing another diaper from hell. But at least this one didn't get everywhere. He cleaned Emory up and blew a raspberry on his tummy, grinning at the little shriek. The little bruise Vicki left on his arm wasn't too bad, but it was definitely noticeable. "Emmers, my man. You got all the chill, and your sister got all the fire."

Emory giggled and cooed, wiggling for him, like he was pure happiness. Mitch put him in a new outfit, something warmer because it was getting chilly and these old New England houses had charm, and in the winter charm meant drafts.

Oh, maybe they could have a fire in the bedroom later. In the fireplace and in bed.

"Your Uncle Dan-O is hot as the sun, Mister Emster," he sang, putting little socks on Emory's feet. They would last about ten minutes. Tops. "Mhm. And I'm going to tear him up later. Doesn't that sound like fun?" Babies didn't care what you said as long as you said it in a high, cute voice.

Emory kicked and turned over, giving him that diapered butt.

Mitch shook his head and patted his tushie. "You're just showing off now, rolling over without falling off the table." He scooped Emory up and headed downstairs. "Breakfast for dinner? That's easy right? You can have pancakes. Hey Vicki? Vic?"

The living room was empty. Dan must have gotten Vicki to go outside. Impressive. He dressed Emory up in a toasty coat and hat and went out the back door.

Vicki and Daniel were obviously learning to do cartwheels. Someone was going to end up with a broken neck. That was the scariest thing he'd ever seen.

Although Daniel's ass was pretty upside down.

Noted.

"Hey, you two. No ER visits today, okay? Emory and I want to stay in and snuggle."

"Uncle Mitch! Did you see? Dan-O can do a cartwheel!"

Do was a strong term. Attempt—that was way closer.

"Uncle Dan-O can do anything. He's a wizard, didn't you know?" He set Emory down in the grass to let him crawl but kept a close eye because the kid liked to try to eat bugs. And sticks. And rocks. Pretty much anything he could get in his mouth.

"Uh-huh. He's cool."

Dan grinned and rolled his eyes, but didn't argue, even though Vicki had been screaming about hating him, an hour ago.

"He's very cool. And he loves you. So we have to take care of him, right?"

"Yes! Dan-O! Play seeky-seek with me!"

"How about Ring Around the Rosie?" Dan held out his hands to her.

"Oh boy." Mitch scooped Emory back up again so they didn't "all fall down" on the baby. "Dizzy Dan should be fun."

"You like to play, don't you?" Vicki asked, and Dan nodded.

"I used to have lots of brothers and sisters to play games with."

Lots? Mitch made note of that, and decided they needed more pillow talk. It wasn't that he wanted to dredge up anything painful but getting to know his new lover meant getting to know all of him.

"You don't anymore?" Vicki asked with pure curiosity.

Mitch winced inwardly. Dan's plain honesty was both a blessing and a curse.

"Nope. I have you and Emmers and your Uncle Mitch."

The kids didn't have grandparents on either side, and Mitch had no one either.

"You're really lucky to have Emory. You two will grow up together and be best friends." Most of the time. But it was true enough for now.

"Yeah. I'd rather have Daddy."

Dan snorted and shook his head. "That's not how the world works, angel. There's no picking and choosing. You get what you get, and you make it work."

Vicki stared at Dan for a long time, and Mitch could see the wheels turning as her little brain worked to figure out how what Dan had said fit into her view of things. Then she took a deep breath, glanced over at him, then back at Dan. "Okay."

"Love you, Angel. Do you know about hopscotch? Chalk drawing?" Daniel's eyes went wide. "Have you seen Mary Poppins?"

She frowned. "No. Where is she?"

"She's in a movie. And in the movie Bert draws magic on the sidewalks. It's one of my favorites." Dan's voice lowered to a whisper. "I wanted to make magic drawings, so bad."

Vicki's eyes went wide. "I want to see Mary Poppins!"

See? You're right, Dan is a wizard. A couple of hours of electronic babysitting was just what they needed.

"Yay!" Dan picked her up and swung her about. "Have you kissed Uncle Mitch and told him happy Friday?"

"No. Happy Friday, Uncle Mitch!" She kept her arms around Dan's neck but leaned toward him with kissy lips.

"Happy Friday, beautiful girl." He stuck out his cheek and she gave him a big fat wet kiss, gross and wonderful, and he kissed her back. "I could make popcorn."

"I like popcorn!" She smiled at him. "It was a bad day today. I'm glad I'm home."

"It was bad, but it's not ruined. We can make it better."

Emory lunged for Vicki going straight for her hair, and

both he and Dan took a defensive step backward. Emory shrieked, laughing and he couldn't help but laugh too.

"Nice reflexes, Dan-O."

"Thanks. Damn." Dan looked a little horrified. "Let's not do that again."

"Yeah. Let's not do that again." Vicki looked at Dan and rolled her eyes. "Take me to Mary Popovers!"

"Mary Popovers, ho!" Dan's laugh chased them inside.

13

"Hey, Daniel."

"Hey. You're on speaker, Ally." Daniel had seen his manager's name pop up on the phone, and he had almost let it go to voice mail, but—It had been a month.

"Am I? Who's listening?"

"The baby. He's a good listener." He talked to Emmers a lot, really.

There was a short pause before she spoke again. "The baby. So...maybe you should catch me up?" That was diplomatic.

"Have I not..." He blinked. "Adam died. He left me his business partner and his kids. I live in Vermont now. Everything is new."

"Well. That's...god. I'm so sorry about Adam. I just have to process here a bit. How does one leave someone a business partner? And Vermont doesn't sound like a good business decision."

"I don't know." He sat down on the floor with Emmers, so thankful that no one was home. "My soul hurts. Adam is the person I would call when I feel like this."

"Oh Daniel, this is so awful for you. And kids? Are you sure you're ready for this? Do you have help?"

"Mitch. Mitch is—he's amazing. He loves the kids. He likes me too, and he holds me, which I need, but I can't tell him how wigged I am. I don't want him to be disappointed in me." It was like someone had turned on a faucet, and now he couldn't shut up.

"He likes you? Are you into him? Why would he be disappointed?" Ally was asking so many questions.

"I do. I like him a lot. In that sex sort of way." He glanced at Emory. *Don't tell Mitch I said that in front of you.* "I'm just—I need my things. I need to work. I need to be okay, and I'm not sure I'm okay, but I have to be okay, because I have a family now!"

And they were all there all time. All the time.

"Okay. Hold on a second, Daniel. Everything single thing about you has changed completely in a month, and you expect to just be okay? You don't have to be fine. If Mitch cares about you he won't expect you to be fine either. Your work is more than a job for you, it's like...your sanity. Does he know that? You need to tell him." Ally's voice was calm but firm. "Where are your things? Maybe you should take a break and go get them. I think you should."

"What about the kids? The baby? I don't—I-I—" He closed his eyes and sucked in a breath as Emmers started to fuss. *Stop, Daniel. Stop. You're scaring the baby.*

"Hey. Listen to me. Okay?" Ally took a deep breath herself. "Daniel, just listen. You said Mitch loves the kids, right? He can keep them for what, a few days? A week at most? Just so you can get your things. He can. The kids will be fine."

"I'll talk to him. Maybe I can take them over the holidays and drive." Maybe they could all go. Would that be weird?

"Or maybe you need a few days to yourself. Think about it. This is a lot." She sighed. "So I guess you don't have anything new for me."

"No. Not right now. I've been making angry things. Hurt things." He'd been sneaking time when the baby was asleep.

"Okay. But are they good? Send me pictures."

Was she serious?

"Really? I'm—they're hurting, not..."

"Daniel, just do it. Don't argue."

"Right."

Ally did the business, and she had never led him wrong.

"Thank you. Now. What can I do? Do you need an advance?"

"I don't think so. Can I call you after I figure out... anything?" What did he spend money on? School supplies?

"You can call any time, Daniel. I'm always here. I know I'm just your agent, but I do care about you, and I have some resources. I think you should think about taking a few days on your own and getting your head straight. You don't sound all that okay to me."

"I am, unless I'm not. I just haven't been able to scream, you know?" He wanted to rage against god, but...he was a dad. His job was to raise these little people into bigger people.

"I do know. Get your...friend to watch the kids for a few days. Go scream. You'll be a better father. And send me those pictures. Tomorrow."

"Tomorrow. I will. Love you, lady."

"Ditto. Call me."

Ally hung up, and the house was quiet again. Emory was busily chewing on his toes, but went after the phone as soon as he put it down.

"Are you going to call Heaven and explain to your daddy

that he sucks?" Daniel nuzzled one baby foot, grinning as Emory cackled.

He'd only been playing dad for a month but, even in that short time Emory had changed so much. He was rolling all over the place now and he was so close to crawling. So damn close. And his eyes would lock on things like he was curious and was trying to understand, not just to stare. There was a little person in there, working on coming out.

"Are you going to know anything about your dad, like in your soul? Are you going to be his, in your genes? God, I hope so. I don't want him to just fade away into nothing."

A little of his dad, and hopefully a little of his mom too. Vicki didn't remember much about her mother, but Emory wouldn't remember either of them. He was all this baby would know. Him, and Mitch.

God. He didn't know what to think, so he tried not to. He loved Emory. Mitch did too. That was going to be what Emmers knew.

Assuming he and Mitch worked out. Assuming this somehow was a real thing and not just what was easy, or just them trying to play at being a family.

He found himself sitting there, staring, just watching Emory chew on his phone—at least until it rang and vibrated, making Emmers drop it and burst into tears.

Mitch.

Lord.

"Is that Emory? Is he having a morning?"

"He was chewing on my phone, that's all. How're you?"

"I am having a very average, normal Monday, and I thought I would call and share that with you before everything went to hell." Mitch laughed. He seemed to be in a good mood. "I was thinking I could leave in time to grab

Vic from school for you and then we'd get home before the snow starts."

"Is it going to?" *I talked to my agent. She thinks I need to go get my shit together.*

"They're saying eight to ten inches. Yeah. I don't mind driving in it, but why do it if I don't have to, you know? I could even stop by the store if we need anything."

"I—I could make green chile stew, but it's spicy..." He needed to work. He needed to remember how to breathe. "Ten inches is impressive."

"Thank you. Oh! Were you talking about the snow?" Mitch cracked up, giggling into the phone.

Daniel felt the tension in his chest relax with a pop, and he started laughing too. Oh. Oh, that felt better. That felt real.

"I love your laugh. Text me what you need for your stew, and I'll grab it on the way home. If Herself doesn't like it, we can make her grilled cheese. It sounds great to me."

"I can do that. I—" *Was having a terrible day.* "Needed a call."

"Yeah? Well, then I'm very glad I did. We'll be home in an hour or so. Maybe I'll put a fire on to warm us up."

"Yeah." He might need to be held. He might need someone to tell him he was going to be okay. "I'd like that."

"Me too. Let me run. We'll be home soon." Mitch hung up, but that was okay. He was coming home.

Daniel looked at Emory, who was grinning at him. "Hey, baby. We're going to have to learn about snow in Vermont. We get it in New Mexico too, so we'll be fine."

Emory's entire body wriggled like snow was the best thing ever.

It had started by the time Mitch rolled in the driveway, and Vicki hopped out, bounding up to the front porch and standing on the steps to let it fall on her face. Mitch scooped her up as he passed her, making her laugh. "Hi, honey, we're home!" Mitch called out.

"We're home, honey!" Vicki echoed happily.

"Emmers and I are also home, my dears," he called back, while Emory just farted like a mule.

Daniel was beginning to suspect this was Emmer's way to communicate.

"Good to see you too, Emory." Mitch shook his head, came right to Daniel and kissed his cheek. "It's snowing." Mitch's eyes were lit up and happy. "I have the stuff for your stew."

"Thanks. Seriously. It's good to see you." He drank up that happiness and let it soothe him. "Yay snow!"

Mitch caught his eye. "Are you okay?"

"Uncle Mitch, are you going to make lunch? I'm hungry." Vicki leaned against Mitch's leg.

Mitch rolled his eyes. "Let me get her fed and put the groceries away. Then I'll start a fire, okay? Then we can talk."

"I'll help. What are you supposed to make for lunch?" He went to put Emory in his high chair.

"She asked for an apple with peanut butter and hot cocoa."

"And pretzels!"

Mitch shrugged. "And pretzels."

"Mmm." He was a fan of pretzels. "I love pretzels and hummus together."

"What's hummus?" Vicki asked, and he hid his grin, answering with a straight face.

"Bean mayonnaise."

"Ew!" Vicki made a stinky face.

"Yeah, that wasn't a very good sell, Uncle Dan-O." Mitch

bumped shoulders with him as he passed by to put the groceries away.

"No? I like beans, and I like mayo." It worked perfectly for him.

Mitch chuckled and set a jar of peanut butter and an apple on the counter. "I happen to like hummus and pretzels too. Also carrot sticks. Yummy. You want to cut an apple or make cocoa?"

"I'll cut the apples. I like your hot chocolate better." Dan loved it cut with coffee.

And Mitch made it for him just how he liked it.

They got Vicki fed and settled in her room for a while. Kindergarten wore her butt out, and she had started crashing for a little while after lunch every day. Usually she'd just go up to play and then crawl into bed at some point and fall asleep. If they were really lucky, like they were today, Emmers would nap at the same time.

"Right on, Uncle Dan-O." Mitch winked at him and got to work on a fire in the den. "Kindergarten for the win, huh?"

"She loves it, most days, and she adores when Uncle Mitch comes, because that's special." Anything different was special, right? That was sort of the definition of special, when you got right down to it.

"She was excited to see me. And she liked shopping for your stew. She said she wanted to try it." The fire was starting small, but he could tell it was going to grow quickly. Mitch stood and moved in close. "Tough day?"

"Does it show?" Because it had been. He'd been...lost and worried and stressed and unsure and anxious. He leaned in, letting himself feel Mitch right in close.

"A little? You just seem...stressed." Mitch shrugged and

circled long arms around him. "Emory is a handful right now, I know."

"No. No, he's good. My agent called. I hadn't—I hadn't talked to her. She didn't know, and I had to tell her everything." And it hurt his soul—even the good parts felt raw.

"Oh. Oh, man. I'm sorry." Mitch gave him a squeeze and then led him to the sofa that faced the fire. It was roaring now, warming his skin. Mitch rubbed his chest like he knew just where it hurt. "It's hard. It was hard for me to talk to people at work too."

"Worse, I'm sure, because they loved him too." Lots of people had loved Adam. Tons. Him? Well, he had fewer folks, but he thought they loved him pretty damn well.

"Are you glad she called though? Was it good to talk to her?"

"She wants me to go and get my trailer, clear my head." His cheeks began to burn. "I sort of had a meltdown."

Mitch leaned back in the sofa and pulled Dan with him. "I'm sorry. I could have come home sooner. You can always call me; you know that right?" Mitch's hands smoothed down one arm.

"I should... I don't want to be a pain in the ass. I have this." Except he didn't. He really didn't. He felt lost, and he didn't want to bitch at Mitch about it.

"You've got this, huh? So, what's the plan?"

"I—I have no idea." He looked at Mitch, shaking his head. "I honestly have no idea what to do, love."

Mitch kissed his temple. "Okay. So stop pretending you're a pain in the ass when you know you're not and talk to me. I assume you want your trailer?"

"It's all the stuff I have in the world. My good coat. My books and my paints—so yes. The stuff. We could travel in the trailer. That might be neat with the kids?" That might be fun, actually.

"Hm." Mitch was quiet for a second, thoughtful. "I can't just pick up and leave work again right now, baby. And Vicki just started school...when were you thinking of doing this? Soon, probably, right?"

"Ally said I should." *Think. Creative thinking. You do this for a living, for fuck's sake, Daniel.* "Maybe... Is there... Do you know if I could hire it done? Is that a thing? I'd hate to drive for hours and hours with Emmers stuck in a car seat..."

"Maybe. Sure, maybe. We could research, or possibly your agent would know. Would you trust someone with your rig? Or... I can hire someone to watch Emory, and you just can go get it if you want. Adam had a sitter he used, so someone might be available."

He sighed softly, weirdly reluctant to leave the kids, to leave things right now. "I'll just keep paying the rent at the place until I find a good solution. Nothing's going to rot. I can buy more paint."

"Let's keep talking about it. I want you to have your things. I think that's important. We'll figure it out. I wish it was easier, though."

"Nothing feels easy right now. Nothing but you. You feel like things will be okay. You make me feel..." Like he could breathe.

Mitch touched his face and took a deep breath with him. "Tell me."

"You make it hurt less." Because he did hurt—he missed Adam. He was scared to be a terrible father. He was scared that he was just wrong—about everything.

"You make all of this easier for me too. I'm...okay, this is going to sound weird, I know. But I'm starting to wonder if Adam knew what he was doing."

"What?" He glanced up, his attention fully caught.

"I know. But...don't you kind of feel set up?"

"I feel confused. Why me? Why did he—" Do this to me? What if Mitch had hated him? What if he wasn't a great parent?

"I asked myself that after the funeral when we found out his custody wishes. Why pin you down? And he had to have known I wouldn't want to give the kids up. But I could see you loved them. I didn't want to take them away from you either. So... I don't know. You were his best friend. I was a friend and business partner...maybe he was trying to push us together?" Mitch shrugged. "I just... I don't know. It's just something I was thinking about."

"I want—My chest hurts." Daniel tried to suck in a breath. Adam was his family. He didn't know who to talk to now. He was in a relationship—his first guy that was a let's sleep together and be together and live together relationship —and Adam was supposed to be here to help him.

Mitch sighed and hugged him tighter. "Fuck, I'm sorry. I was... I shouldn't have said all of that. I didn't mean to freak you out."

"No." No, Mitch didn't understand. He stood up, beginning to pace, his heart fluttering in his throat as he fought the urge to cry. "No, I'm not freaked out. I miss him. I want to tell him about you, about Vicki and school. I want him to laugh at me and tell me that we're like Mutt and Jeff and perfect for each other, and that I will be able to paint here."

"I miss him too." Mitch stood but didn't stop his pacing. "I get up from my desk all the time like I can go into his office and ask his advice on something. Work, Vicki...mostly though, I just want to thank him. For you."

"For me?" He had to confess. Had to. "I'm a fuck up.

Adam was the only person who thought I was worth anything."

"Hey." Mitch stepped in front of him, cutting him off. "You're solid, Dan. I didn't really know you before this, but you haven't fucked up a thing since you got here. You're kind and funny, and you're way handier than I am for sure. You're fantastic with the kids. You're right there for them. And you're there for me."

"I—" He reached for Mitch, because he didn't know what else to do. He simply didn't know what to do. "Help."

"Dan. No one is asking you to prove that you deserve this." Mitch caught his nape and kissed him, following up his words with an undeniable, physical truth.

The connection was enough to stop the rushing worry, and the inhalation he took was flavored with Mitch. He could imagine it—their molecules melding together, balancing each other.

"Better." Mitch whispered, still just a breath away.

"Yes." So much better. Mitch's eyes were warm, the look happy, admiring him.

Mitch pulled him back to the couch where the fire was cheerful. "I may not know what next week looks like, but I do know a few things. We're allowed to miss him. We're allowed to wish we could talk to him. Things are going to be okay. And you will be able to paint here."

There was something so comforting about those sure, solid words. Something that he could believe in. "I need to. My work is important to me."

His work was part of the air he breathed.

"Whatever I can do to help make it happen, you just let me know. Do you want me to watch the kids Saturday so you can get whatever you need? Give you some time to get set up? It's a really nice space you have for your studio, maybe you just need to be in it for a little while."

He wasn't sure what he needed, but just the offer was a balm. "Maybe. I may just need to get in the studio and remember how to work."

"There's a solution. We'll find it for you." Mitch's warm hands felt both soothing and protective as they slid over him. "You take Saturday and close the studio door. I went back to work, so you should too. Maybe after you've had some time we can talk about how to make it work for you long term, you know?"

"Yeah. I've never tried long term before. I'll have to practice a lot." He tried the wink out, the tease, and he found it didn't feel like a lie.

"I haven't either. Practice makes perfect, right?" Mitch smiled at him again, looking completely relaxed. Did he ever worry about anything?

Maybe not. Mitch had worked with Adam, and god knew that man was the king of split-second decisions.

"We just had a grown-up conversation in the middle of the day without being interrupted." Mitch chuckled softly. "To think—you could have had a blow job."

"Dammit!" He rolled his eyes and cracked up. The blow job would have been way more fun. Maybe not more necessary, but...way more relaxing.

"No more talking for us, right? It's a waste of precious time." They just laughed together, Mitch's abs vibrating against him.

"No shit on that. No talking. No stress." He rested his forehead against Mitch's, tickled as anything.

"What's your favorite place on earth?" Mitch put his feet up on the chest that served as a coffee table, eyes on the fire.

"Taos. There's magic in the air there that's nowhere else." And the Taos hum was happy making.

"Taos?" The name sounded rich when Mitch said it. "Tell me about it."

"It's higher than Santa Fe, a little old West, a lot Native American, but there's magic in the light. Art." He took one of Mitch's hands and told his lover about this amazing pizza place, about buying wine glasses in Arroyo Seco, about the way that the bobcats came down off the mountain.

Mitch listened, nodding slowly and smiling, not humoring him or just letting him talk, but really hearing what he was saying. "Well, you have to take me there one day. It sounds...just like you said. Magical. I love the light in your eyes when you talk about it."

"I'd love to show you around. I love traveling, and going with you would be magic. Do you think the kids will like it?"

"With you as a tour guide I can't imagine anyone who wouldn't. The poop monster likes everything, and you know Vicki loves an adventure." Mitch slipped out from behind him and got up to stoke up the fire.

"The poop monster loves everything but pureed sweet potatoes." That had been a terrible experiment. One he never wanted to repeat.

"And peas. Oh...the peas." Mitch shuddered and flopped back next to him on the couch. "So, Colchester isn't Taos I guess, but it can be very pretty. Maybe with a dusting of snow you'll get inspired."

"There's going to be a whole new world to explore." He leaned against the back of the couch with one cheek. "Ally wants pictures of what I've been working on."

"She's your agent? I guess that's her job..." Mitch must have gotten a look at them at some point because he seemed to understand why her request was kind of awkward.

"Yeah. Those are different. Personal. I'm not ready to sell them." He might not ever be ready.

"Isn't art always personal?" Mitch mirrored him, lying his head on the couch too, and played with a lock of hair near his forehead.

"Yes, but personal art and personal pain aren't the same, right? Like writing a truth and writing *your* truth."

Mitch squinted at him. He could tell Mitch was trying to understand. "Your truth is bigger than the truth itself. So, Adam died is the truth. But your truth is that Adam died and left you with a new, complicated life you're not sure you...um." Mitch nodded. "I mean I get that."

"That I'm not sure I understand." Daniel wanted that to be clear. "That I'm not sure I'm good enough to manage. What I do know is that I'm enough to try."

Mitch relaxed a little. He could see it. "I don't really know what I'm doing either, but we're not alone, right? I just had a couple of months head start. And I have to tell you, everything has been easier since you arrived."

Oh. Oh, damn. That felt so good to hear. Like Mitch had hugged his soul. "Yeah?"

"Yes. Everything." Mitch's sigh ended in a soft laugh, and he rolled his eyes. "I guess you thought I was a natural parent, huh? I had no idea what I was doing. I had Adam, you know? He taught me things, told me about the kids, showed me how to bath time and the way Vicki likes her sandwiches cut. But I was on my own and already in over my head by the time you got here. When you showed up and Vicki went running out to you? God, I was so relieved."

"I'm still scared, but not like I was. When I found out, I couldn't even feel anything. I'm so glad you didn't walk away from me."

"I wanted to." Mitch caught his eye and gave him a wink. "For a minute."

Shit. It had so been longer than that, but Mitch had put the kids first. Him too. He couldn't have done this alone. "I bet you were furious and hurt. I know you were. I'm not sure I could have not been hurt at me. I love that about you."

"I was…" Mitch looked thoughtful for a breath and then nodded. "I was hurt. But I knew Adam well. Very well. Every client we ever had he would say to me, 'Okay. Suppose this were my business?' you know? He never made a decision without thinking about other people. So, I knew he had a reason. I knew eventually I would understand." Mitch shook his head. "It wasn't like you had any idea. I could see that. There wasn't any point in being mad at you. He loved you."

"He did. He was my best friend. He saved my life." No one on earth had ever believed in him like Adam had. No one had ever thought he could be more than he was before Adam had. Now, Vicki did. Mitch did. Even Emmers.

Mitch tangled their fingers and then covered them with his other hand like that connection was something precious. "I didn't think he'd want me to take it out on you. And now I can't imagine doing this without you."

"No. No, we've made a family. We're in this together. I—" He stopped, frowned. "We need to talk to the lawyer."

"Oh." Mitch blinked at him, looking surprised. "Well… are you sure? I hope you don't think I'm—it should wait until you're sure."

"What if something happens to one of us? We need to make sure we're settled." What if Mitch needed to take Emmers to the ER? What if he passed out? What if Mitch had an accident?

"Right. Well, you can have him draw up a letter so I can make medical decisions for them, that's easy."

He shook his head. That didn't work for him at all. "No. We're a family. You. Me. Them. Right?"

"Yes. We are..." Mitch watched him carefully.

"Then...marry me."

The words fell from him, but he meant them. It wasn't romantic, but it was truth, and that was the most important thing.

"No." Mitch shook his head. "I mean, maybe. Maybe yes even, but no. Not like this. Like that. No."

Oh.

He let himself sit with that for a second, then he nodded. "Fair enough. I'd like you to be a guardian for the kids, one way or the other, so they have that."

Daniel would figure out his feelings later with a few canvases and a shit ton of paint.

He felt the weight of Mitch's gaze. Mitch hadn't stopped watching him. "I would love that. Thank you. Do you want me to make an appointment with Adam's lawyer?"

"Works for me. I'm assuming it's not a huge deal." If it was, they could deal with that too. Daniel glanced out at the snow, smiling. It was warmer in the house than in his trailer. "It's really coming down."

He was tired of talking now.

14

Mitch stood at the bedroom window wrapped in a blanket and watching the snow fall. They'd gotten close to a foot, but it was slowing down now, and in the morning they'd be squinting into bright sunshine. Dan was buried under the down comforter asleep—at least he hoped Dan was sleeping and not just trying to and failing like he'd been. Dan needed the rest; it had been a long day.

Every day had been a long day lately, for one of them, or both, or one of the kids, or all of them at the same damn time. This just wasn't easy. But maybe it shouldn't be. The hard things were what forced you to pay attention, live in the moment.

And there had been some moments.

That afternoon, he and Dan had managed some really good ones. They'd connected on so many things. He'd let Dan in on his own anxiety a little. He'd made Dan smile. God, that had been an exceptional moment.

But he wasn't wide-awake and worrying over Dan's smile. He was playing over what he'd done to make it disappear again.

Maybe he should have just said yes.

That proposal had shocked him, honestly. It felt like it had come out of nowhere. It had come right from Dan's heart, and it had been absolutely sincere; he knew that. But he just couldn't say yes yet.

Dan hadn't thrown a fit or even acted off, when he got right down to it. Dan had played with Vicki in the snow, had helped with dishes, chatting idly, but Mitch could tell that Dan was totally going through the motions.

Small wonder. He'd hurt Dan's feelings, and he knew it. Which meant they needed to talk. Again. More. Assuming Dan would.

He glanced back at the lump under the covers—his poor frozen cowboy. Well...still his? Hopefully. Frozen, probably. Cowboy for sure.

He went to sit on the edge of the bed, and Dan sighed softly.

"You okay? You're all restless."

"I'm sorry, am I keeping you up?" Mitch tossed the blanket onto the foot of the bed and climbed back in, which his frozen toes appreciated.

"Nope. I've been dozing. You're cold. C'mere." Dan snuggled into him with a quick inhalation.

"Just my feet mostly." Dan was warm and relaxed, and he tucked his arms around that lean body. He sighed, letting himself just be with his lover for a minute, breathe with him.

Dan was good at quiet, at still. Mitch could understand it —Dan had spent so much time alone that it was inevitable. Mitch wasn't though, and he was especially bad at holding things in that he needed to let out.

"I know I hurt your feelings today, and I'm sorry." He

had reasons for turning Dan down, but apologies needed to be just what they were first.

"You don't have to apologize. You told your truth. That's all I can ask."

"No, I didn't though. I said no because my gut said no. I didn't tell you anything. But I do have a reason, and I think it's...it's kind of a romantic reason, as silly as that sounds. And...well, when you're ready to talk about it, I can explain. You deserve an explanation." That was the truth. Or the beginning of it at least.

Dan kissed him on the cheek. "We have a plan now, though. So it's okay. I have your back."

They had a plan for the kids, which was important. It would be good for them to both be able to make decisions and handle all the legal things. But a plan as a couple? They didn't have that. "I have your back too. I meant everything I said today, I hope you know that. We're a team. We're a family."

"We are. I might need a dog."

He angled his head so he could see Dan's face in the dim light. "A dog?"

"Yeah. A dog. Do you like dogs? We can talk about cats, if you'd rather, but I like animals."

"I...know nothing about dogs. Or cats. But I like them both. You want a dog? Let's get a dog." A dog. Because they didn't have enough chaos in the house. But Dan was the one home all day and if he wanted a dog, he should have one.

"Yeah? Okay. I'll start looking. It needs to be the right dog, because of the kids. Did you have critters when you were a kid?"

"No. I didn't have pets. Unless you count the field mice and the occasional bear." His grandparents hadn't been into warm and fuzzy on any level.

"A real bear? I would love to touch a real bear. I grew up with a ton of pits. Good beasts, for the most part." Dan's face was relaxed, fingers idly tracing patterns on his skin.

"These aren't touchable bears. But they do look soft— the black bear coats? They look like you could just snuggle right in." He didn't have an opinion on pits or any other dog. He was completely clueless. That was definitely on Dan. "Are you thinking a puppy?"

"No. We aren't up for that. A dog. Something with a little training and a good temperament." So that was definite and sure.

He nodded. "Sounds reasonable. There are a couple of shelters around. I can help you look them up tomorrow." He just held Dan, trying to appreciate how easy it was and not worry about the things he needed to explain.

"Good." Dan opened his eyes. "You can relax, you know. I'm not a bastard. I had a rough day, but I got over myself. I swear."

Mitch huffed a soft laugh. "If I thought you were a bastard I wouldn't let you anywhere near the kids." He rolled so he was hanging over Dan, looking down at the kindest face he'd ever known. "You're allowed to have a rough day. It's okay not to be okay. You are enough, Daniel McCaverty. I said it earlier, but it's worth repeating. And I'll tell you again every time I think you need to hear it. You're everything this family needs."

He bent and kissed Dan's sternum, drew a line with his tongue to one sweet nipple and from there up to the hollow of Dan's throat. "You're everything I need."

Dan sucked in a deep breath, the tiny sound pure need. "I like how you show it."

"Mm. Good." Sometimes talking wasn't enough. "I'm going to appreciate every inch of you." He tasted Dan again, this time behind one ear, the flavor a little salty, a little wild. He tried a kiss, a short one, which was nowhere near enough, so the next one was longer, hungrier.

Dan stretched, rubbing up against him in a long, lazy motion, that Mitch felt from his balls to his bones. As their hair caught, his nerves began to tingle.

He loved that Dan was kind and sweet, but right now he was more interested in the part of Dan that was hot as fuck and had no shame. He licked Dan's throat and nipped at his collar bone, fingers sliding under Dan to get a handful of that perfect ass.

"Yeah. Yeah, I need you. Like all the way." Dan's fingers tangled in his hair, keeping his biting kisses where they belonged.

"All the way. Uh-huh." He worked a knee between Dan's thighs. It was so pretty, the way Dan spread like a hot knife through butter. Mitch felt it stretch his spine, loving how Dan needed him.

He felt his cock stretch too, the friction so right against Dan's hip. He let Dan guide him, teeth moving down to nip and pinch. He drew that pretty nipple up between his lips and rolled with his tongue.

Dan's body told him that he was giving his lover what he needed. That hard body and the sweet, strangled sounds. And that was what he wanted. He wanted to focus on Dan, watch him move, and drive him mad.

He slid his hand from Dan's ass to cup his balls. Mitch slid a finger along the sensitive line of skin to a perfectly puckered hole, stroking up and back as his palm pressed into Dan's hot, heavy sac.

Dan leaned into his touch, lips parting as he rocked, the friction between them stoking the fire.

"I want you, Dan. I want inside you." His balls grew tight just at the idea, making him moan. "I need you."

"Yes. Yes. I want—" Dan reached down, cupped his cock and squeezed it. "—you."

Lightning shot up his spine. He loved seeing Dan as hot as he was. Hotter even. He dove for the nightstand, dug up supplies, and slicked his fingers. "I got you." Mitch pushed Dan's hand aside and replaced it with his own, and the slippery fingers on his other found Dan's tight muscle and teased their way in.

Dan was deliciously heated, muscles rippling around his fingers, squeezing him rhythmically. "Oh, damn."

Mitch was completely enthralled, eyes studying Dan's face and his needy expression. "Good? How do you like it, baby? Deep? Fast? Easy going?"

"Been a long time. But I like it deep. I want to feel you tomorrow."

Mitch answered by pressing his fingers in deeper, until his knuckles were right up against Dan's ass. "I can give you something to feel." And Dan would walk around here tomorrow while he was at work unable to forget him.

"Yeah..." Dan began to move, riding his touch with a steady rocking rhythm, focused on him, on his fingers. Damn, that was pretty.

Mitch could watch this for a while, keep Dan right here until he begged. He kept a good hold on Dan's prick and glided his thumb over the head, dipping into the slit with his thumb.

"Oh fuck yeah..." Dan's body clenched around him like vise.

His cock jerked and his balls drew up, and Mitch knew there was no way he could wait Dan out. He just wasn't that guy. Patient everywhere but in bed. He was craving Dan, he needed more, and he needed it now. "Are you ready for me?" He let Dan's cock go and grabbed the condom, tearing it open with his teeth.

"You want me like this or hands and knees?" Dan grabbed one knee and tugged, spreading himself wide.

He pulled his fingers back and rolled on the rubber, mouth going so dry he had to swallow and lick his lips before he could speak. "Jesus, Dan. Just like that. You're fucking gorgeous." And he could get deeper this way.

Dan smiled at him, and it lit him up all the way to the bone. "Thank you."

That was the smile he'd chased away earlier. It was back, and he was going to be more careful with it now. He lined up, his impatient cock pressing firmly against Dan's body. "Oh, thank *you*." He leaned a little and let up, then tried again, giving Dan time to adjust, to relax.

When his cock popped in, it was like being hit by a wall of heat, and he groaned, his sound joining Dan's as they connected.

"Oh, fuck, Dan. So tight." He ducked under the leg Dan had pulled back and caught it with his shoulder, bending Dan even more as he leaned in, sinking deeper and deeper with each careful thrust.

Dan's lips parted, and he sucked in air, each breath evident around Mitch's prick, Dan tightening and relaxing again and again.

Mitch was going to lose his fucking mind. He took a breath and puffed it out, focusing on Dan and everything he wanted to give his lover. He groaned as his thighs pressed tight against Dan's ass and gave one more quick thrust. Any deeper and his balls would climb right inside.

"Yes. Again." That was a clear demand, firm, needy.

He did it again and it forced another groan from him. He

quenched a little of his own need by turning his head and sucking up a dark bruise on the inside of Dan's thigh.

"Marking me. Fuck that's hot." Dan fought to get the words out, the sound rough and husky.

"Tomorrow," he said, on a panting breath. "I want you to remember you're mine." His voice was rough too. Possessive, which was unusual for him, but he didn't hate it. He rocked into Dan, giving them both more to feel, more to work with.

"Fuck." Dan grabbed at his shoulders, clinging to him. "Fuck, that's hot."

He could feel that compliment in his bones. And he was just getting started. Mitch walked his knees up a little closer for a better angle and thrust deep, picking up a steady, patient rhythm that he thought he could hold onto for a while.

Dan met his thrusts, rocking with him, joining them so they worked in tandem.

"That's it." He kept one arm braced on the bed but caught Dan's thick cock in his other hand and let the motion push all that length through his fingers. "Good, baby?"

"Perfect. Gonna beg for this over and over, hear me?" Those were words that suited him to the bone.

"I hear you." He ducked his head and picked up the pace, letting Dan scramble to catch up despite his lack of leverage. "Come on, baby."

"Come...fuck, I—" Dan groaned, his body beginning to milk Mitch's cock as the heavy ball sac drew up.

God, Dan was so sexy when he was flustered. Mitch took it up another notch, listening to his own need now, hips slapping into Dan's. Dan's lips pulled away from his teeth, his shoulders leaving the mattress as they rutted.

With Dan just in reach, Mitch took a breathless kiss, their lips barely catching for a moment between their harsh pants. He wouldn't trade their rub-offs and their blow jobs for anything but this—this was what they'd been missing. This connection was undeniably them.

Their gazes locked, and he could see the universe for a second, he swore it.

Perfect.

Then he thrust in again, and Dan whimpered, his eyes rolling.

"Dan..." Mitch swallowed and found that same spot again, keeping his hips steady and concentrated on driving Dan crazy—on making Dan come.

It didn't take much longer before Dan began to shatter, his lips parted, his entire body working to shoot. "Soon."

Yeah. Soon was right. He was barely holding on. "Show me, beautiful."

Dan reached up, cupped his jaw, thumb sliding over his lips, then it was all over, Dan shooting between them.

Dan's scent was heady but the grip around his cock made it hard to breathe. He shuddered and groaned, hips useless for a long moment before Dan began to relax. An unsteady breath later, Mitch came hard, hips jerking and arms trembling under his own weight.

Dan pulled him down into a sloppy, lazy kiss, thanking him in a very direct way.

He indulged in the kiss, in the lazy hormone fog until his arms finally protested and he flopped onto the bed beside Dan. Good things—right things—were going through his mind, like ditch the rubber and make sure Dan was okay, but his body wasn't having any of it yet. He was heavy as lead.

"Damn, man." Dan got it, he could tell.

"Uh-huh. You good?" There. He asked. Go him.

"Mmhmm. Good." Dan's eyes rolled before they closed. "So good."

He managed to tie off the condom and drop it in the bin by the bed. Then he curled around Dan, one arm over his side. *I love you*, he thought as his eyes slid shut. *Shit.* He should have said that out loud. He'd remember in the morning.

15

The music was slamming into him, the paint flying as he poured himself out—love, fury, pain, joy, need. Everything.

Daniel painted, using the snow as his muse—blues and grays, creams, and then the universe was punctuated by pure white.

By the time that the sun was sinking, he was lying on the floor, soaked in sweat, utterly exhausted.

Daniel couldn't have moved if he wanted to.

He had no idea what Mitch had done with the kids, but no one had interrupted him all day. He hadn't heard anything over his music. He'd just been focused. In the zone.

It had felt like sex, but deeper, because he couldn't live without this. He'd done without sex.

He was just starting to catch his breath when there was a soft knock on the door. "Dan? Dinner's just about ready. No pressure, but I heard your music shut off and I thought—you okay?"

"Uh-huh. 'Mon in." Supper sounded like a great idea.

The door opened and Mitch came in, along with a rush of cooler air. "Warm in here. Whoa." Mitch stood back taking in his work. Or his mess. Probably both.

"Hey. Oh, man. Feels good." He closed his eyes and let himself breathe, let himself float. He didn't ask what Mitch thought.

Mitch was suddenly on the floor beside him, one hand resting on his belly. "Tired? You've been busy."

"I have. I poured it all out. Every ounce."

Mitch rubbed light circles on his stomach. "Excellent. I love them. I really like that one, all the snow...it's really beautiful."

"Thank you." That touch echoed all the way through him. "Thank you for today. I needed it."

"Did it feel good? Are you happy with what you got done?"

He had no idea what he'd finished, but he knew he was happy and empty and right inside. "It felt amazing."

Mitch leaned down and kissed him. "Perfect. I've got Vicki setting the table. I'll make sure she sets you a place. You want a hand up?"

"Please? I'm sore." And tired. But happy.

"I bet." Mitch got to his feet and offered him a hand. "Come on up, baby."

He took the offer, and Mitch pulled him up, right into that hard body. "Oh. Hello."

Mitch tucked a hand over his ass and smiled. "Hello, handsome."

"Handsome and colorful, right?" He loved the way the art colored him.

"Yes. Colorful suits you. It's a good look." Mitch's kiss was quick but hot, and those blue eyes flashed at him. "I'll wash you off in the shower later if you want."

"Oh..." Hell yes. "I want. I so want."

That won him the sweetest laugh and Mitch pulled him along. "I missed you today. Come on, let's go eat."

"What's for supper?" He was happy to leave the room behind, along with all the emotions he'd spent.

"Vicki requested spaghetti and meatballs, and I made garlic bread. And I finally got up the nerve to raid Adam's wine stores in the basement and dug out a Chianti."

"Spaghetti!" Vicki came running over. "Did you paint all your feelings, Uncle Dan-O?"

He grabbed Vicki up and spun her around. "I did, my beautiful angel. And I'm starving. Did you tell Uncle Mitch that garlic bread is my absolute favorite?"

Vicki wriggled. "You're all painty!"

"I am. I was busy making things. What did you do today?"

"Played Candy Land three times."

"It was awesome." Mitch winked at him. "Go sit, baby girl. I'll get your brother. You want to pour the wine, Dan? I want to hear all about your paintings after dinner." Mitch disappeared into the living room, where he probably had Emmers in his playpen.

"Mmm..." Daniel poured two generous glasses, the scent of the Chianti making him think of velvet curtains, drugged kisses.

"Look Ems, it's Dan-O."

"Oooooo..." Emory repeated making grabby hands for him.

Mitch handed the baby off and picked up the wine. On the table were two covered dishes and a big plate covered in foil. Mitch uncovered all the food and started serving Vicki while he got Emmers into his chair.

"You think we can mush up a meatball for Emory? Because you know he's going to want what we're having."

"Sure, why not? If he wants it, let him try it." Daniel liked the idea that the kids could be adventurous with food. He was going to travel with them, so they needed to learn about different textures and flavors and shit.

They served up big plates of spaghetti and drank their wine, and he and Mitch ate half a loaf of garlic bread between them. Vicki talked for most of the meal, telling them stories about school and movies, and her dolls, until Emory started to fuss.

"Oh, look at that, Vicki. It's bedtime." Mitch gave him a wink and stood.

"Already? No fair!"

"Do you want me to get Emmers ready for bed, or Miss Vicki?" He got it—they needed sleeping children to get in the shower and start to fill up all his empty spaces with Mitch's need.

"Me, me!" Vicki ran around the table to him. "It's my turn Uncle Dan-O. It's been *all day*."

"There you go. You guys head on up. We can do dishes and whatever after we get them in bed." Mitch scooped Emory out of his chair, quieting him instantly. "You and me, Ems." Mitch danced Emory around the kitchen, making the baby giggle.

"Did you miss me so bad all day?" Vicki asked. "I wanted to go paint with you, but Uncle Mitch said you had to work." She stuck her tongue out. "Work sucks."

"Does it? I need to do it." He scooped her up and carried her up toward the bathtub.

"Did you paint about Daddy?"

"A little bit. I painted about you and Emmers and Uncle Mitch too. And about moving to Vermont."

"Do you like them? Uncle Mitch said you are going to sell them."

"That's something someone else does." He didn't care about them now. They were done. They didn't belong to him anymore. What he cared about was the process, not the product. "I want them to go where someone likes them."

"Somebody will love them." Vicki got undressed and ran buck naked for the bathroom. "I want the pink bubbles! Lulu at school has the same bubbles as me. Can she come play sometime? We both like snow too. And cupcakes."

"Sure. Sure, why not?" How did that work? Did he have to make nice with her parents? That was Mitch's job. The nice part. He could provide cupcakes, and the snow happened without his say-so.

"Yay!" She hopped in the tub as he filled it and they splashed around for a while until the water got chilly. She loved her baths. If they didn't let the water get uncomfortably cold, she'd never get out of it.

Mitch poked his head into the bathroom and held a finger to his lips. "Emory is down, okay Vicki? So shh."

"Dan-O says Lulu can come to play and eat cupcakes!" Vicki stood up and Daniel wrapped her in a towel.

"Oh yeah? I guess Dan-O will have to talk to Lulu's mom after school and figure out a day that works." Mitch shot him a knowing grin.

Wait. What? Him? He wasn't good at that. "We'll figure it out, me and Uncle Mitch."

Together.

Because talking to moms wasn't his strong suit.

Mitch chuckled and left the bathroom. "I've got dishes. See you downstairs, Dan-O."

"I'll be down as soon as books are read." They had a thing now—teeth and hair, nightie and one last pee, a bit of a chat and a story. It was neat practice, and he loved the weird questions, the little truths they shared together.

Vicki did well with routine, it helped her settle, and by the time they were done with her story, she was yawning. "Can I see your painting tomorrow?"

"If you want to, yes. Can we go get doughnuts for breakfast?"

"Yes! Doughnuts and coffee and the newspaper. And can we go see the puppies?" Vicki hunkered down into her pillows.

"If Uncle Mitch is cool with it, sure." It sounded like a fun morning.

Not as fun as tonight promised to be, but fun, nonetheless.

Her eyes were already closing when she whispered, "I hope he says yes."

"Me too, angel girl." He kissed her forehead and headed down to help with the dishes and steal some kisses.

Mitch had music playing in the kitchen and seemed to be just finishing up with the dishwasher. "Hey, there. All good?"

"Perfect. She wants to go look at dogs tomorrow after doughnuts. I told her I'd talk to you." He wiped down the stove with a bleach cloth.

"Dogs, huh? Have you two been conspiring? I already said yes, you know." Mitch gave his ass a pat. "This Sunday doughnut thing is going to give me a belly if the garlic bread doesn't get me first."

He wouldn't care if Mitch had two bellies, but he was

willing to work out together. "We'll have to find something to do together for exercise. I like hiking, yoga, swimming."

"Sex. Sex is good exercise. And in the shower there's steam, right? So that's good for us too."

"See? I like how you think—heart rate up, releasing toxins? It's perfect."

"It's the Chianti, it makes me smarter." Mitch caught him around the waist. "We're done in here, right? Will you show me your paintings?"

"We're done in here, and of course." He snuggled in, leaned a little. "Thanks for wanting to see them."

"Are you kidding? I've been so curious all day. But dinner, kids...it needed to wait a minute. Are you exhausted? You looked totally wiped out when I came in." They moved slowly, staying close as they headed for the little art studio.

"It's a hard thing. I know it doesn't seem like it, but it's emotional. Just being with you and the kids starts to fill that well up." He wasn't sure if that was the right way to explain it, but he was the best way he knew how.

Mitch seemed to get it. "What would fill it up before you were here?"

"I slept a lot. I cried sometimes. I went up into the mountains." He'd called Adam and talked for hours.

Mitch's arms tightened around him. "Maybe this could be better."

"I think it might be. I know that I feel...better." He felt real. He felt like he could honestly breathe and relax, already.

"I hope I can keep it that way." Mitch's smile lit up the studio as they went inside. "Do you consider these finished, or in progress?"

"This side here—they're done for sure. The others are waiting for me to decide how I feel and how Ally feels."

"Did you send those pictures to her after all?" Mitch looked them over. "They say so much. This one especially, all the color and the movement through this part." Mitch waved a hand over the lower corner of one of his paintings.

"Thank you. I wanted to bring the outside in here on the canvas. This place is so different." The colors of everything were new, rich, different.

"This one is all the snow right? It's so neat. It feels like a blizzard but... I don't know, less cold."

He let one hand rest on the small of Mitch's back. "Because you're looking out from the heat."

Mitch inhaled and leaned into his touch, the way his lover wanted him so clear in that sound, in Mitch's body language. "Mmm. It is warm in here."

"It is." He might just start sweating. "Tell me when you're ready to go upstairs. I want our shower."

Mitch turned to face him so his hand slid over one hip and settled over his abs. "I wanted to see your work. I want to know all of you. But I'm ready now."

He was too. He wanted to be clean, strip himself down, and give himself over to Mitch.

They moved upstairs quietly so they didn't wake up the kids, and Mitch closed the bedroom door behind them. "We had a good day today, but I was surprised how much I missed you even though you were just on the other side of a door." Mitch reached for him and worked his t-shirt out of his jeans, fingers finding his skin. "The kids would do something, and I'd want to turn and laugh with you, or I'd want to touch or hug you. I guess it's good to want a little, but I'm not used to feeling that way."

Daniel loved to hear that; it was—more than sweet. More than good. Those words resonated inside him and left him lighter. "Thank you. I'm glad that I'm part of our family."

Mitch just nodded and kept undressing him slowly, leaving patches of clean skin and patches still covered in paint.

Every so often the paint would tug his body hair, and every time he jerked, wiggling a little bit.

"You're a little dirty, Daniel." Mitch's tone was low and teasing.

He snorted softly, doing a little bump and grind that was either ridiculous or sexy. "Butthead. I might be a lot dirty."

"I'll take it." Mitch's clothing landed piece by piece with his in a pile. "It's hot, I can't wait to give you a good scrub."

"I'm all in." He led Mitch to the tub, starting the water going while Mitch pulled out big fluffy bath sheets.

"Hop in, Picasso." Mitch grinned, using their height difference to muscle him into the tub.

"Ha." The water poured over him, and he rubbed his hands over his arms, the paint beading up on his skin.

"Hey, I want to do that." Mitch took his hands and pushed them behind his back, then soaped up a washcloth. "This is my job."

He chuckled and let himself feel sensual and wanted. It was easier now, because he'd left the rest on the canvas. The pain and the mourning and the fear would creep back, but it wasn't here with them now.

Mitch grinned and kissed him playfully, leaning hard enough to push his head into spray where the running water broke them apart. The cloth in Mitch's hand was warm as it moved over his skin, washing all the colors of his work away. Mitch took his time, scrubbing in places, touching him everywhere.

Well, almost everywhere. Mitch seemed to be

deliberately avoiding his cock, and every hot spot and sensitive area he had.

It was fascinating and maddening at the same time, so he let Mitch touch as he would, focusing on the sensations.

"There." Mitch hung the washcloth over a shower knob. "All clean. You're beautiful, Dan. I just wanted to...worship, a little."

"Have you—are you a bathing kind of guy?" Because he totally was. Hot water, hot man—it worked for him, balls to bones.

He got a slow smile. "I haven't since I was about five. But I bet a grown-up bath is more fun."

"Oh, they're amazing. Sensual and lovely. Wanna?" He could luxuriate in Mitch for days.

"Sensual. I like the sound of that." Mitch reached around him and flipped the lever so that water was coming from the tap. "How do you put the...plunger thing down?"

"Poor, unbathed man." Daniel got tickled and started chuckling, getting the tub filling. He set them up with a huge towel, padding his back as he sat. Then he patted the water. "Come sit here and lean back against me."

"Ooh." Mitch sank into the water, scooching back to lean against his chest. "Mmm. Hey, this is really nice."

"Right?" He thought so. He had warmth, access, and he could relax. He started stroking Mitch's belly, fingers dragging over the flat belly.

He heard Mitch's sigh and felt Mitch relax, shoulders sinking as Mitch grew heavier against him. "This feels so decadent."

"Mmhmm. You understand." Daniel got them settled and relaxed, and he hummed as he stroked and caressed.

"We don't get to just relax together much, huh?" Mitch ran his fingers up the inside of his thigh.

"No. No, we're...is it okay to say we're dads, do you think?"

Mitch chuckled. "With the amount we've been pooped on and the number of five-year-old tantrums we've endured, we have earned that title I think, don't you?"

"I think that Emory's going to never know any other fathers." He wasn't sure if it was terrible or wonderful that Vicki would. Maybe both.

"I think we can say dads. No matter what they call us. It won't be long before Vicki will have spent more years with us than anyone else, you know?" Mitch took his hand and kissed his fingers. "So...we're parents."

"Yeah. We are. Poor babies." He chuckled and kissed Mitch's temple.

Mitch's head tipped back and landed on his shoulder. "I want to be a *we* though too, you know? A you and me. An us. Somehow."

"Yeah." He didn't know how to respond to that with more. He'd already fucked up with Mitch, and he wasn't going to do it again tonight.

"I'm talking too much, huh?" Mitch turned his head and kissed the side of his neck. "It's good to be alone."

"We can talk all we want, but you're right. It's amazing to be alone." And together.

Mitch pushed his hand lower, across tight abs, over a smooth hip and tucked it up against heavy balls. "Mmm."

"Yeah. You feel good to me." He stroked, petting Mitch nice and easy. "You're so thick."

"You think so? Thanks." Mitch sighed again, finger sliding over his thighs.

"I've had you deep inside me. I know so." He nuzzled the join of Mitch's shoulder.

"That's heaven, being deep inside you." Mitch's cock

swelled in his fingers proving the truth in those words. "I'd return the favor if you're into that."

"I am. I catch and pitch, both positions." Daniel chuckled at himself. "You into that? Both positions?"

Mitch huffed out a soft laugh shoulders moving against his chest. "Both, any, all. I'm into that."

"Yeah? Good." He rolled Mitch's balls, pushing just a little.

Mitch arched into his fingers. "Mhm. Good." He liked the gravel in that tone, it was hungry. Needy.

"Uh-huh. I like the sound of that." He so did. He started exploring, fingers pressing against this hot spot, stroking another one.

Mitch's fingers searched and fumbled for a minute, trying to return the favor but from this position Daniel was pretty much had all the access. Mitch finally seemed to accept that, and reached for his nape, pulling him down for a kiss.

"Mmhmm." He groaned, his cock growing, caught against the small of Mitch's back, the top of his ass.

Mitch rocked back and his cock rubbed against all that warm, wet skin, sliding easily under the water. "I'm going to want some of that," Mitch whispered against his lips.

"You can have it all. Everything." He was all in. Bath. Orgasms. Snuggling. Sleep.

"All of it. Fuck yeah." Mitch's tongue pushed past his lips and glided along his, headed for his tonsils. He eased Mitch around, bringing their bellies together, scooting forward so Mitch's legs wrapped around his waist. "Damn, Dan. You're an expert at this bath thing."

Mitch hands went to his chest, touching him with the same hunger that had been in his voice.

Good. He wanted this to be one of those things they did

over and over. He wanted bathing to be something special and theirs and hot as fuck.

Daniel tilted Mitch's head and drew him into a wild kiss.

The needy sound Mitch made was just for him, and Mitch's fingers wrapped around his prick, squeezing and stroking.

Oh damn. He bucked up, grabbing hold of Mitch's hips like he was a drowning man. The water splashed around them, and Mitch rolled his hips too, bringing their bodies tighter together before sliding back again.

"Dan...want," Mitch managed around the kiss.

"Yeah. Yeah, fuck, I need you." Now. Now would be good.

Mitch pushed back and climbed carefully out of the tub, reaching for the towels. "Come on."

That cock was right there, and the temptation to lean over and lick it was huge. Gigantic. His mouth even opened, and Mitch's eyebrow lifted.

"Come on, Dan." Mitch's hand shot out, offering a hand up. "Not that I don't love your mouth."

"That's good to hear. I want you to love my mouth, my cock, my ass..."

Mitch ran a towel over him before pulling him toward the bedroom, but it was more of a gesture. They were both still damp. "I told you. I'm into it all. As long as it's with you."

"Come on. Bed. I want to love on you." He took Mitch's hand and led them to the bed.

"I love how you say that." Mitch's smile was warm, touched. "Love on me."

"That's what we have. It's better than a hard fuck. It means something."

Mitch climbed onto the bed, watching him with serious eyes. "It means a lot, Daniel. You're...the best thing in my life."

Daniel doubted that, but it was lovely to hear, one way or the other. Absolutely perfect, and he was going to pretend it was the truth.

"Come here." Mitch reached for him and tugged him into bed. "I'm all yours."

"All mine." And all clean and tasty and yeah, his.

"Mhm." Mitch caught his nape and arched up, kissing him hard.

Oh. Oh, hell yeah. He leaned in, covering Mitch totally, diving right in. One long leg snaked around his hip over his thigh, bringing their hips tight together. Mitch groaned, teeth nipping at his lower lip.

That little sting made his cock jerk, and he had to hump against Mitch, the act instinctive and immediate.

"Yeah." Mitch sucked in a breath and arched, giving him something to work his aching cock against. "Want you Dan. Need you."

"Uh-huh." He grabbed the lube and the condoms, but instead of using them he plopped them on the bed and moved to nuzzle Mitch's fuzzy sac, tilt his lover up, and spread that sweet ass with his thumbs. "This first."

Then he licked a long line over Mitch's hole, listening for a response.

"Oh. Oh! Oh, Fuck." Mitch gasped and grabbed his knees, hauling them up toward his shoulders. "Holy fuck, Dan..."

Oh yeah, baby. Bingo. He smiled and started licking, intending to make his lover dizzy with it, open and relaxed before he took him.

"Fuck...oh, fuck." It was gratifying how Mitch totally shorted out, moaning and arching toward him. Mitch dropped one hand dropped to his balls and squeezed, then higher, fingers curling around his own cock.

He began to hum, slicking his lover up, giving them both the visceral ache they needed. Dan heard Mitch's deep cry, and he shook, his cock jerking from the sound.

"Please." Mitch's groan was imploring. "More, Dan. I need..." Mitch hauled one knee even higher, so wide open for him.

"Need." He grunted and grabbed the slick and the rubber. "Let me...shit, let me get you ready."

"Got it." Mitch snatched the lube from his hand and managed to get some on his fingers before he fumbled it, then two fingers slipped shamelessly through that tight hole while he was watching. "Mmm. Pretty fucking ready."

"Fuck, you're so pretty..." His eyes rolled, and Dan got the condom on, even with shaky fingers.

"You...you've got me so..." Mitch planted his feet on the bed and reached for him. "I need you inside me."

"Oh, thank god." He muscled up between Mitch's thighs, his cock in hand. "I'm aching for you." He pressed close, his cock sliding against the slick hole before he tried again, the tip popping in.

"Yes." Mitch gasped, fingers gripping his arms hard, but relaxed as he got a breath. Their eyes locked and Mitch gave him a heated smile. "Yeah. So good."

Thank fucking god. Dan tightened his abs, then he got to work, intending to give Mitch the ride of his life.

Mitch rocked up and met him as he thrust in, heels catching him under his ass, fingers gripping and catching his arms and shoulders. The sounds were pretty, but the blissed-out look on Mitch's face was everything.

It was the easiest thing ever to rock in and out, finding a steady rhythm that he could hold onto forever if he had to.

Mitch wasn't giving him that much time though, moaning as that sweet ass tightened around him, gripping him tight. Fuck, that was unbearably good, making his rhythm hiccup, his pleasure flare.

"More, Dan," Mitch implored him breathlessly. "Please... harder."

Harder he could do. He slammed into his lover, his hips slapping against Mitch's ass.

Mitch muffled a cry with his fist and rocked under him, then dropped a hand to his own cock again to stroke every few thrusts. "Yeah...yes."

It was the hottest thing he'd ever seen, Mitch jacking himself, writhing underneath him. Fuck, it was goddamn inspirational.

Their eyes met and Mitch stared into him. "Dan. Love."

"Yeah. Yeah, love. Come on." Mitch was so fucking pretty.

"Yes. Fuck, yes." Mitch nodded like he was totally on board with that and pumped his cock a couple of times before he shivered and shot, striping his belly, ass working Dan's cock with each pump.

"Fuck..." He watched as long as he could, before he couldn't hold on anymore. His body demanded that he focus and shoot. Now.

Mitch trapped him with a soft moan, heels curling around his thighs, and arched up, letting him sink deep into that amazing heat. It was all he needed and more, and he shot, shaking with his entire body, whining as his balls emptied.

Mitch yanked him down and they sucked in harsh breaths between needy kisses. "So good. Fuck, Dan, So fucking good."

"Uh-huh." He was a little dizzy with—well, everything. Absolutely everything.

They settled together, pressed close and feet tangled

with Mitch's head resting on his bicep. "I didn't think this would be possible for me. Not really. I wanted it, I welcomed it, but I've never had...anything like this."

"No." Shit, he could spend months at a time without speaking to anyone else. Months. He never thought he'd be sleeping with someone at night, full-time.

"No?" Mitch chuckled softly and kissed his chest. "That's a lot to ask of two letters. Or did you short out a few brain cells while you were nailing me?"

He blew out a laughing breath. "Yeah, I may have. I just —I didn't believe I could have a thing with someone. I like this thing we have."

"Me too. I like it a lot." Mitch shifted up on an elbow meeting his eyes. "I love it. I love *you*."

His cheeks heated, but he didn't look away. "You think so?"

"Well." Mitch smiled at him. "It's a first, so I guess you could doubt me but I'm pretty certain."

"If you know, that's good enough for me." In fact, it worked for him all the way to his core. "I know a few things about that myself."

"Do you?"

"I do. I'm very in touch with my emotions, you know?" He drew a line down Mitch's nose, tapping the end. "Very."

And he knew that he was going to hang with Mitch, no matter what.

"Must be an artist thing. I'm more known for keeping my emotions at arms length and proceeding with caution." Mitch shrugged. "I'm not very...in touch."

"Sure you are." He brought Mitch's hand to his cheek, letting himself deliberately misunderstand. "You touch me deep."

"Deep." Mitch snorted but nodded, on to him. "I do want to marry you, so how's that for deep?"

His breath caught in his chest, and he forced himself to stay relaxed. "You don't have to. I get it. I want you to know that I get why you said no."

"It wasn't really a no, Dan. I just wanted to slow us down. I wanted that proposal to be about us. Everything else is about the kids, or Adam, or work. But not this. I'm not marrying all of that. I'm marrying you. All of that is big...it's important. But it's...beyond you and me."

He almost asked if Mitch would have been into him if it hadn't been for Adam, but that was a stupid question. How many people came together because of someone else? Lots. "I hear you. I don't—I don't know how all this happened, or why, but I'm here for you."

"Right? I don't know how you ended up with an anal-retentive ad-man over some hot cowboy or something but here we are and I'm all in for you." Mitch kissed him, the touch of their lips like a promise.

"I never looked. Adam sort of saved me, again, bringing you to me. Me to you. Whatever."

"Whichever." Mitch chuckled. "So I guess we're engaged now?"

"I guess we are." It felt weird and wonderful all at the same time. Mostly wonderful, when it got right down to it.

"Good." Mitch lay down on his chest again. "Somehow —maybe because of the kids or the house—I already felt married, but now I can say you're mine for real."

"Vicki will be pleased, I think. She's very into happily ever after."

That made Mitch laugh. "We'll tell her you're my handsome prince."

"She'd believe that, I bet." He gave Mitch his best

princely expression, whatever that was. "I'm totally principetic."

Mitch drew a circle around his navel. "Stick to painting, Dan. Making up words is more my line of work."

"Principoligetic? Pricipetual?" He couldn't stop grinning, not now.

"Tsk. Those will never sell." Mitch blew a raspberry on his belly, still laughing.

"Butthead. God, I do love you, silly man. I love you so much."

Mitch sat up on his elbow again and smiled. "I love you too. Honestly. I don't know what I'd do without this crazy life we have now."

"Sleep more? Jack off more? Uh...there would be more lonely beers." Imagining shit was his job.

"I'm so done with lonely beers." Mitch bent and kissed him and then slid out of bed. "Time for rated G pajama pants."

"I'm going to buy you fuzzy Cookie Monster pants." Then he could rub Mitch's butt and create static electricity.

"Listen, you. My cookie addiction is none of your concern. I can stop anytime I want." Mitch pulled on a pair of striped pajama pants and returned to bed with a pair for him.

"Tell that to my Nutter Butter budget."

Mitch laughed as he climbed back under the covers. "Our budget. Which now also includes Oreos. Aren't we supposed to share everything now that we're engaged?"

"Absolutely. I promise to share my fudgesicles, if you share your cookies."

Once he dressed, Mitch snuggled in again with a yawn. "To have and to hold until eating the last fudgesicle doth rent our love asunder." Mitch was warm and heavy, resting on his chest.

"No renting or asundering." He hummed, taking a deep breath and letting it out.

"Nope. None. Nothing. Nada." Mitch sighed again, the sound soft and sleepy. "I hope the kids let us sleep."

"Shh...don't beg trouble. Sleeping." What would happen would happen. He'd worry about that later.

Right now, he needed to rest.

16

Mitch closed the dishwasher and grabbed a sponge to wipe down the countertops while Dan put the clean pots he'd dried away. Their little after-dinner routine had become very familiar and easy. Neither of them thought much about it anymore, they just did it.

They usually talked more though.

When he and Dan needed to work something out—a parenting thing, a money thing, whatever—they would talk about it, make a decision and figure out how to get it done. They were really good together that way.

But if they had a bigger issue, something more emotional, and especially if it had to do with Adam, well... they didn't quite have that down yet. The silence in the kitchen was getting awkward though, and Mitch knew they were going to have to talk.

As soon as one of them got up the courage to address the elephant in the room.

Maybe it was more realistic to call it the turkey.

Thanksgiving was coming next week, no matter what they did, and they had to do something. Vicki deserved a holiday. Hell, both of them did too. Adam had loved the holidays, had driven the celebrations at the office, here, everything.

He tossed his sponge in the sink and dried his hands, then reached for Dan, tangling his fingers into the hem of Dan's sweater. "So...my office is closed Thursday and Friday. And school."

Okay. That was lame, but it was a start.

"Is it already that time?" Dan winced. "I was sort of hoping it just was a little later this year."

He couldn't help but snort softly and shake his head. They'd both been in such deliberate denial. "Okay. So this really is as big a thing as it feels, huh? I have no idea what to do. I don't think I have the spoons to host the big employee potluck thing that Adam always did."

"Do your people need you to do it?" Dan's question surprised the hell out of him. "I mean, I'll help. I know how to make a list."

Did they need it? No, probably not. It was just a fun office thing. "Maybe we can do something smaller in the office on Wednesday. We should probably...what do you usually do for Thanksgiving?"

"Not much. I came here for December a lot, but not Thanksgiving. The flights were too full. I usually slept through, I think."

That sounded like a great idea. He'd love to just go to sleep on Wednesday and wake up on Friday and skip Vicki's first holiday without her father altogether. "I don't think the kids will be on board with that plan."

"I don't think so either, and it's not fair. I guess we need to see what she wants. If turkey is important or pizza the night before. If she cares about the parade, or if that's just for old people. I'm not sure what their traditions were."

"I was only here for the party so I don't know about those things either." There was turkey at the party and always a handful of kids including Vicki. He didn't remember if she liked all the chaos or slept through it. She'd only been four last year after all. "I guess we need to talk to her." He shot Dan a quick grin. "Flip you for it?" He was joking, this was something they needed to do together, but the air in the kitchen was so fucking heavy.

"Bah. No flipping. She talks. We listen. I go work out my shit in the studio."

And he'd work his shit out...somehow. He'd go have a drink. Or play his guitar. Or he wouldn't. He was good. He'd just...get over it. "When do we want to do this?"

Dan sighed and moved into his arms, surprising him with a hard hug instead of an answer.

He was stiff for a second, only just then realizing how tense all of this was making him. He circled his arm around Dan and sighed, trying to let some of the tension go. He didn't know a hug was what he needed but Dan did, and it felt really good. It was all the answer he needed right then. "Mm. Thank you."

"Thank you too. I bet Adam's laughing at us. He would think this was funny as hell."

"I hope not. There's nothing funny about his little girl trying to be thankful for something after losing her dad." There were things to be grateful for, he knew, it was just hard not to let losing Adam overshadow them. "Sorry. I'm just—I don't know. Maybe I'm making too big a deal of things."

One thing was for sure; he wasn't letting Dan go yet. Dan was solid and his arms were a comfort.

Dan chuckled softly, though he didn't say anything else, just held onto him tight.

"Shut up," he said, knowing he sounded petulant. "You paint, I babble. Hugs are good though." He gave Dan one last squeeze and let him go. "Okay. When? Tonight? Now?"

"Let's just do it." Dan took a deep breath and then hollered, "Vicki! You want to come down so we can talk on turkey day, girl?"

Well, that was a way to do it.

"Subtle. One of the things I love about you." He kissed Dan's cheek.

"Coming!" Vicki sang, feet thundering on the stairs. "What's turkey day?"

"Thanksgiving? You know gobble, gobble, gobble, and wobble, wobble, wobble?" Dan scooped her up and hugged her. "It's our first one, the four of us, and the baby is too little to plan."

Vicki sat up in his arms like she'd just remembered something. "Daddy has a party."

"That's right. He liked to invite the whole office, and we'd all bring food." And kids. And dogs.

"Are we having a party?"

Oh boy. If she wanted a party... "Do you want to?"

"No. None of my friends ever came."

"Okay. So what do you want to do? You want to cook a turkey and stuff?" Dan got a pad of paper and a pen, then took Vicki to the table.

"I don't like turkey." She wrinkled her nose and Mitch started to worry for a second, until she smiled suddenly. "But I like the gravy on mashed potatoes! And pumpkin pie."

"I also like pie," he added, winking at her.

"Okay. So, if I like turkey, I can have some?" Dan asked, drawing a picture of mashed potatoes, gravy, and pumpkin pie.

Vicki gave him a look like he'd asked a silly question. "Yes. Where else will the gravy come from?"

"The gravy fairy. What's your position on cranberry sauce?" How Dan managed that straight faced was beyond him.

Vicki shrugged. "Daddy liked it."

Mitch nodded. "I always brought a cranberry-apple sauce to the party for him, do you want me to make that?"

"I'd try it." Vicki nodded.

"I like sauce. We all like bread. Uncle Mitch, what's your favorite part of supper?" A bowl of goo appeared on the paper.

"The wine?" He grinned.

"Uncle Mitch!" Vicki gaped at him.

"Sorry, sorry. I have to agree with Vic, the mashed potatoes are kind of the highlight for me. Smashed, with some garlic and a little pepper...or whipped until they're fluffy and creamy...there's no bad with potatoes."

"I like the munchies before—so dip and veggies and crackers and cheese ball." Those appeared on the paper too. "Do you like the parade with the big balloons?"

"Daddy says if you miss Santa then he won't come at Christmas. We watch it with...oh! Cinnamon buns!" Vicki tapped Dan's paper telling him to draw them. "And cocoa. Daddy liked coffee better though. The balloons make Emory laugh."

This was going much better than he'd expected so far. "I am so in for the cinnamon buns." And something about Emory's laughter was good for his soul.

"Cinnamon buns. Hot cocoa. I'm in. We can buy them, right? They seem hard to make."

"Daddy smacked the thingy on the counter, and they'd pop!"

"Those are my favorite." He leaned into Vicki like they were sharing a secret. "And if you don't use all the frosting you can scoop it out of the tub with your finger."

"Frosting is the best!" Vicki beamed at him. "Did you hear, Dan-O? Don't use all the frosting!"

Mitch winked at Dan. "Aren't you going to draw that?" He loved Dan's Thanksgiving drawing; it was fun, and Vicki was into it.

"It's okay to miss Daddy though, right? Daddy always said it was okay to miss Mommy."

"It is. It's okay to miss him. It's cool to talk about him. It's good to think about it."

Vicki smiled, obviously very happy with that answer and Mitch was so grateful for Dan, yet again, who always seemed to know what to say to her. Her question was hard, and he didn't process that fast.

Maybe he needed to take up painting.

"Cool. I miss him a lot, but I'm glad you're both here. I would be scared taking care of the baby alone."

Dan blinked, glanced up at him, and he shrugged. Where had that come from?

"We're glad to be here too. We have a great little family, right? But your dad had plans for you, baby girl. He would never have left you alone. He knew all along that Uncle Dan would be here for you."

"And you, right? You're here too."

He gave Vicki a hug. "I am here for good. And I'm so happy about that. I'm grateful. Perfect for Thanksgiving."

"Okay, good, because I love you too." The simple words heated him all through.

His next breath was so much easier than the last one. Easier than they'd been all day long. "I love you so much, and Emory and Uncle Dan-O. This holiday might be sad sometimes, but we'll have fun too. We have each other. We've got this."

"Can we have waffles for breakfast tomorrow?" And just like that, what he had stressed about, she pushed away, like a doll that she only needed to take out and play with every so often.

"Regular ones or the fat Belgian ones?" She could have anything she wanted. He took Dan's hand and squeezed his fingers.

"Ones with squares for the syrups, please."

"And the butter!" Dan sounded ridiculously happy.

Of course Dan was happy. This was ridiculously perfect. There was no other way to be. "I will make everyone waffles for breakfast tomorrow. I'll even make a squishy one that Emory can gnaw on."

"Sounds perfect to me. Thank you, Uncle Mitch," Dan prompted.

"Yes! Thank you, Uncle Mitch! I'm going to ask Santa for a puppy when I see him. I'm going to play in my room now. Bye!"

He watched her go, then glanced at Dan. "When she sees him?"

"You know, Santa on his throne? Ho, what do you want, little girl? Pictures by an elf, candy cane. Next."

"Oh. Shit. I totally forgot about all of that stuff." Christmas morning, presents from Santa, cookies and milk. He'd better do some research. He pulled Dan close, sliding an arm around his waist. "One holiday at a time."

"No worries. I spent a goodly number of Christmases here. All of the kids'. Those traditions I know." Dan kissed his temple. "I just need to learn yours."

He shrugged. "What was it you said? I think I slept through." He hadn't; he wasn't really able to do that, but he'd spent a lot of time watching Christmas movies in a Santa hat and eating take-out Chinese food.

"Well, you won't get to do that for another twenty-some-odd years. Maybe longer. At some point we'll be grandparents."

He blinked at Dan. "Oh. God. Will you still love me when I'm toothless?"

"Yes." Dan's lips twisted. "I mean, think of the amazing blow jobs."

"Just imagine." He laughed. He laughed a lot with Dan, a lot more than he ever had.

17

"Dan-O? How bad do you miss Daddy?"

Daniel glanced over at Vicki. Seriously? He had his arm up to the elbow in a turkey's mostly frozen asshole. "Lots. He was my best friend."

Vicki nodded like that made sense in her five-year-old mind. "Kammy is my best friend. She likes purple like I do. Why was Daddy your best friend?"

"Because we loved art, because we made each other laugh, because we both liked steak sandwiches with pickles, and Bruce Willis movies." There was more—Adam had believed in him, and he had trusted Adam without question. Adam understood his demons, because Adam had them too —but none of those were for a little girl to know.

Vicki wrinkled her nose. "Ew. Pickles. Uncle Mitch says you make him laugh all the time. Are you best friends now instead?" She watched him cleaning the turkey with interest, always so curious.

"Yes. Uncle Mitch is one of my best friends. Also, I'm in love with him." He worked the neck out of the ice, finally.

"Are you going to marry him? Like people do when they

love each other? I think you should. I could be a flower girl like when the prince got married. Did you see that? It was on TV. She had on a pretty dress and had flowers in her hair."

"I am going to marry him, yeah. I think you'd make the best flower girl too." Jesus, his fingers were cold. Next time, he was buying a precooked turkey. "You'd have to decide what color the dress should be."

"Purple, Uncle Dan-O." She sighed, like he should have known that. "What do I call you after you're married?"

"You can call me whatever you want to. Dan-O is good, but I'm easy." Next, the innards. Gross. He hoped Mitch didn't want them, because ew.

"Mitch-O doesn't sound good though." She sighed. "I'll talk to Emory, and we'll figure it out."

She'd talk to Emory. Because of course she would.

"Well, let me know what y'all decide, hmm? I'd love to know."

"Decide about what?" Mitch came in with Emory on his hip. "Ew, are those innards? Please tell me you're tossing those out for the bears."

"I was intending the trash..." Because feeding bears was bad, right?

"Me and Emory need to talk about what to call you after you get married."

"What's wrong with Uncle Mitch?" He asked Emory, like it was a perfectly reasonable conversation. Emory blew a raspberry at him. "Oh."

"See? Are you really our uncles?"

"Well, no. Not technically." Mitch shrugged at her.

"What are you?"

"Your...guardians, I suppose."

Vicki scowled. "A what? Guardy Mitch is icky."

Mitch laughed. "I'm not so guardy. Stick with Uncle until you and Emory work it out. There's no rush, okay?" Dan figured Mitch could be uncle forever.

"You can decide what you want to call us, angel girl. You can pick. No matter what, we're still going to be family." He wasn't sure what Vicki needed, but they'd figure it out.

Emory made a dive for the turkey carcass, grabby hands out in front of him and Mitch caught him in the nick of time. "Whoa, tiger. No raw bird for the poop monster."

"God no. Gag. No raw bird. Full stop. Only cooked." Daniel didn't even want to go there.

"What can we do? Give us a job, Dan-O." Mitch kissed his shoulder, avoiding the raw turkey and went to sit Emory in his chair.

"Can you put the veggie tray together? That would be great." They'd bought everything cut up, so Vicki could help.

"Definitely. Come on, Vic." Mitch opened the fridge and started handing her veggies. "Carrots, celery, peppers, cucumbers, radish...put everything on the counter, okay?"

"And there's cheese and pickles and ranch!" Vicki bounced over. "Chee-ee-ee-eesy cheese!"

"Chee!" Emmers crowed.

"Did he just say cheese?" Mitch glanced at Dan, pulling the cheese out and handing it to Vicki. "His first word is cheese? Seriously?"

Daniel started laughing—the sound built inside him, growing and growing, until he was cackling with merriment. Emory laughed along with him.

"Not what sound does the cow make, or some version of Dan-O without consonants. No. Cheese. Huh." Mitch shook his head and closed the fridge, brandishing a bottle of ranch. "Found it!"

Daniel got another look from Mitch, this one warmer, with a great smile. "You okay there, baby?"

"I'm buying precooked turkey next year, but yes. I'm having a ball." And he felt...real. Solid. Damn near capable.

Mitch chuckled as he opened the bag of baby carrots for Vicki. "You do seem to be wrestling a bit. That thing is a monster. You think Adam has a veggie plate?"

"I haven't the foggiest. Surely there are platters, right? He was a dinner party type."

"Surely." Mitch started opening and closing some of the higher, out-of-the-way cabinets.

Vicki got up and opened a tall, thin cabinet next to the fridge. "Platters like that?"

Mitch looked inside and pulled out a large, round, ceramic platter with a mottled blue glaze on it. "Just exactly like that. Aren't you a smart cookie?"

"I am. Smart peanut butter cookie." Vicki looked totally pleased with herself. "With ice cream."

"Mmm." Mitch kissed her cheek. "Delicious. Come on, let's get these veggies out. Dan-O's going to be hungry once he gets that bird in the oven."

"And we have to hurry! Santa's coming! Wait. I'll go check." Vicki headed out like her butt was on fire.

That girl was something else.

"I can't get her to put her laundry in the hamper but when it comes to Santa? She is on it." Mitch laughed.

"Can you blame her?" Daniel started rubbing butter all over this carcass. This was hell on earth. "You know she wants a puppy?"

"Yes. And I know you want a dog." Mitch chuckled. "No influence there, I'm sure. And I already said yes."

"Well, we need to discuss the particulars, given that Santa is involved." He wanted her to be excited, but he wasn't sure they needed a brand-new puppy. There were many details.

Mitch caught him around the waist and leaned against his back. "Have you told her a puppy or a dog? Because you know I'm clueless about dogs in general, so a puppy would be all on you."

"Like I said, we'll need to discuss it later, plan." He needed to understand what he was getting into.

"Like you planned for that turkey?" Mitch kissed his nape.

"I will shove this huge cold dead bird where the sun don't shine, my gorgeous lover." He thought he was doing... okay-ish.

"I'm teasing, baby. You're doing great. And that is not what I want where the sun don't shine." Mitch purred the last bit in his ear.

"Oh..." His hands slipped as he stuffed vegetables in the turkey, but he caught himself. "I do like how you think."

"I will be very grateful tonight for all the work you're putting into making Thanksgiving amazing for everyone. I love how important it is to you." It was important to Mitch too, he knew.

"I just want it to be a good memory. We all deserve that. Goodness." Something new and fresh.

"We do, and it will be." Mitch let him go and checked the oven. "You're all preheated over here."

"Okay. You want to put it in while I wash up?" He felt like a bout of salmonella ready to strike.

"Sure." Mitch picked up the roasting pan with a groan. "Turkey sandwiches, turkey soup, turkey pot pie..."

"Turkey broccoli casserole. Turkey tacos. Green chile turkey burritos."

"Santa is coming!" Vicki shrieked from the living room.

"Oh." Mitch closed the oven and went to the highchair. "I got the poopster. Go."

"Coming!" Daniel dried his hands on a dish towel and made a run for the front room. "Yay Santa!"

"Yay Santa! Dan-O! Santa!"

She grabbed his hands and they bounced together in a circle.

Mitch hurried in and plopped down onto the couch, perching Emory on his knees. "You two are crazy!"

"Chee!" Emory repeated his first ever word, making everyone laugh.

"No, Em. Santa." Vicki bent nose to nose with her little brother. "Saa-nn-ta!"

"Chee!"

So that totally was a non-accidental first word. Cool. A little weird, but cool.

"Sit. Sit, you guys. There's his sled!" Mitch leaned forward, totally into the parade, looking young with his eyes glued to the TV as he bounced Emory on his knees.

Vicki ran to the TV, eyes huge. "Santa! Santa, tell Daddy I love him, and that Dan-O came to help Uncle Mitch just like he promised!"

Mitch's hand found his and held it tight. "Hello, Santa! Merry Christmas!"

Daniel tried to speak, but there was a frog in his throat. He hoped Adam already knew.

Mitch had obviously caught on and was keeping Vicki distracted for him. The hand holding his was firm and steady. "Look at that sled, Vic. Isn't it amazing?"

"It's so tall and fancy. Look at all the presents!" Vicki was so close to the TV it was a wonder she could see anything.

"That bag is huge. Do you know the reindeer names?"

"Dudeolf!"

Daniel snorted, and then the laughter hit him, hard and happy, just filling the air.

Emory joined him, giggling like a fiend.

Mitch leaned in. "That one has a red nose for an entirely different reason."

Daniel laughed so hard it hurt. Fuck, this was why they did this. This is what they would remember when they were toothless grandpas.

The parade ended and they spent the afternoon playing cards and board games and watching the snow fall, taking breaks to prep dinner and check on his turkey, which looked fabulous, if he did say so himself.

It was late afternoon when they sat down for their meal. Vicki had insisted they dress nicely, so he'd helped her do her hair and she had on a cute dress with party shoes. Emory was in a onesie that looked like a tuxedo and Mitch was looking hot in his crisp button-down shirt, even despite the goofy tie that had turkeys all over it.

He wore a sweater he'd bought a few days ago, plus decent jeans. That was the closest to dressed up that he did. They all three got to the table, and Vicki looked at him, a little teary.

"It's okay that I wish Daddy was here?"

"Yes." He didn't hide his tears either, because you had to practice the shit you preached. "I wish he was here too, but I'm happy to have you and Emmers and Uncle Mitch."

"How about we toast him?" Mitch raised a glass but paused and caught his eye. "Or...did you want to do Grace first, Dan-O? Adam used to say Grace on Thanksgiving. I wasn't brought up that way, but I bet you were."

"I was. I do." Daniel took Vicki's hand, Mitch's. "Just real quick."

"Can I do it?" Vicki asked, shocking the living fuck out of him.

Could she? Hell, why not. "Of course, angel."

"Dear god, thank you for food, and Santa, and letting Daddy in Heaven. Thank you for Dan-O and Uncle Mitch. Thank you for snow and puppies and bubbles. Amen."

Mitch put his glass down and moved around the table to Vicki to kiss her cheek. "Amen. Do you know how amazing you are?" Mitch was holding it together, but Dan could hear the emotion in his voice. "Your daddy would be so proud of you."

"He loved me and Emory more than anything. He said. That's why he gave us you and Dan-O."

"I miss him. I wish he was here too. But we have each other." Mitch gave her a big hug, and he did see the tears then. "He gave us to you too."

"Yep! Turkey time, Dan-O!"

Daniel snorted, but he nodded. "Right on, chickie-mama. Let's eat."

"She means mashed potato time, Emory. Don't you worry, I've got your number." Mitch wandered back to his seat and sipped his wine. "I am going to watch you carve, Dan-O. I leave these things to the experts."

"Yeah. We're going to hope the YouTube video is helpful. I've never cooked anything this big. Ever." But he had done it. He'd cooked a turkey, and it looked turkey-tastic.

"It looks amazing, and it smells even better, baby. I can't wait." Mitch smiled at him.

Then he got to work, hacking at the bird. Somewhere, Adam was laughing his ass off at him. He knew it.

Happy turkey day to them.

18

"Vicki. Baby girl. We're going away for like, a week, tops. And Dan-O's trailer is really little. You don't need all these dresses. Pick four. And two pairs of shoes." Mitch understood that Dan didn't want to go get his trailer alone and leave them behind during the holiday season. He understood that it would be a neat family thing to do together. And until they started packing, he'd been totally on board.

But packing to take a baby on the road was like packing for the apocalypse, and Vicki was not understanding the concept of "small trailer".

"Four. Is there a potty? Can I go potty in the trailer? Can I play with my babies? Are there games? Is it a long way? Is the baby coming?"

Like she hadn't asked those questions a hundred times.

"Yes. To everything. We're going to have so much fun all of us. We get to see New Mexico, and drive through some cool places, and eat all kinds of neat food. Dan-O is going to show us everything." He was excited about that part, seeing the country. Seeing it through Dan's eyes.

"And we're going to sing in the car and laugh a lot."

"A lot. I'm bringing my guitar so we can sing at night when we're camping too." He hadn't told her that he had a folder full of kindergarten schoolwork she'd have to do before going back to school in January, but he'd figure out how to make that fun too. "Are those your four?"

"Uh-huh. I love them best." Vicki kissed his cheek. "I've never been on a vee-venture before."

God. This little girl made him smile every day. "Honestly, I haven't been on many myself." He closed the top of her suitcase and zipped it up. "Perfect. Let's go check on Dan-O."

Dan was in the bedroom, singing to Emory, laughing as the little one yodeled nonsense.

"I'm packed Dan-O. When are we leaving? Now?"

Hopefully not now; the only person that wasn't packed was him. Mitch put his suitcase on the bed and opened it.

"Don't you think we ought to let Uncle Mitch pack too?" Dan grinned at her. "I think he'll get stinky without clothes."

"I can help." Vicki went over to Mitch's dresser and opened his underwear drawer.

"Oh, uh..." He followed her quickly. He was so picky about packing, just the idea of her helping could give him hives. "How about you sit with Emory? I bet he's missed you. You've been busy all day."

One of her eyebrows went up, the look clearly unbelieving. "Missed me?"

"Sure. I miss you when I go to work and don't see you. Makes sense, right, Dan-O?" He pulled his own favorite underwear out to pack and a bunch of socks and put them in his suitcase.

"Totally. Let's get the bags downstairs, girlie. We have to

be at the airport around three, and the car will be here soon."

"Thanks, Dan. I'll be down in a few." They were so fancy. Burlington Airport was practically the size of a postage stamp with one restaurant, maybe ten or fifteen gates, plus a walk-out tarmac for smaller flights, but they were getting a car to take them. It really was an adventure.

He packed quickly. It wasn't that difficult; he wasn't working, and it was winter. He was good at casual snow day attire. Then he closed his suitcase and took it downstairs.

"You ready?" He found Dan and caught him by the elbow.

"Fridge is empty. Note is left for house sitters. We have paperwork for flying the kids. We'll go from the Sunport to the airport hotel, eat and sleep. Take a car to pick up my truck in the morning." Dan was, surprisingly, good at this.

"You're amazing." He kissed Dan's cheek. "I packed the poop monster's go-bag. I'm prepared for on-board natural and unnatural disasters. Plus, I have snacks." If this dad gig had taught him anything, it was that kids needed snacks at all times. It was still weird to him that they would just be holding Emory on their laps for the whole time. "We can restock in Denver if need be."

"Yeah, and the hotel has twenty-four-hour room service, so we can eat whatever." Dan grinned at him. "Are you ready to travel with babies?"

"No. Is that something anyone is ready for, do you think?" He kind of thought it was something parents just did. Ready or not. He wasn't ready to get barfed on either, but that had happened several times in the last few months.

"God no. Let's do it."

The car pulled up and honked, and Vicki squealed. "Vee-venture!"

He had no idea what that meant, but it was cute as hell.

He let Dan put their luggage in the back, and he settled Emory in the car seat they had to take with them for Dan's truck and tucked Vicki into her booster. He would never have remembered that detail, or half of the others Dan had taken care of so naturally. The division of labor here was clear.

For the hundredth time, he had to wonder if Adam had known. If Adam had guessed somehow how good they would be together.

He sat in the back seat with the kids, listening to Dan talk with the driver in the front. Though he wasn't listening so much as watching, admiring, being a little awed by how easily Dan talked to people. The only thing he could say for sure is that Adam had known them both very well. He'd heavily influenced Dan's career path and helped Mitch turn his wild idea into a thriving business. Adam had been observant and intuitive, and it wouldn't surprise him one bit to learn for sure that this was Adam's grand plan.

Not that it mattered at all. One way or the other, he was happier than ever.

"Uncle Mitch, we go in the airplane, then another airplane, then we're there, right?"

"That's right. Did Dan-O tell you that? We have to change planes in Colorado, in a city called Denver. It will be my first time anywhere near Denver."

"Dan-O says we can get a snack there, and maybe a book."

"Oh, a book sounds like a great idea. We could read it together on the way to Albuquerque. That's a city in New Mexico. We get to go up above the clouds, where it's always sunny. It's so cool. You're going to love it." He did anyway; he loved flying.

"So cool!" she parroted, while Emory squealed.

"Chee!"

He snorted and grinned at Emory. Two kids, two planes, and they'd land around midnight local time. Two in the morning east coast time. Piece of cake, right? He hoped to hell the kids would crash on the second flight. And maybe they could sleep in at the hotel some.

What the hell was he thinking?

Dan looked over at him and winked. Right. Time to get his lover all the way home, where he belonged. Whatever craziness they were in for, it would be worth it. It was an adventure. Their first family vacation.

Checking their luggage was an adventure in itself. Keeping Vicki from running into every little convenience store and gift shop on their way to the gate was another. Glaring back at judgmental passengers was fun. But pushing Emory in his stroller was like walking a cute dog. They got compliments and smiles and Emory ate it all up like a champ.

Hopefully they'd all remember how cute Em was when they took off.

"So other than sleeping forever, what's the plan when we get there?" Mitch kicked back, resting his feet on the wheels of Emory's stroller and sipped a coffee. "We will get there eventually."

"We'll grab the trailer and the truck, and then we'll head to Santa Fe. Then we start wandering back this way. It'll take us five to six days, depending on weather and stops and fun moments." Dan winked at him. "I think Vicki will need some fun moments with her Dan-O and Uncle Mitch."

"Lots of fun moments." He laughed softly. "That's what this is about anyway, right? Fun moments." He knew what Dan meant, because parenting wasn't always fun. But he wanted Vicki to remember this fondly. He wanted them all to.

He watched as Vicki climbed into Dan's lap. "When do we go up in the clouds?"

"In about an hour. It's going to be so much fun." Dan rubbed their noses together.

"An hour?" Vicki sighed and flopped dramatically over Dan's arm. "This is taking *forever*."

Oh man. They hadn't even boarded their first flight yet.

"It wouldn't be an adventure if it went by in a hurry, baby girl. Why don't you go look out the window at the planes? Maybe you'll get to see one land."

"Okay!" She went to the window, hands against it as she stared.

"So, I have a bag here. It's full of weird little things— nothing major, a ball, a puzzle. I read to do it—keep filling it up and rewarding her. Is that cool?" Dan was a good dad.

"Were you on Pinterest?"

"Shut up."

He reached over and gave Dan's knee a squeeze. "I'm sure I can find you a twelve-step program."

"Don't make me beat you. I have lots of time to plan wickedness."

Mitch leaned closer. "Ooh. Is there a Pinterest board for that too?"

"I—" Dan tilted his head, eyes wide. "I don't know..."

Mitch laughed and gave Dan a quick, impulsive kiss. "Jesus, you make me happy."

"Good. Good, because it would suck otherwise." Dan squeezed his hand, holding on tight. "You looking forward to our holiday trip?"

"I am. I'm ready for a break. I'm ready to see something

new." A voice came over the loudspeaker and the plane started boarding. He was excited. He wanted to Vicki and started gathering their things.

19

Daniel sat at the window, staring over at the mountains. The kids were asleep still, and so was Mitch, so he was sitting and watching the desert wake up.

The sky here was special, and he smiled as purple turned to pink turned to bright blue. Perfect.

Mountains were definitely home, though the mountains in Vermont were so different. Greener. Even when it snowed they were greener.

Still, home was good. He wanted to show off New Mexico, and then get on the road, head north.

"Good view?" Mitch's voice was raspy, tired. "You okay?"

"Fine. Considering ordering coffee and breakfast. Go back to sleep, love. The kids are still napping."

"Mm. Coffee. Come nap with me. I bet you're chilly." Mitch patted the bed beside him.

How could he possibly turn that down? He crawled back into bed, snuggling into Mitch's warm arms.

"Are you glad to be here? You must be." Mitch curled around him. "Right this minute I'm just glad not to be on an airplane."

"They were pretty good, though, and they're crashed out." He kissed Mitch's jaw.

"Oh, they were good. They did great. And I've had some sleep now, so... I'm feeling pretty good." Mitch's warm hand slid over his bare chest.

"Mmm... I am too." He cuddled right in.

Mitch kissed him, soft and lazy, one hand moving around to his back to pull him closer. "What were you looking at out that window?"

"The mountains, the sky—the desert is special, you know? So different from home."

"All I've seen of it was on the ride from the airport. I've never been out here. But I love that you just called Vermont home." Mitch's hands kept wandering, slipping under his kid-safe pajamas to settle on his ass this time.

"It is. My whole family is there." Oh, that sent goosebumps along his skin, and he arched back into the touch.

"Yeah? Mine too." Mitch tugged on his ass and rolled into him, grinding their hips together.

"Mmm..." They couldn't get busy, but this was perfect— heated and happy, sensual. He was learning how to be Mitch's.

"I don't have to go to work. For a good reason this time. I like feeling lazy, having time to just enjoy you."

"You and me and vacation." He took one kiss, letting it slip into another and another. His world was melting.

The way Mitch simply met him there and didn't push, letting that kiss, that heat just simmer between them, was everything. To be able to just want and not have, the whole lack of urgency. They'd find some time to themselves somehow, but this little hotel room wasn't it.

"I want to show you everything here," he whispered, the words muffled against Mitch's lips. "I want you to see it all."

Mitch smiled, tracing the line of this cheekbone. "I hope it will help me know you even better. You, your art..."

"You'll get to see where I've lived for ten years. Me and my trailer."

"Mhm. I bet I'm going to learn all kinds of things when I see that trailer. Uh-oh. A gremlin is climbing up."

"What are you talking about?" Vicki's sleepy face popped up over Mitch's back and Mitch's hand disappeared from his ass.

"Breakfast." He smiled at her, wrinkling his nose. "Good morning."

"Morning. Where are we? Can I have pancakes?" Vicki rested her head on Mitch's shoulder with a sigh.

"We're in Albuquerque, and yes, you can. You can have pancakes *and* bacon."

"Oh, I want bacon. Will you share with me, Vic?" Mitch had to turn awkwardly to look at her.

"Okay, but I'm hungry. Is your trailer in Alberkey, Dan-O?"

"It is. We'll go get it and the truck today and then drive it to Santa Fe and explore. Sound good?"

"What's there?"

"We can shop, look at art, play in the snow."

"I want to look at art. Cool." Vicki sat up, waking up slowly.

"Okay, Dan-O. I think we better start moving toward breakfast before we get hangry." Mitch rolled onto his back and stretched out long. "I'm definitely not used to the time change yet."

"Time change?" Vicki said. "Did you move it, Uncle Mitch?"

Mitch laughed and sat up, pulling her into his lap. "No, baby girl. I'm not that magical. But it's two hours later at home than it is here. Isn't that cool?"

"Why?"

Daniel was glad that she'd asked Mitch, because he had absolutely no idea why. He guessed there was a reason, but he didn't know what it was.

"Well, it's complicated." Mitch looked at him a little panicked but must have figured out that he wasn't going to be much help because he got a grin and an eyeroll. "Okay. Well. There's a trick my science teacher did once with a tennis ball and a flashlight, and I'll show you all about it later, okay? It's hard to just explain. Maybe Dan-O has a flashlight in his trailer. You want to get dressed?"

"Nope. I want to eat in bed in my jammies like I'm fancy."

"Good save, Uncle Mitch," he whispered, fighting his chuckles.

"We can absolutely make that happen, right Dan-O?" Mitch shook his head and whispered back, "I think I stopped breathing for a second."

"Thank god for Google." He waggled his eyebrows. "What do you want for breakfast, honey? Bacon and waffles?"

"Whatever you're having. And coffee. Please." Mitch kissed his cheek. "I'll get us set up in here. Should we let Em sleep or wake him up do you think? Sleep for a bit?"

"I'll order him an egg and some milk but let him sleep." It was going to be a little bit of a transition, and they were fixin' to have to be flexible, he thought.

Mitch nodded agreement and started smoothing out the bed, tucking the comforter around Vicki. Look at him, making parenting decisions, and Mitch just totally trusting him.

He ordered a huge breakfast, knowing that Mitch would feel the altitude in Santa Fe, and would be hungry.

By the time he was done ordering, Mitch had set Vicki up with *Frozen* on his iPad with headphones on and then hopped in the shower. Emory was sleeping like only a baby who'd been uncomfortable all of flight number two could sleep.

And there was a text from Ally on his phone.

Made a sale. Congrats. Check your PayPal.

Woot. In town. You want to meet for supper?

His bank account was a blessedly happier place right now. Excellent. The paintings from Adam's house were selling.

You are? Could do. Get settled, then text me a time and place. Do I get to meet the family?

Yeah. I'm thinking Plaza Cafe, but we'll see. I have a place at a park for 2 nites. Then they'd get on the road.

Can you squeeze them all in? Should be fun. I'll watch for your text.

"That was okay, but I already miss our shower. I guess I better suck it up because this is probably our last hotel room for a bit, huh?" Mitch passed behind him, the scent of hotel shampoo and soap filling his nostrils.

"Yeah. There's a decent shower in my trailer. It's a nice one. And the trailer parks are going to have playgrounds, firepits, that sort of thing. We'll be comfortable." He'd been happy in the trailer. It was actually sort of luxe.

Mitch dried his hair and dug out a comb. "Firepits and playgrounds sound pretty perfect. Wow. Look at the mountains." Mitch froze by the window, mid-comb.

"Aren't they beautiful? They're the Sandias. They're an isolate. Seventeen miles of beauty."

"Neat. Have you hiked them? Do you paint them?" Mitch finished combing and put the comb down. "I guess you must. They're amazing."

"They are. There's a tram up to the top." Next time they came out, when Emmers was older, they'd go up, all of them, and enjoy the view.

"Oh. Ooh. I'd love to but..." Mitch glanced over his shoulder at the little travel crib. "A reason to come back, right? Do you have anything showing in Santa Fe? Like, in a gallery or anything?"

"I do. I have a number of pieces around. I'll show you. We'll walk Canyon Road together." They could take it nice and easy.

There was a loud knock at the door, which had to be room service. The sudden noise woke Emory, who started fussing, just a half-hearted cry. "I got the door, you get the little man?" Mitch kissed his cheek and went for the door.

Daniel scooped up Emory, kissing his little cheek. "Hey, cowboy! Good morning. How are you?"

"Stinky," Vicki said. "He's always stinky."

Emory flopped onto his shoulder, face pressing into his neck. He was stinky, and wet. But mostly unhappy to be awake.

"You sit tight Vic, and I'll bring you your pancakes. Since you're so fancy." Mitch chuckled and got to work.

"I'm going to change him. I bet he dozes off again." Daniel had this early morning diaper change down these days. They'd had some catastrophes, but he was a master.

"Okay, Miss Vicki." Mitch whispered, bringing her pancakes on a tray. "Breakfast in bed. Move your movie over. You're hungry I bet."

"Sooo hungry."

"You eat, I'm going to see what else Dan-O ordered. There's so much food."

"Dan-O is hungry too. He has an empty leg. He told me."

Mitch laughed softly. "Oh, well that explains it."

Emory was asleep again before Dan even got him down. Mitch had climbed into bed on one side of Vicki with a plate of waffles, bacon, some eggs and fruit. "Can you pour me some coffee, baby?"

"I can." He poured coffee and juice for both of them, then put Mitch's on the bedside table. Breakfast looked delicious, and he fixed himself a plate, feeling decadent.

They'd have to stop at Smith's, get food and snacks on their way out. He was looking forward to this—to hamburgers on the grill, sitting around a fire pit, snuggling together in the bed.

"You're a genius with that little man." Mitch gave him a smile and popped a bite into his mouth. "Mm. Yum."

He sat near the window, enjoying the view and the bacon. This was pretty damn perfect, to be honest.

"Got those mountains on your mind, huh? I call you a genius and you don't even tease me?"

"I want to get and show off the trailer. I bet we travel around in it a lot. Camping, touristing—the whole thing." He was excited and a little bit scared. What if Mitch thought it was tacky? What if the kids hated it? What if it brought him down in their estimation?

"Okay, so we finish stuffing our faces, pack up and go. You're in charge. I'm just along for the ride." Mitch took another bite, looking happy with his breakfast order. "We could travel. We go up to Montreal or Maine even."

"Yeah. I love the idea of traveling without needing motels and constant restaurants. This is another home."

"It'll be fun. I haven't done much traveling at all so I'm clueless, but I'll learn." Mitch took Vicki's empty plate. "You want more, Vic? Or are you full?"

"More! More!" Vicki stole a strawberry from Mitch's plate.

"More, *please*." Mitch set his plate down on her tray and went to fill hers up again. "Manners."

"Please!" Vicki sang and stole a piece of bacon before Mitch made it back with more pancakes.

"It's getting bright out there. Look at the blue sky, Vicki. Pretty, right?"

"Uh-huh. Nummy bacons." Vicki didn't even look up, and Daniel couldn't help but chuckle. Five was not big on landscape, apparently.

Mitch's hands landed on his shoulders, and Mitch bent to kiss his cheek. "I promise to be way more impressed."

"God, I hope so." He turned his face for his cheek. "I want you to enjoy this. It's crazy important to me."

"It's already amazing, and we haven't walked out the door yet." Mitch looked right into his eyes. "You should see the way you look at those mountains. I can hear it in your voice too. It's a special place. I know it."

"It is." It was the first place that was home. It was where he had belonged, where he was welcome.

Mitch stole a piece of bacon off his plate and grinned wide. "Do I get to take turns driving the trailer?"

"Sure. Absolutely." He beamed at Mitch. "Although I park it the first time. Fair?"

"More than fair. You can teach me in some huge warehouse parking lot somewhere on the road. I've never driven a trailer."

"All done!" Vicki slid out of bed and ran for the bathroom. "Potty."

"She's done." Mitch's eyes were lit up, happy. "Let's get ready to go."

"Let's wake Emmers up and get something in him, huh? We can pack as he eats." He stood and grabbed a stray sausage before pulling on his jeans.

"Are there still some eggs left?" Mitch went over, leaned into the crib and rubbed Emory's back. "Hey, hungry boy. Time to wake up now."

Emory whined softly, snuggling into the covers, thumb popping into his mouth.

"Come on, kiddo! Food then we can go bye-bye." Daniel knew Emmers loved to go.

"He's so snuggly." Mitch scooped the baby up. "Dan-O has eggs." They danced over to him. "Maybe once he gets a whiff of breakfast?"

"Egg-os for Em-o!" Daniel kissed Emory and got himself a grin.

"Oh, good one." Mitch sat on the end of the bed and cleared a spot on the breakfast tray for him to put a plate of eggs down. "Human highchair."

"I'll pack us and then trade out." Daniel handed Emory over before he pulled out clothes for the kids and filled the laundry bag up with their dirties.

"I'm good."

Mitch helped Emory shovel in the eggs while Vicki climbed back into bed, and it wasn't long before everyone was dressed and ready for the day. Dan had put Emmers in the cutest pair of overalls and Vicki actually wore everything he'd picked out for her.

Score.

It was time to explore and show his family where he'd become an artist.

Daniel couldn't wait.

20

Mitch had to admit, he was a little bit in love with New Mexico.

One day in, and he was already loving this trip. The scenery was the complete opposite of Vermont. Where home was green and lush, everything here was dry, and colored in the rich browns, oranges and reds of the desert. At home with all the trees, the only time you could see more than a couple of miles was when you were up high. Here it felt like the land and the blue, blue sky were wide open. Even the architecture was different. What Dan had shown them so far of Santa Fe was so neat.

And it was more than all of that. It was Dan too. He was so relaxed, so in his element. Mitch already knew this would be a favorite place to visit. Maybe even retire one day.

"So when Adam told me about you, that you were an artist, he left out exactly what that meant. Maybe he assumed I knew, but I don't buy a lot of art. Those galleries are amazing."

"Aren't they? I love Leland Holliday's stuff. Those ravens and bears and coyotes. I'm tempted to buy a couple and hang them in the hallway by the bedroom." Dan was stretched out on one of the recliners holding Emory. They'd stopped to buy a little Pack and Play for Em to sleep in, while Vicki got the single bed in the loft.

This place was amazing—a table, a sofa, two recliners, a queen-sized bed for them. It was going to be amazing to vacation in this thing.

"Let's do it. That's the perfect space for them." He'd been wandering around the trailer opening and closing cabinets and doors, poking his nose in everything. "Also? This was not what I'd imagined when you said you had a trailer. This thing is crazy. It's huge—I mean, for what it is, it's...wow." He could stand up in the shower. There was a full oven. Crazy.

"It was my home. Now it can be ours to play with. It's so much nicer than hotels with the kiddos. They can bring toys, be loud—and we can relax." Dan looked so pleased, so relaxed and open. It was amazing to see.

"We can go where there are no hotels." Mitch glanced up at Vicki who was playing with her dolls in the loft, then sank down into the other recliner with a sigh.

"Yeah. Yeah. Man, I wish we hadn't agreed to supper out. I'm lazy." Dan winked at him, eyebrows waggling. "But I am craving the cashew mole."

"I have no idea what that is, but I do like cashews." Mitch chuckled. He was feeling the day a bit too, and the hour, the altitude. All of it. "We can sleep in tomorrow, be a little lazy then."

Emory crawled around in Dan's lap and gave him a huge smile before settling again. Mitch reached over and rested a hand on Dan's arm.

Dan lifted his hand and kissed his knuckles. "Mmm... and yes. We should plan our route in the morning, enjoy ourselves."

"Perfect." He let that little bit of affection warm him right up. "Do I need to dress for dinner?"

"Jeans and a sweater. This is a diner, honey, and Ally isn't fancy. She'll probably bring her twins."

"That I can do." He was glad she might bring her kids, so she didn't get impatient with theirs. Vicki had been going all day. If he was tired, he knew she was. "I'm looking forward to meeting her."

"She's a good person. Hard as nails where business is concerned, but she treats her artists with kid gloves." Dan helped Emory stand up, bounce on his thighs. For a man that had been terrified of Emory, he'd sure figured it out.

He didn't know why that was so hot, but it was. Dan had been determined to figure out kids and Vermont and diapers, and he had. He just...did it. Dan was much more capable than he gave himself credit for.

"That's nice, that gives you room to be creative I guess, right? Letting her deal with the business details?"

"Yes. I don't love the money part. It stresses me out. Adam watched her the first few years, made sure she wasn't fu-screwing me over."

That sounded so much like Adam. He'd always been totally transparent when it came to finances at work. Everyone always knew exactly how well they were doing as well as when things got rocky. "Trust is important, especially when it comes to money."

"Yessir, it is. Are you getting hungry, angel girl? You want to run into town and meet my friend?"

Vicki peered down from the loft at them. "Yes, please. Tacos, right? Real ones."

"Real ones. What do you mean? Vermont doesn't have real tacos?" Mitch knew the answer to that question damn well.

"Not like Dan-O's! Dan-O's are yummy!"

"I agree. Dan-O's are the best." He was ready to try anything as long as it came with a margarita. He hauled himself out of his chair, groaning with the effort. "Wow. I'm up. You want me to take Emory so you can get ready?"

"Please." Dan stood and handed Emory over, before going to the bedroom. "Get your shoes on, mi'ja. You'll need your coat too."

"Okay! Are we taking our house with us?"

"Nope. We're taking the red truck."

He chuckled. Vicki was so fascinated that the house moved with them. He bounced Emory in his arms, cooing and distracting him while Dan got himself and Vicki ready, then he changed the poop monster and pulled on a sweater. It was as much winter here as it was back home, just less snow on the ground.

They piled into the pickup and took off, heading back into the town. Santa Fe was lit up with thousands and thousands of lights in paper sacks—they lined the roofs, the sidewalks, everything, and it was beautiful.

"Dan-O! The lights!"

"Those are pretty cool, Dan. Is it a celebration?"

"This happens for the holidays every year. In the rest of New Mexico, they're called luminarias, but here, they're farrolitos." Dan found a parking space. "We've only got a few blocks walk, y'all."

"It'll be a pretty walk with all the lights. Uh. Farrolitos." Mitch hopped out of the car and grabbed Emory's stroller from the back.

They wandered into the plaza, the square filled with lights and trees and people. It was charming, and Vicki watched wide-eyed as they entered a busy little cafe.

"Daniel! Daniel, I got us a table!" A wild-haired lady with a pair of little girls around Vicki's age stood and waved.

"That's us." Daniel smiled at the hostess, and they all made their way over. "Mitch, Vicki—this is my good friend, Ally and her little girls Mariposa and Flora."

Ally was pretty much exactly what he'd expected after visiting the galleries today, and her enthusiasm made him smile. He offered her his hand. "Hello. It's great to meet you."

"Mitch, Vicki, and Emory is adorable." They all got handshakes, and Dan got a huge hug. "Oh, honey. It's so good to see you! I've missed you so much."

"Same here, lady. Same here."

Vicki ran right to the other girls, who pulled her over to the table. He followed Dan and Ally and found a good parking spot for the stroller. "Vicki has been talking about tacos all day long."

"Oh, they have a decent one here. She should be happy. My girls want tacos too." Ally sat down. "Have you two had a good day? Good flights in?"

He glanced at Dan. "The flights were a little challenging with the kids, but really they were very good, and everything was on time so I can't complain. And Dan gave us an amazing tour of some of the galleries today. I'm having a great day."

"Santa Fe is a special place, for sure. I love it." Everyone got settled, with Ally grabbing Dan's hand. "Speaking of love. The new work is stunning."

He couldn't help but feel proud. And he couldn't agree more. "Isn't it? He's been working hard."

"It's stunning. I was worried when you moved, but your talent just took a new turn."

Dan shrugged and blushed, looking uncomfortable. "Good. That's good."

"It was a tough adjustment. Vermont, the kids, me, school, his work...everything." Mitch slipped a hand into Dan's. "Don't shrug, baby, you can own this. I'm proud of you."

Ally beamed at them. "Oh. Oh, that's—Yay!" She bounced a little in her chair. "Just yay."

Dan chuckled softly and squeezed his hand. "I owe Adam a lot."

Ally's gaze sharpened as she shook her head. "No. Adam owes you. You are the one who took the babies. You are the one brave enough to fall in love. You moved. You created a new family that functions, and you are still creating art. I'm so proud of you, honey. I can't tell you how good it is."

Mitch gave Ally a knowing nod. He liked her. He'd known he would, just not how much. She cared, and she really had Dan's best interests at heart. He turned back and leaned into Dan's shoulder. "Have we embarrassed you enough? You want a shot of something? I think we're celebrating."

"I'm driving. I'll have a glass of wine. Something that goes with mole." Dan's cheeks were bright red, but that expression was pleased.

"He's really got me sold on this mole." He decided to take a little heat off Dan for a bit and looked at Ally as he leaned back in his chair. "Do you live in town?"

"I do! My husband is an attorney here. He's meeting with a client right now. I'm hoping he gets done in time to have dessert with us." She winked at Mitch, like she was telling a secret. "I'm one of those rare birds—a native New Mexican. So is Christos."

"Neat. I'm a Vermonter with deep roots. I've never been

to New Mexico before, and it couldn't be more different. Do you have lots of clients? How did you find Dan?"

"I have about a dozen. I saw Daniel selling his painting for fifteen dollars a piece on the plaza. I knew immediately that he was special."

He'd known almost immediately too. "I'm really not knowledgeable about art. I tell Dan that all the time, but there's something about the way he uses color, and his paintings always feel like...like they're moving. I'm so fascinated by them."

"Good. Good! You should love them; they're the essence of him!"

He thought he had a pretty good handle on the essence of his fiancée but he knew what she meant. And he did love them. "What do you tell people when you're hoping to sell a painting?"

"That these pieces scream with emotion, pure and simple. They're inspired by landscape but filtered through a uniquely different eye."

Then she glanced at Dan, and they both spoke together. "These are not hotel lobby landscapes."

He chuckled. "No. That's for sure." And Dan had plenty of emotion to pick from in their crazy little wonderful family home. "I'm sold."

"You don't have to pay, love."

"Dan-O! Where are the tacos? Did you see I have new friends? Emory is sleeping." Vicki looked totally tickled with the world.

"Tacos are coming. Are you sharing with the girls?" Mitch picked up a menu and lowered his voice. "We better order before Vicki marches herself back there to find the tacos herself."

"Right on. Two moles, three tacos, and an enchilada plate with Christmas, right?"

"You got it." Ally chuckled and waved down the waiter, the food order going easy as pie.

"I had to learn about Christmas. And I hear pretty regularly how hard it is to get green chile in Vermont." he teased Dan, poking him in the arm.

"And they're not Christmas anyway. Christmas is Santa," Vicki added, like she knew more than all of them.

"And that's coming up, isn't it? So much fun." Ally didn't even blink. "I'll mail you a bunch of frozen chile when you get home. We have an entire freezer full."

"Score. That will keep him happy for a while." The wine arrived and he poured them each a glass.

"Dan told me you were Adam's business partner?" Ally picked up her glass and sniffed it.

"Yes. We had a little advertising and marketing firm. Have. It's all me for now."

"Well, if you ever need graphic artists, holler at me. I meet tons, and I can give you some names."

"Thank you. I'll do that." He had a couple, and he didn't think they were going anywhere, but it was a kind offer. "Did Dan tell you we're engaged?"

"Oh my god!" Her squeal cut across the chatter in the restaurant like a knife. "No! Congratulations! When? When are you doing it?"

Dan cracked up. "We haven't talked about dates yet and thank you."

Mitch laughed, loving her joy and Dan's laughter. "We haven't talked any details at all. We don't even have rings. It's just happening. Somewhere. Somehow. Soon." Rings. He needed to start shopping. Or they did. "Maybe New Years. Maybe Valentine's Day. Maybe tomorrow."

"If you get your license tomorrow, I'll marry you tomorrow night at the house. I'm totally ordained!"

"Oh. Wow." He was kidding right? He was just kidding about tomorrow. Sort of. He looked over at Dan. "I mean…"

"We'll talk about it, lady, and I'll text you. This is something we have to figure out."

"Well, of course you have to talk about it. The offer stands, though. Daniel's been to the house."

"Thank you so much. We'll talk about it." He could do tomorrow. He could do it any time. But yeah, they should talk.

Just when he thought things might get awkward the food arrived, and Vicki stood up on her chair. "Tacos!"

"Sit down, girl!" Dan snorted and got her set up, checking on Emory, who was still out like a light.

"That's a girl who likes her tacos." Ally looked over his way as Dan got up to finish helping Vicki get settled. "He's good with her. I always knew he should have kids."

"He's great. It almost makes me wonder why he was so unsure of himself at first. When he isn't sure about something he just figures it out and does it. He's braver than I am."

"He was alone for a long time. That messes with your head. People need other people to love."

"Well, I plan to keep him. He's…perfect." Mitch shook his head. "Not perfect-perfect, but perfect for me. And forgiving, because I've hurt his feelings a couple of times." *Speaking of which*—"Listen. I love your offer. I've just learned we have to look each other in the eye and discuss things because we both just want the other guy to be happy, you know?"

"Totally. You'll learn that I'm impulsive." She watched Dan as he sat back down again. "You'd think that was a terrible quality in an agent, but I follow my gut, and it works."

Dan nodded to Ally, spoon of food halfway to his mouth. Someone loved his dish. "It does. Art is all about the gut."

"I think my kind of art needs more planning. But that's okay. That's part of why we work." He picked up his spoon and took a bite of his mole, the strong, rich flavor making him do the happy food dance in his chair. "Mm. Oh. Yum."

"Right? I love a good mole. It makes me happy." Dan licked his spoon clean.

"It's my first. It's amazing." He glanced down the table. "How is your taco, baby girl?"

"The best." Vicki's satisfied little face said it all. "The best taco ever."

"Is he always so good?" Ally peered into the stroller at Emory.

"Actually, yes. But right now I think he's all off his schedule and sleeping is easy."

"I bet it's partly the altitude too. We're about three thousand feet higher here."

Oh. He hadn't thought about that. "I bet that's it. But he's a happy kid anyway. We're lucky."

"We are. Both of them are good kiddos. I like hanging with them both."

Mitch wasn't sure if Dan intended Vicki to hear them, but she did, and she sat up that much straighter.

"Which is good, because you're kind of the default kid-wrangler on weekdays when I have to go to the office." He winked at Ally. "He took them both shopping for Vicki's school supplies before he even really knew his way around yet."

"Oh, that's a madhouse, isn't it?"

The conversation became what was obviously normal

for parents—school and how fast they grew, holidays and activities.

He guessed this was going to be his life for the next twenty years.

Maybe it didn't have to be the next twenty minutes though. "We're still working on our itinerary for our trip back home. Dan has a couple of great ideas. Any suggestions?"

"I don't. I've never made that drive. I do love the trailer, though. You two can really make it easy and slow."

"It's amazing. Another first for me. It's my turn to let Dan show me around."

"It'll be nicer than a hotel room with weird bedding and foreign pillows for sure."

"Oh my god. It's gorgeous. I don't know what I expected exactly, but it wasn't this luxurious thing." He slid a hand over Dan's thigh. "Dan likes to downplay everything."

"It was a good home, and I think we're going to make use of it." Dan looked at their hands like he was fascinated.

"It's still home. When we're in it." He squeezed Dan's fingers.

Ally tugged her phone out of her purse, texting quickly. "Christos is on his way. He wants the coconut cream pie. As if he needed to tell me that."

"Mmm...coconut cream pie sounds luscious." Dan looked so relaxed, so in his element. Mitch intended that his fiancé learned to look like this all the time. He could make it happen, he just needed to pay close attention for the next week or two.

"Split one with me?"

"Totally. Then we'll head back to the trailer and let Vicki get some rest in her loft bed."

"And so you two can have a beer before bed?" Ally teased, and Dan's grin wasn't hesitant and all.

"You know it."

He didn't dare hope *beer* was a euphemism for something much more fun, with Vicki in the loft he was a little worried his balls might shrivel into raisins before they made it back to Vermont.

"I bought a six-pack of Shiner at the store when I ran out for supplies. Shiner, Cokes, Doritos, grapes, cheese, hamburgers, pickles, buns."

"Sounds like a cookout is in our future." He swallowed down his last bite of mole with a sip of wine. "Well, we have things to talk about while we sip our Shiner." Which he had never had. He ought to start writing all of this down.

"We do. Christos! Hola!" Dan stood and shook the hand of an incredibly handsome Latin man. "I want you to meet my family. This is my fiancé Mitch, and our kids, Emory and Vicki."

"Hello. Life moves fast when it needs to, doesn't it?" Christos sat and stole a bite of Ally's leftovers. "I'm glad I didn't miss you. What do you think of our amazing city, Mitch?"

"I am completely enchanted. It's fascinating to me, and so beautiful." He wasn't exaggerating. "Dan is a really good tour guide too."

"This is where Dan-O used to live. He moved away." Vicki sounded so serious, so very adult.

"Did he? That's very exciting. Do you like it here?"

"Uh-huh. I like the moving house very much. There's toys."

He smiled at her. "Vicki really enjoyed the art galleries today, right baby girl?"

She nodded. "Yes. I'm going to be an artist too."

"Are you?" Ally asked, and Vicki nodded.

"We put our feelings into the colors so we can see them together."

Ally's eyes went shimmery. "That's right, honey. That's exactly right."

Christos put an arm around her shoulders in quiet support, and Mitch squeezed Dan's fingers for the millionth time. "She already is an artist, if you ask me. She and Dan have a lot in common."

Dan's cheeks went red hot, and he waved the waiter down. "We need some dessert here please."

They ordered, and the plates were removed. The little ones all got a scoop of ice cream, and then they got three pieces of pie.

He kept his chuckle to himself; he'd embarrassed Dan enough tonight already. But he got a hunk of pie on the end of his fork and offered it up to his fiancé. "Bite?"

"That looks amazing." Dan leaned forward and took the bite, meeting the challenge, head-on.

He couldn't help his smile; he was ridiculously pleased.

"Oh my goodness, you two are so...ah! I'm so happy." Ally took a bite of her own. "Mmm."

"You're not going to feed me?" Christos asked.

Ally stuck her tongue out at him. "Eat your coconut and leave me the chocolate."

He watched as Dan glanced over at Emory, who was starting to stir in his stroller. He'd noticed also. It might be time to make a friendly but quick escape. He took another bite and handed Dan the fork.

Dan took a couple of bites, and then started making "sorry, but it's time to leave" noises, getting the check, and getting Vicki's hands and face cleaned up.

He followed Dan's lead. "It was so great to meet you

both. I've really enjoyed this." He stood up and started tucking a warm blanket over Emory. "I'm sorry we have to cut it a little short, but he's not going to be too restaurant friendly when he wakes up."

"No problem. It's the girls' bedtime soon, and they need baths." Ally stood too and hugged Dan tight. "You look good. Seriously. I'm so happy for you."

"Thanks, lady. I'll text later. I swear."

"You better." She turned to him and surprised him with a hug too. She gave really good hugs. "Will you be in town a few days or are you moving right on?"

"I think we're in a campground near here for a couple of days while we make the rest of our plan. We'll be in touch." He offered Christos a hand. "Good to meet you. You have beautiful girls."

"I do. Thank you. Your family is glorious. Have a nice night." Christos shook his hand before they all got moving, heading for the truck.

"I see why you like her. She's great." Mitch looped an arm around Dan's hips as they walked, Dan pushing Emory's stroller and Vicki holding his hand.

"Isn't she? She's my best friend."

The snow fell in huge flakes, and it was a little like a fairy tale.

"I'm glad y'all are here. I wanted to share this with my people."

"I know I kind of made you wait, but I hope it's worth it." He leaned over and kissed Dan's cheek as they got to the truck.

"You're worth everything." Dan's eyes gleamed in the streetlights.

He loved the kids. Their kids. He really did. But right now Mitch wanted them to disappear for a minute. Just a minute. Just long enough for him to kiss Dan breathless and make sure he knew the feeling was mutual.

Words would have to do, so he poured everything he had into them. "You're beautiful, Dan. Especially right here and now. And I love you."

"I love you. Come on, let's get everyone to the trailer so we can...talk."

That worked for him.

Emory woke up before Mitch could get him into his car seat, so there was a diaper change break and a scramble to find a binky before they could head back to the campground. They made it back in time for meltdown number two, but he made a bottle and Dan scrounged up food, and Emory ate so much he thought the kid might pop.

Then it was Vicki's turn because she liked baths and was a little afraid of the shower, but Dan was brilliant as usual and somehow managed to convince her that all the coolest people took showers.

Probably the first time in his life he'd ever been cool.

Eventually though, Vicki had been read to and tucked in, Emory was awake but sleepy and entertaining himself in his play crib. Mitch took a breath and pulled two Shiners from the fridge.

"Hooray for day one!" Dan said, plopping down on the other recliner. "What did you think?"

"I'm exhausted. But in that completely satisfied and happy way." Mitch handed over a bottle of beer. "And I could get used to putting my feet up with a beer at night for sure."

"Yeah. It's just a good way to unwind. Together. I'm glad you liked Ally. She's important to me."

"That makes her important to me too." He reached across the armrest between them and took Dan's hand. "We haven't talked about how to get married at all, have we?" All they knew about their wedding was that Vicki wanted a purple dress.

"No. No, we haven't. I mean, the important part is settled, the yes part." Dan's grin was part naughty, part joyful. "Do you want a big wedding?"

Oh, boy. He had to answer questions first? What if he said he didn't want something that Dan really wanted? He really didn't want to hurt Dan's feelings again. "If I'm being honest, which I guess is important, I don't think so. I was thinking maybe just a family thing. I mean, a party could be fun later but the ceremony... I kind of want small. What about you?"

"Small works for me. I don't need a to-do. I just want you and the kids there, you know?" Dan took a deep breath and relaxed. "God, I'm so glad you didn't want a huge thing. I don't have any friends in Vermont yet, and I don't like white cake or spending a ton of money on flowers that are going to die."

He turned a little in his chair to look at Dan, grinning. "Right? I mean, cake is cake, and I'm not going to turn it down, but chocolate is so much better. And have you ever worn a tux? They're the most uncomfortable things ever."

"I'm not really the tux-y type. I love carrot cake and lemon pound cake a lot." Dan chuckled. "You want to get married when we get home?"

"You want to get married tomorrow?"

"We...we could. It would be a neat story—married by my agent in Santa Fe at Christmas time."

It would be a good story but there was more to it than that. "Married in Santa Fe by your best friend. She's your family."

"She is. She's my only friend now." Dan looked down

into his beer. "I guess I'll need to work on that, when I get home."

"Adam was my best friend. Now I have you. And we're talking about our wedding so no looking for the answers in your beer." He put his beer down and took Dan's chin in his other hand. "Ally is full of love and joy, and that's exactly what we need. That, some rings and a purple dress."

"Yes. Yes, a license, some rings, a purple dress, and some champagne and biscochitos!"

"So. We go into town in the morning and get a license, then we go find some neat rings that scream, 'New Mexico'. Maybe Ally would like to take Vicki shopping for her dress?" There must be something in the water out here, or the air. He'd been here a whole day and already felt so...free.

"I'll text her." Dan beamed at him. "God, I want to kiss you right now. You ready?"

"I'm so ready." Nothing made him happier than that smile. He didn't wait, leaning in to meet Dan's lips halfway.

Dan kissed him like he was storming a beach—the mixture of joy and passion and desire heady. He'd never been kissed, quite like that.

He caught Dan's jaw and held him there, offering himself and all that passion right back. He needed to be closer, and he found himself climbing out of his recliner and into Dan's lap.

Dan's hand found his ass, squeezing it and dragging him in closer, as Dan fed from his lips.

Yeah, that was just right. He rocked into Dan's hand and slid his fingers under Dan's sweater. "Please tell me the master back there has a door."

"The master has a sliding door. I wouldn't do that to us." Dan winked at him. "I need you more often than once every ten days, honey."

Oh, thank god. The bedroom had a door. Perfect. He could absolutely learn to love this. "Yeah. Like now. Right now." He slid off Dan's lap and moved backward toward the bedroom.

They checked on the now sleeping Emory, covering him up, then headed to the master. Dan pulled the door too, clicked the little plastic lock.

"Ooh. A lock even." Mitch kept his voice down because the door would likely be far from soundproof, but he'd take what he could get. He didn't waste time and shoved Dan's sweater up and off. "Mmm. That's the view I wanted. Well, part of it."

"Mmm... You got what I need." Dan hummed and returned the favor, stripping Mitch's shirt from him.

"I've wanted you since I woke up to you staring out the window at the Sandias." He slid his fingers over Dan's warm skin and took another kiss, craving the connection.

Dan worked his jeans open, fingers sliding in to cup his cock, rub him nice and firm.

Fuck, yes. He let their kiss muffle his moan and stuffed his hands into Dan's back pockets, giving that sweet ass a squeeze before going to work on his belt. Dan was so confident and in his element here, and it had Mitch hard and wanting. It was the hottest thing ever.

Dan sat on the bed, lips dragging over his belly, moving south toward his needy prick. When the barely-stubbled chin brushed the tip, he went up on tiptoe.

"Shit," he whispered, threading his fingers into Dan's hair. He watched intently, anticipating, toes curling. "Fuck, I love your mouth."

"I love your sweet prick." Dan opened up, lips wrapping around his cock and sliding, slow and steady down his shaft.

He let a deep sigh replace the moan that wanted out and

his head rolled back on his shoulders. Fuck, that heat was everything he needed. He squeezed Dan's shoulder to let him know, not trusting himself to speak quietly enough.

"Mmhmm." Oh, that sound was utterly delicious, vibrating along his prick, the sensations rolling in his balls.

This was going to be the perfect ending to a perfect day. He rocked a little, letting Dan know he wanted more.

Dan's fingers wrapped around his balls, rolling and tugging, driving him higher and higher.

He wanted this to last longer than it was going to. Dan knew how to bring him right to the edge and keep him there, and Mitch knew how much he enjoyed doing it. "Yes, Fuck." He tugged on Dan's hair and pushed a little deeper, knowing Dan could take it, knowing he would. Dan swallowed over and over, throat closing over his tip.

That was it, he couldn't hold off another second. His thighs trembled, his ass clenched and he stuffed his knuckles into his mouth to keep from shouting as his balls drew up. His orgasm crashed over him like a tidal wave, making him shake and gulp for air.

Dan swallowed around him, pulling good and hard until he was spent and shaking.

"So good. Love you." He tilted Dan's chin up and kissed him between panting breaths. He shoved his jeans and briefs the rest of the way off, kicking them aside, then pushed Dan onto his back and opened Dan's fly.

"Yes." Dan arched up into his hand, a low, needy cry filling the air. "God yes, please."

The way Dan wanted him gave him goosebumps, and he focused in on his soon-to-be husband, determined to make sure Dan got what he needed and more. He dragged Dan's jeans and briefs down and off together, then nuzzled into one thigh, kissing and nibbling his way back up.

Dan opened up like he'd pushed a button, and wasn't that pretty as hell? It was such a high to be with someone that needed you that much.

He sucked on one finger, then pressed it against Dan's hole with just enough pressure to tease. "I love you," he whispered, and drew his tongue from balls to tip of that heavy cock.

"Love..." Dan rolled up, curling toward him with a soft sigh, abs tight as he clenched and bore down. "Yes."

He let his finger pop inside sinking up to his knuckle and took Dan into his mouth, the salty, bitter taste a hint of things to come.

Dan grunted and fought to push up into his mouth and back onto his finger at the same time, the jerky motions making him smile.

He scrubbed his tongue along Dan's shaft and swirled it around the head for another taste of precome, then let Dan push deep into his throat. After another few seconds of frustrated movement, Mitch finally braced his other hand on Dan's hip and took over, head bobbing in earnest.

"Mitch." The whisper made him suck harder and Dan's cock swelled before he shot, filling Mitch's mouth.

He loved the way Dan's ass rippled around his finger, but he slipped it free as soon as Dan was spent so he could climb under the blankets and get his arms around his man. They lay there, fingers exploring each other as they caught their breath.

"Mmm...hey." Dan offered him a sloppy, lazy kiss.

He took it, and a couple more. "Hey. You make me crazy, you know that? I wanted you. So bad."

"We're lovers. That's how it's supposed to work, right?" Dan grinned at him. "So, we're going to get married tomorrow, huh?"

"Mhm. That was your last BJ as a free man." He chuckled. "Are you happy?"

"I am absolut—" Dan's eyes went wide. "Shit! I didn't text Ally back!"

Thank goodness it was before nine.

All he could do was giggle as Dan got out of bed. "Where's your phone? Wait...you need pants."

Dan looked like a circus bear as he pulled on a pair of sweats and stumbled out into the main room, hunting a phone.

He should help. He probably should. But watching Dan scramble was too entertaining and he couldn't stop laughing. Quietly. Trying not to snort. And he was pretty sure Ally would be all over their plans no matter what time Dan texted, so he wasn't going to stress this.

Dan was chuckling by the time he got back to the bed, plopping down with the phone. "Jesus."

He leaned against the headboard and pulled Dan back into him, grinning. "Hi, Ally, Mitch just gave me a mind-melting blow job so I've decided we should get married right away."

"Ally, listen. I'm going to bind him to me ASAP while we're both cum-addled. Tomorrow is good."

Mitch nipped at Dan's shoulder. "Also, can you take the kids so we can do it again only louder?"

"There you go." Dan's fingers were flying over the phone, the texts moving fast and furious.

"What did she say? Are we good? I want to go get neat rings, you know? Something that reminds me of this every time I look at it. Silver and turquoise maybe or...a neat stone. Something different."

"Turquoise instills calm. I like that. We need calm with Vicki." Dan waggled his eyebrows. "And with me."

"Mmm. I like you not-calm." He licked Dan behind the ear and pulled him closer.

"Do you?" Dan wiggled, teasing him with that tight little ass.

"Like you don't know." This time he bit Dan's shoulder a little harder. "Be good."

"I am good! Like gold. Ask Emmers." Dan's laughter made him stupidly happy.

"He's not talking. But when he does, he'll tell me all your secrets." He peered at Dan's phone. "Maybe she's already in bed?"

"I doubt it. Probably putting the twins to—" Dan's phone buzzed, a—YES YES YESYESYESYESYES! —popping up.

"So...that's a yes, then?" He cracked up—as quietly as he could manage—and hugged Dan tight.

"It seems she approves, yes. So, we'll get a license, rings, and a purple dress tomorrow morning."

"I can't wait. It'll be such a fun day. You're good? It's not too fast for you?" They deserved some fun and some spontaneity, something that was just theirs, that wasn't dictated by kids or work or...or Adam.

"What's fast? I love the idea of someone I care about marrying us."

"Good." He nodded. "Me too. I love it. What are we wearing?" He didn't bring a suit. He didn't want to wear one anyway. "Purple isn't really my color..."

"Jeans and nice sweaters? We can buy some tomorrow." Dan didn't look terribly concerned. "Something we can wear back home and remember the day."

"Works for me." He took Dan's phone and set it on a little ledge by the bed, then scooched back down into the pillows. "We were snuggling."

"We were having post-O-face bliss." Dan plopped down, wrapping around him like a koala bear.

"Not that it wasn't amusing to watch you almost bolt out of here in your birthday suit and then stumble around like you were walking on hot coals." Mitch chuckled. "But I prefer this."

"This is just right." Dan stroked his belly. "I swear to god, this is just right."

"It is." Just right. Dan had been right beside him through one of the worst times of his life to the eve of what he knew was going to be one of the best he'd ever have, and he was finally ready to look forward—only forward—toward an amazing future with his family.

21

One wedding license, one black sweater, one green sweater, two rings, one purple velvet dress, and a little purple baby-tux later, they were standing in Ally's living room with her husband and one of the gallery owners who had given Daniel his first shot as witnesses.

"Wow." The house was gorgeous, all decorated for the holidays, the huge tree covered in ornaments and lights strung everywhere. Daniel was totally in awe.

Mitch had his phone out and was taking pictures of Vicki, twirling in front of the Christmas tree, making the skirt on her dress flare. "You're going to make yourself dizzy, pretty girl."

Vicki slowed and smiled at Mitch, only stumbling a couple of steps. "I am pretty, and we're getting married!"

He watched as Mitch scooped her up. "We are."

"Oh, give me your phone, Mitch, let's get a family picture by the tree." Ally held her hand out and wiggled her fingers. "Go on, Daniel. By the tree. Grab the baby."

"Yes, boss." He scooped up Emmers, who was chewing

on a bunch of plastic links. "Family picture of our wedding, buddy."

How friggin' amazing was this—a picture of his family, his man, his wedding day.

Mitch moved close and put an arm around his shoulders. "This is a dream."

"Say cheese! Oh you're all so cute. Smile!" Ally snapped a zillion pictures in a row, tapping the phone over and over. "One of those will come out. You never know with babies, right?"

"Right. Children and animals." Daniel chuckled and kissed Emmers' head. "Okay, so should we go ahead and do this? Is there a mandatory groomzilla moment?"

"Ugh! I know you're not looking at me," Mitch teased.

"Really, boys? I think we'll do it over here by the fireplace. Vicki, would you like to stand between them?" Ally looked beautiful in a deep green dress, and the whole family was watching like this was magical, which it was, so—

Yeah.

Yeah. Pure magic.

Vicki moved to stand between them, and Christos took Emory from him. Mitch pulled the little box that held their rings out of his pocket and handed it to Vicki, then tangled fingers with him.

"Keep those safe for us, baby girl."

She nodded and held the box in both hands.

"You ready to do this?" he asked, holding Mitch's gaze.

Mitch squeezed his fingers and gave him a happy smile. "I am so ready."

"Me too. Let's do this."

Somehow Adam had done it—in his last acts, the bastard had saved him again and found him a family.

Daniel smiled at Mitch and sent up a prayer of thanks. *Thank you, Adam. I love you. It's all going to be okay. We have this, me and Mitch.*

Then he let Adam go and married his lover while their children watched.

WANT MORE BA & JODI?

Interested in learning more about our East Meets Westerns?

Join BA & Jodi's Newsletter
https://lp.constantcontactpages.com/sl/nzvRTTy

Patreon: https://www.patreon.com/BATortuga
There are lots of tiers to chose from, and also free serial stories.
Discord: https://discord.gg/Vba5P5Qv
BA's Discord server has a channel for BA/Jodi related chat and info.

Hey, Y'all!

We want to thank you for giving Bigger Than Us a try. We hope you enjoyed the story and want to check out the rest of the series.

If you can spare a few minutes to post a review at the retail website where you made your purchase, we'd very much appreciate it!

Yeehaw and thanks for reading!

BA & Jodi

ABOUT JODI

JODI takes herself way too seriously and has been known to randomly break out in song. Her queer MCs are imperfect but genuine, stubborn but likable, often kinky, and frequently their own worst enemies. They are characters you can't help but fall in love with while they stumble along the path to their happily ever after. For those looking to get on her good side, Jodi's obsessions include nonfat lattes, basketball (go Celtics!), and tequila any way you pour it.

Website: jodipayne.net

Newsletter: https://readerlinks.com/l/2317334

All Jodi's Social Links: linktr.ee/jodipayne

ABOUT BA

Western to the bone and an unrepentant Daddy's Girl, BA Tortuga spends her days with her hounds and her beloved wife, having mother-daughter dates, and eating Mexican food. When she's not doing that, she's writing. She spends her days off watching rodeo, knitting, and surfing Pinterest in the name of research. Following their own personal joys, BA and Julia heard the call of the high desert and they now live in the New Mexico mountains. BA's personal saviors include her wife, her best friends, and coffee. Lots of coffee. Really good coffee.

Having written everything from fist-fighting cowboys to rural single dads to werewolves, BA does her damnedest to tell the stories of her heart, which is committed to giving everyone their happily ever after. With books ranging from heart-warming stories of found families, to rodeo cowboys that are fighting to make a mark, to fiery passionate love affairs, BA refuses to be pigeon-holed by anyone but the voices in her head.

BA loves to talk to her readers and can be found at http://batortuga.com/ and her newsletter signup link is http://bit.ly/BAJulianews

AVAILABLE FROM JODI & BA

East Meets Westerns

The On the Ranch Series

Tending Tyler

Roped In

Diamonds in the Rough

Outfoxed

The Wrecked Universe

Wrecked

Flying Blind

Special Delivery, A Wrecked Holiday Novel

Seeds and Sunshine

Pickup Man

Cowboy for Sale

The Merry Everything Series

Window Dressing

Cowboy Protection

Cowboys and Cupcakes

Thawed Out

A Present for Parker - Coming January 2026!

The Higher Elevation Series

Heart of a Cowboy

Keeping Promises

Bigger Than Us

Home Free

BDSM/Kink

The Cowboy and the Dom Trilogy

First Rodeo, Book One

Razor's Edge, Book Two

No Ghosts, Book Three

The Soldier and the Angel, a Cowboy and Dom Novel

The Sin Deep Series

(set in The Cowboy and the Dom Universe)

Sin Deep

Trouble with Cowboys

The Triskelion Series

Breaking the Rules

Making a Mark

Making the Rules

Les's Bar Series

Just Dex

Hide Bound

Wholly Trinity

New Tricks

Lost Boy

The Barn Series

Zeke & Wesley

Other Titles

The Collaborations Series

Refraction

Syncopation

Puzzles Series

Cryptic

Single Titles

Temptation Ranch

Land of Enchantment

———

Summit Springs Sapphic (F/F) Romance

Christmas Bizarre

Honeymoon in the Cards